Phantoms of the Pharaoh (A Lady Marmalade Mystery)

by

Jason Blacker

PUBLISHED BY:
Lemon Tree Publishing
Copyright © 2013
Jason Blacker

Visit www.JasonBlacker.com on the web to stay up to date

Editing: Andrea Anesi

ISBN: 9781927623473

For my wife and son. My beacons and yardstick for everything good and pure

Table of Contents

One

The summer of 1895 was hot in Cairo, and especially here in Giza, as most summers were. But this particular summer was especially annoying to Howard Trenglove. For weeks he and his companion, Arthur Vipond had been trying to find the hidden chamber in the Pyramid of Menkaure. It had been rumored to exist but no one had ever found it.

Richard Vyse who had first discovered the upper antechamber in 1835 and then the basalt sarcophagus which he believed carried the remains of Menkaure, never made mention of a secret chamber. Nevertheless, Trenglove had it on what he believed to be good authority that such a chamber existed, and it was filled with treasures that men like him can only dream of.

How had he come to believe in something that nobody had ever claimed to have found? Like all good pirates and other rapscallions he had paid for the information. A sum of one hundred and fifty pounds he had paid to a man named Leith Walker who had been on the dig with Richard Vyse when Vyse had uncovered the basalt sarcophagus in 1835.

Walker claimed that later that evening on that fateful day when Vyse found the sarcophagus, Walker went back into the pyramid and discovered a secret chamber filled with so much gold and jewels the likes of which man had never seen before. Or so the story went. Walker also claimed that it was booby trapped. He had tried to steal a gold chalice when the small hidden entrance he had entered into this chamber started to close in on him.

He managed to escape with his life, but not without breaking both his legs as he tumbled down the steep shaft that had led him to the chamber. And this was why he sold the information to Trenglove. When Trenglove had found him at a retirement home in Manchester the year before, Walker was a feeble man of seventy-seven, stuck in a wheelchair, and babbling on about his glory days.

But there was something about Walker and the way he told the story that Trenglove believed him. He had to believe him, for he had paid Walker what was for him a large sum of money. In fact, it had been his life savings to that point.

Trenglove sat across from Vipond at an outdoor cafe in the middle of Giza. The odd fly buzzed around, and when it landed he hammered his fist down upon it, though he kept missing, and this was infuriating him as much as the oppressive heat.

It was mid-afternoon and Vipond looked at Trenglove with bemusement on his face.

"What's so funny?" asked Trenglove.

The two of them were dressed the same. Khaki pants and a short sleeved khaki shirt. Sweat rolled down the side of both Vipond's temples as he took off his safari hat, and placed it on the table. They were in the shade, if a threadbare canopy that hung sagging above them could be considered shade. Vipond took a damp handkerchief from his trouser pocket and mopped his brow.

The two of them were slim which was about the only thing in common they shared. Vipond was a few inches shorter than his tall and gangly colleague. They both had brown, damp, short hair though Vipond's was curly. He looked at Trenglove through green distant eyes.

"You're only making it worse on yourself. This oppressive heat is going to drive you mad if you keep your anger up like that."

Trenglove looked at his friend through brown, beady eyes as he sipped at his coffee in a small white cup. He turned his chair at a ninety degree angle to Vipond and looked out at the busy market square. Hagglers were everywhere, and all sorts of things were being bought and sold. Trenglove took off his hat and rest it upon his knee.

"We've been out here for three weeks now," he said, as if talking to some imaginary figure in front of him, "and we still can't bloody well find what we're looking for."

Trenglove didn't look at his friend. He took another sip of coffee. And for the love of God, he couldn't remember why he had chosen coffee on such an oppressively hot day. He put his cup down on the saucer on the table, and stared at the merchants while he ground his teeth.

Vipond watched Trenglove's jaw bulge and sag, as if it helped Trenglove move the mechanisms of his brain.

"Well, I asked you if he thought the information was good, and now I'm doubting you," said Vipond.

Trenglove didn't look at his friend, he kept his eye on the busyness of the market.

"Walker was here back in '35. He knew what he saw."

"But you don't know that what he saw is what he told you."

"A hundred and fifty pounds says I believe he told me what he saw."

"Or a hundred and fifty pounds requires you to believe."

Trenglove slammed his hand down on the table and coffee leapt from his cup in fear and dashed itself upon the brown table. Vipond leaned back in his chair, calmly watching his friend. He had seen outbursts like this before, but they were becoming more frequent. Vipond couldn't decide who was the greater fool.

Trenglove for paying a hundred and fifty pounds for the information, or himself, for having paid that amount to get the two of them here.

"You don't have to stick around if you don't want any share of the spoils," said Trenglove, looking at a merchant arguing with a customer over a pair of trousers.

"In for a penny, in for a pound, and I'm in as much as you are now. But I won't go any further," said Vipond. "By the end of this week, if we haven't made progress, we're finished with this wild goose chase."

"We'll find it by then, I'm sure of it. I have a feeling."

Trenglove and his feelings. It had been his feelings that he had used to hoodwink Vipond into coming onto this expedition. Though if truth be told, they both needed a spot of good fortune. Vipond was just about broke. He'd taken the last of his savings to fund this fool's errand, and if it didn't pay off he'd be destitute, with nothing to his name. Same was true of Trenglove, though he was a better swindler than Vipond and would find his way into some other scheme. For Vipond though, this was the end of the road, and if it didn't work out, well, he didn't like to think about the options available to him.

"After all this time, you're still full of bounding optimism even though your demeanor says otherwise."

Trenglove turned around to face his friend and his mouth turned down.

"What other choice do we have at this stage? You know my situation, and I know yours. We're beggars if this doesn't work out for us. And nobody likes a beggar. You can leave if you want, but I won't. I've spent my life savings to get to this point and there's no turning back. If we don't find the bloody chamber we'll make one."

Vipond looked at Trenglove steadily. He mopped at his brow again.

"Tell me why you still have so much faith in this man, Walker?"

Trenglove sat back in his chair, facing the market. He waved off the fly that he could not kill.

"I've told you that at least a dozen times."

"And you'll tell me a dozen more if you want my continued assistance," said Vipond.

Trenglove looked at Vipond for moment and glared at him. Then he went back to watching a tourist getting robbed, not aware of the proper approach to haggling. When your life, your very existence is a haggle, you learn the art very swiftly. Trenglove grabbed his hat and fanned his face with it. The air wasn't even cool, it felt like hot dog's breath. He reached into his trouser pocket and pulled out his own damp handkerchief that had been white not long ago. Now it looked as if it had been washed in weak coffee. He dabbed it at his forehead and at the sides of his temples.

If there was a hell, he was surely living in it, and its name was Giza. What had started out about a month ago as a trip full of friendly hope and shared dreams had turned into the bitter, sour dregs of dashed chances. Vipond had seemed like such an amiable chap, but he had become a turncoat, and a coward. Ready to leave at the first sign of trouble. At least that is what Trenglove felt. This also happened to mirror the thoughts that Vipond had about Trenglove.

"Leith Walker was an honest man..."

"And he took your hundred and fifty pounds," said Vipond, with a bit of bile in his voice.

Trenglove smirked towards the marketplace as the tourist walked away with a dress, smiling as if she'd gotten a deal, when in fact she'd just been robbed in broad daylight. But the smirk was not meant for her, it was meant, rather, for Vipond.

13

"If we find this chamber, and I believe we will," said Trenglove, turning to look at his friend with eyes as hot as the blazing Egyptian sun, "I will never forget to remind you of this moment."

"And I'll be happy to be reminded."

Trenglove looked back over at the merchant counting out his piastre coins and grinning wickedly. If he was sure of one thing, it was that the Egyptians were shrewd business men, and they had already cost him the equivalent of tens of pounds for information that had been highly suspect. No, this week, he and Vipond would venture out on their own to access the Pyramid of Menkaure.

"You see that man over there," said Trenglove, pointing with his chin in the direction of the merchant. Vipond nodded. "He just robbed that woman in broad daylight."

"Really?" asked Vipond, sounding somewhat incredulous.

"Well, not really, but he might as well have done it. She didn't haggle him and he charged her five times the regular price for a dress she bought."

"Interesting, but how does this have anything to do with Walker?" asked Vipond.

"Everything," said Trenglove, talking towards the Egyptian merchant. "We're going to find this chamber and its gold and we're going to rob these people blind. They have no idea what riches are right in front of them, and because of that we're going to take it."

Trenglove wiped at his face again. Then he wrung out his handkerchief and lay it flat across the table to dry out. Vipond sipped on his tea. It was now warm, but at least it was hydrating.

"That's a nice sentiment," he said, "but it still doesn't bring me comfort in what Walker told you."

"I told you," said Trenglove. "Walker was an invalid, he was in a wheelchair and he showed me the scars and the deformities on his legs. I don't know how else he would have gotten those except in some serious accident the kinds of which he spoke about in finding the secret chamber in the pyramid. He showed me papers written between him and Richard Vyse, and the last one where he was dismissed from Vyse's employment. He worked for that man and he was there in Cairo working at those pyramids in Giza. His passport confirms this. You don't think I'd just hand over my life savings to any man without a good and thorough check."

Vipond chose not to respond to that. He had known Trenglove for a few years. They had worked together in the coal mines of Barnsley, South Yorkshire. Trenglove was a dreamer, he had said he had heard that there were still lots of treasures to be uncovered in Egypt, though at that time it was all rumors.

"Of course Walker wanted to get paid. His information is valuable, and I think I got quite the deal actually. We could have access to tens, maybe even hundreds of thousands of pounds worth of gold."

"We could if we ever found it."

"We will, I believe our Egyptian guides have been misleading us, and perhaps they've been doing so on purpose."

"Why?"

"So they can find the treasure for themselves. Walker told me you had to be careful with what information you share. I had to develop a relationship with him for over a year before he was comfortable telling me about this secret chamber and the treasures it hides."

"That sounds all good, but one could argue he was just a lonely old man, happy for any sort of friendship, and he was just milking it out for as long as he could."

Trenglove picked up his hat again and fanned his face. The sun would soon be dipping below the canopy and they'd be in the heat of the afternoon sun. That wasn't somewhere where Trenglove wanted to be.

"I never told you this, because I thought it might prevent you from supporting this trip."

Vipond now leaned in, and rested his elbows on the table and looked at Trenglove with a frown.

"What do you mean there's something you didn't tell me. I'll walk now, I tell you, and you'll hear from my solicitor."

Vipond's voice was getting louder and as it did it hit the squeaky tones in his otherwise tenor voice. Trenglove tried not to smile, but whenever Vipond got upset his voice hit the high register quickly. It was comical, and hard to take him seriously. Trenglove put up his hand.

"It's not like that. There is just one small item that I have withheld, and I'm sure you'll not hold it against me when I tell you what it is."

"And what is it, damn you, tell me now!"

Vipond slammed his hand down against the table, rattling their cups as they shook in fear on top of their saucers. This also drew looks from others who were nearby. Trenglove leaned in.

"Listen," he said, quietly, "if you continue this outburst I won't say."

He stopped and looked at Vipond for a long while. Vipond crossed his arms in front of himself.

"Fine, tell me, but I warn you..."

He didn't finish the sentence. Trenglove fished a folded and damp piece of paper out of his shirt pocket, and held it in clammy hands.

"This is perhaps the most important reason as to why I believe Walker is telling the truth."

Trenglove waved his hand around with the paper as he spoke.

"And what is that exactly?" asked Vipond, still folding his arms crossly in front.

Trenglove smiled with delicious anticipation.

"Not only did Walker get me to pay him that large amount of money, but he also demanded that I share the spoils of this find with him at fifty percent."

"My God," said Vipond, becoming unhinged and dragging his hands through his hair. "Are you completely mad?" He managed to keep his voice down, but there was anger and bewilderment in his voice. "What were you thinking?"

"It's not that bad," said Trenglove, "I haggled him down to ten percent. That's all we have to share with him, a measly ten percent of our find, and of course we'll not itemize everything we find. Listen, the thing is, why would he ask for fifty percent of nothing? Perhaps even more telling, why would he be willing to settle for ten percent of nothing?"

Trenglove watched Vipond for a while as Vipond started to think through what he had just heard. Fifty percent was indeed outrageous, but ten percent wasn't that bad. If there was even a fraction of truth to what Walker had told Trenglove, then their share would make them millionaires, even if they had to pay Walker ten percent. Vipond looked up at Trenglove after some time.

"I suppose you're right," he said at last. "Why would he settle for ten percent if he knew there was nothing there."

Trenglove nodded.

"What's that in your hand by the way?" asked Vipond.

Trenglove looked at the folded piece of paper in his hand and delicately unfolded it and placed it face down on the table for Vipond to see, careful to find a dry spot for it.

"This is the agreement our barristers wrote between Walker and me," he said.

Vipond nodded.

"I see, then we better make sure we find the treasure," said Vipond, reading the document, "or it looks like you'll owe him another one hundred and fifty pounds, which I'm certain you don't have."

Trenglove folded up the piece of paper and put it back in his pocket where it had come from. He shrugged and looked at his friend.

"O ye of little faith. We'll find that treasure by the end of this week or my name's not Howard Trenglove," he said.

Vipond smiled at last and looked at his friend with the first sign of kindness that Trenglove had seen in over two weeks.

"A celebration is on me then. Tonight we eat and drink our fill and tomorrow night we'll get that treasure."

Trenglove cocked his head.

"We will, my doubting Thomas. We will."

Two

The boat ride across the Mediterranean had taken Lady Marmalade two days. It was glorious and wonderfully relaxing. She had been accompanied by her very dear friend Florence Hudnall.

It was Lady Marmalade's idea for the two of them to visit Egypt. Frances hadn't been to Egypt for over ten years, and Florence had never had the chance to visit.

Frances had wanted to come over to Egypt for a bit of rest and relaxation. The past years had been trying, what with the Second World War barely behind them. Eric had been gone just over eight years, and yet she still missed him terribly. But she knew he'd want her to carry on, 'to live darling, as if your life depended on it', as he'd say.

It was a very warm afternoon on that particular Wednesday, October the 1st, as Lady Marmalade and Florence Hudnall debarked from their boat onto the docks of Alexandria.

"It's amazing what difference a day makes," said Florence, smiling at Frances with her hand on her wide brimmed hat to keep it on. Though why she did that, when there was hardly any wind in the harbor was perhaps more out of habit than necessity.

"What do you mean by that, Flo?" asked Francis.

They walked over to the side of the dock where a porter was unloading the suitcases from the boat for the travelers.

"Well, I noticed yesterday, or perhaps an even better example is when we left Athens. The weather was pleasant, just on the warm side wouldn't you agree?"

Frances nodded.

"And yet, yesterday afternoon on the boat, and now here especially, in Alexandria, it feels so much warmer. At least a couple of degrees warmer, wouldn't you agree?"

Florence watched the porter with the bags. He was straining with a couple of heavier ones, dragging them across the path to where the others were.

"I quite agree, Flo. I see now what you mean. But it's not unpleasantly hot though, is it?"

Florence turned to look at her friend, and nodded.

"No, not at all, I did not mean to suggest that. In fact, I find the weather just about perfect. Not too hot, and not too cool."

"Good, I chose October for just that very reason. There shouldn't be too many tourists, though I see plenty about, but it's not achingly hot like it can be in August and even the early part of September."

"I can't imagine," said Florence.

"I was here in July, many years ago," said Frances, "when I was a much younger woman, and it was well into the high thirties. Unbearable really. I didn't get to see much on that occasion."

"You don't say?"

Frances nodded.

"What on earth brought you here in the height of summer?"

"I was here with Eric, at that time he was looking at some business opportunities. It didn't work out that way, thankfully. I wouldn't have wanted to visit Egypt again in the middle of summer."

"I can't blame you," said Florence.

Frances looked over at some of the other passengers who had joined them on the boat ride over. There was a couple who looked like they might be married. Both were fat and dressed inappropriately for the weather. He had on a three piece brown suit and hat, and she had on long woolen dress with a matching jacket, that was gray. He helped her off the boat and they came and stood not far from Frances and Florence.

Frances looked around and saw that there were many other young Egyptian men looking to offer their help in carrying bags and fetching taxis for those just debarking from the boat. But the porter was not finished with unpacking the bags yet.

Frances and Florence were both somewhat seasoned as travelers, but more than that, they were considered frugal woman. As such, they had both only brought the bare necessities. No need for extraneous clothes that weren't suited to the climate or for more makeup than the bare necessities. They were here as intrepid explorers, hoping to enjoy some sightseeing and learning about the history of the ancient Egyptians and Pharaohs.

Ancient Egyptology had held a special fascination for Florence ever since she had been a schoolgirl with Frances at St. Mary's. Frances on the other hand was not as interested in ancient Egypt as she was in the weather. As much as history, and especially Egyptian history intrigued her, she took any reason to explore parts of the world that were warm.

She had visited Florence up in Puddle's End in the early part of summer and their conversation had somehow turned to ancient Egypt. Florence had been reading a book on the subject and wanted to share some of the interesting bits with her.

At that time, Frances had thought about a trip to Egypt with her friend and had expressed that thought. Florence had thought it a wonderful idea, though she could by no means afford such extravagance. At least not without saving for a few years first.

Frances had decided then and there that she would pay for a trip for the two of them. Florence had politely tried to refuse but had eventually acquiesced, because she knew that arguing with Frances when her mind was made up was a futile effort.

And so they found themselves at the beginning of October standing in Alexandria and watching their bags get unloaded from the boat that had brought them here from Athens. A boat that had been quite full, much to Lady Marmalade's surprise. The tourist season didn't really start in full force until towards the end of October, and there was no reason that she could think of as to why tourists would be arriving earlier. Perhaps it was just an anomaly.

Florence noticed a military man step off the boat, helping a young woman who might have been his wife. He had the confident and crisp deportment of an officer, and he was dressed in his dress khakis including peaked cap. His wife was extraordinarily beautiful, though perhaps several years older than him. She was dressed in white summer clothes, a long dress and she carried a parasol to protect her brown curly hair and pale complexion from the sun.

"That's a clever young woman," said Florence, looking over at her and her military companion.

"Indeed," said Frances, following Florence's gaze. "Good thing we packed ours too. I'm sure we'll need them for the remainder of the trip."

The two of them, the military chap and his companion, walked over to where the rest of the passengers were now gathered, not far from the bags that were still being unpacked.

Soon, a clot of passengers from the boat were huddled around waiting for the rest of the cases to be unloaded. Lady Marmalade and Florence found a porter who took their bags, one each, and carried them over to an awaiting taxi. They were soon on their way to one of the finest hotels in Alexandria. A five story hotel, whitewashed, which had rooms facing the Mediterranean Sea.

Its name was 'The Palace', at least that was what Lady Marmalade had been told its name meant in translation. When they arrived, a bellboy from the hotel, smartly dressed in his dark blue uniform with red tassels and piping, opened the door as the taxi came to a stop, and he took their bags out of the trunk.

The inside of the hotel's foyer was large, with tiled floors that were off-white and streaked with the natural minerals of the stone. The walls held elaborate painting and art from Egypt and there were a few statues of pharaohs and sphinxes around the foyer. The center contained a fountain. The front desk clerk was a handsome Egyptian with dark complexion and warm, brown eyes. He was dressed in a dark blue suit with a red tie and white shirt.

"Welcome to The Palace," he said, in perfect English.

"Thank you," said Frances. "I'm Lady Marmalade and I've booked a suite on the fifth floor, for my friend and I."

The young clerk looked at his register and smiled.

"Yes, my Lady, we have you in our finest suite. The Royal two bedroom."

The clerk looked up and noticed that the bellboy was hovering close by with their two bags. He nodded at him. The clerk reached around and grabbed two separate keys for the suite and handed them to Lady Marmalade.

"Do you wish us to open an account for you, my Lady?" he asked.

"Not this time, thank you. We're here only for the night, and I wish to pay by cash."

"Very good," he said.

Frances signed the register and paid for the room. Florence watched quietly as Frances signed a traveller's check for one thousand Egyptian pounds. The clerk smiled upon receiving the check and issued a receipt.

"I do hope you'll enjoy your stay. I am Ahmed, and if there is anything I can do for you, please do not hesitate to contact me. Abdul will show you to your room."

Ahmed put out his arm towards Abdul, the bellboy with their bags, and he escorted them to the elevator. It was not long before they were comfortably ensconced in their suite, and Abdul had left with an Egyptian pound that Frances had given him for his efforts.

"That's a very generous tip you gave the young lad," said Florence.

"Well, I believe in greasing the cogs of human goodwill," said Frances, smiling.

"I must say again, how very dear and kind of you to take us on this trip. I think I shall always remember this tour as a highlight of my life."

"Not at all, my dear Flo," said Frances. "I have the means, and I'm happy to do it. Besides it wouldn't be the same spending four weeks and not having anyone to share it with."

Florence sat down on the couch next to Frances and pulled out the itinerary for their cruise.

"This is such a treat," said Florence. "We're going to hit all the spots I've ever dreamed of. The pyramids, Amarna, Abydos, Dendera and then Luxor, and finally Aswan. This is truly, Fran, a dream come true."

Florence's eyes twinkled as she read some of the highlights about the excursions they would be taking. Frances sat back and enjoyed the enthusiasm of her friend. It was calming and freeing to be away from the increasing noise and busyness that had become London after the war. This respite was exactly what she needed. A carefree and relaxing holiday away from busyness and chaos of any sort.

France got up and walked out onto the balcony. It was a long balcony that took up half the top floor, and wrapped around the one side. It looked out onto the sea, and off to the west she could see more boats coming into the harbor and others resting on the soft blue belly of the water. It was a picturesque and serene scene. The air was warm and humid with the salty scent of sea and fish. Frances breathed deeply.

Florence came out and joined her on the balcony. They both leaned against the wooden top of the metal railing. They were in the shade, and the weather was perfect. The noise was a dull hum of human activity. After a while, Frances turned to her friend.

"It doesn't seem to have changed much, since the last time I was here."

"When was that?"

Frances looked off across the sea and towards Greece, which could not be seen.

"I think it was with Eric, back in '37. Must have been March or April I think, as the weather was a bit cooler. Now that I think of it, it must have been in March sometime, because I remember our anniversary from that year was in India."

Florence looked over at her friend, and smiled sadly.

"He was a great man, Eric," said Florence.

Frances looked back at Florence and smiled at her, and rested her hand on her friend's forearm.

"He was, Flo. I still miss him after all these years."

"As you should, you were married, what, forty years wasn't it?"

"Almost," said Frances, looking back out across the sea, and thinking how it never seemed to change. Never seemed to grow old and die. The sea just consistently blue, and rippled upon its back as if the idea of life's constant change sent shivers across its soft skin.

"We were married in '03 as you probably remember, considering you were my maid of honor."

Frances looked at her and winked. Florence chuckled.

"I do remember, I'd never seen you so nervous about anything at all, before or since."

Frances nodded, and looked back over the sea, smiling at it, as if they alone shared the sad secret of life's death march into the quicksand of time.

"He passed on the 25th of September 1939. The following April, the 1st of April would have been our fortieth anniversary."

The withered winds of time had long ago dried her tears, but the memories still ached and squeezed her hearth and got caught in her throat. Florence squeezed Frances' hand.

"I'm sorry," is all she said.

And what could you add to that. Platitudes? They were as useless as dry desiccated leaves, long dead and rotting at the severed stump of a long ago chopped down tree. After some time, Frances turned back to her friend and put on the bravest smile. A smile that only the British had perfected after the centuries of difficulties both self-imposed and externally imposed.

"We should freshen up and get ready for dinner. We are after all on a vacation and not on the ferryman Charon's boat crossing Styx."

Florence laughed, and that helped Frances chuckle too. They walked back into the living room of the suite, arm in arm and smile by smile.

Three

"Are you ready?" asked Trenglove.

"I am," came the answer from Vipond.

It was just after eleven at night, and the two of them left their bedroom in one of the cheap hotels on the outskirts of Giza. A good thing it was on the outskirts for they wouldn't have to walk far to get the camels that Trenglove had arranged with one of the local discreet thieves he had managed to find. Birds of a feather did, after all, stick together, or at least recognize their own kind.

They crept down the stairs which creaked and groaned as if the two thin men might have weighed twice what they actually did. It was comical to see them, prancing down the stairs as if they were ballet dancers on their tippy toes. The clerk at the front desk was already asleep. His head bobbing up and down as if attached to some ironic puppeteer. Next to him was a flask of cheap wine, and a glass that held but just a splash of the dark red liquid.

They crept along stealthily until they were just about to cross the front desk, when the clerk's head which he had been perching on his fist flopped off and he jerked awake knocking his glass of wine and almost sending it to the floor. Trenglove and Vipond stuck themselves as flat as they could against the wall and column just to the side of the desk.

The clerk looked around sleepily. Picked up his glass and finished its contents. He had a round face, which was likely ruddy except for his dark brown complexion. He was probably in his fifties and at least fifty pounds overweight. His head was rimmed with a salt and pepper ring of hair leaving his bald shiny pate brown and somewhat freckled on top from too much sun. He yawned and put his head back down onto his crossed arms which were across the hotel's register.

Trenglove and Vipond waited for several minutes until they started to hear the clerk snoring. Without saying anything to each other they walked across the dimly lit front desk and out the main doors of the hotel.

There was no reason for them to have to sneak out, except that neither of them wanted to be seen leaving. Questions might be asked if they ever found the blasted secret chamber and were able to pilfer its contents. And they'd rather be far away with nobody the wiser about their whereabouts to cast any suspicion their way.

The evening was still warm and humid as they travelled down the mostly empty streets of Giza. It was a weekday and most everyone was indoors if not already asleep. Only the occasional group of men could be seen on balconies or gathered around closed shops smoking shishas and drinking coffee. They paid no attention to the two lanky Brits.

Down the last dark alleyway at the very edge of Giza, they found their man. He was a small, thin Egyptian with a wide grin and furtive eyes. The practiced vigilance of a career thief. He saw Trenglove who he recognized not only by his height but by his khakis and safari hat. The Egyptian lit a cigarette to indicate that he had seen them.

"That's our man," said Trenglove.

"And you trust him?" asked Vipond.

"I do. All he knows is that we wanted to visit the pyramids privately for a better look."

"And you think he believed it?" asked Vipond, a dash of incredulity in his voice. Trenglove looked at him.

"Doesn't matter, that's the only story he's getting. Besides, he only knows our first names. Don't worry about it, I'll handle it."

"Ahlan," said Trenglove, as he stepped up to the small Egyptian.

"Ahlan wa sahlan," said the Egyptian in return.

"This is Alfred," said Trenglove, turning to his friend.

"Hello," said Alfred, shaking the Egyptian's hand.

"Ahlan," said the Egyptian, "I am Khaemhet."

"Do you have the camels as I asked?"

Khaemhet turned back to Trenglove.

"They are just around the corner."

"And the other supplies?"

"They are all there."

"Take us to them."

Khaemhet turned and walked down the rest of the alley and then turned right. They followed him along a dirt path that was dark and unlit, except for the full moonlight. A few minutes later, under a large and tall Sycamore tree was another man with two camels. Khaemhet and the other man greeted each other. He was just as small as Khaemhet but younger.

"This is my brother, Menna," said Khaemhet.

Trenglove and Vipond looked at the younger man and nodded at him. Trenglove then went up to take a look at the kneeling camels. They were not the healthiest he had seen. Flies buzzed and dived against their ratty, and in places, flea bitten fur. But he had not expected much more for the price he was paying.

Attached to the camels' saddles were two long poles that trailed out behind them which ended on a wooden sled on top of which contained a large wooden box about four feet on each of its three dimensions. Attached on top of these boxes with strings were blankets and an average sized rucksack. Trenglove walked back to Khaemhet.

"Everything is in there? Torches, kerosene lanterns, twine and rope, tools. You got everything on the list?"

Khaemhet nodded.

"I did, but some of it was more expensive than what we originally agreed on. I have to ask for more money."

Khaemhet grinned salaciously like a weasel who had blackmailed many an innocent tourist. Trenglove didn't smile back. Instead he fiddled with something in his front trouser pocket and pulled out an Enfield revolver, pointing it at Khaemhet's chest.

"Are you sure you didn't miscalculate?" asked Trenglove.

Khaemhet shrugged his shoulders and smiled even wider.

"Yes, Mr. Howard, now that you make me think about it, I think you are right. I miss calculated."

"Good," said Trenglove, and he put the revolver back in his pocket.

Vipond looked as white as a sheet. He had not known about the revolver. In fact he had insisted that this mission was strictly about robbing a Pharaonic tomb. He most certainly was not interested in violence, let alone murder in cold blood. He looked on in horror until Trenglove had put the revolver back in his pocket, but Vipond was still unsteady.

Trenglove put his hand into his other pocket and pulled out a wad of crumpled and still damp British pounds. He counted out ten one pound notes and handed them over to Khaemhet. Khaemhet took his time to count them for himself.

"Anything else I can do for you, Mr. Howard?" asked Khaemhet, quite happy with his new found fortune.

"Point us in the direction of the Pyramid of Menkaure."

Trenglove could only see one pyramid that was off at forty-five degrees from where he stood talking with Khaemhet. Khaemhet turned around and pointed at the pyramid.

"That big one there, is the Great Pyramid of Giza. You can't see the Pyramid of Menkaure because it is hidden. Behind this Pyramid of Giza is the Pyramid of Khafre, and behind that is the smallest one, the Pyramid of Menkaure."

Trenglove grunted his appreciation and started to walk off. Khaemhet grabbed him by the arm. Trenglove looked down at the Egyptian's hand and then at Khaemhet.

"Do not go inside, Mr. Howard. The Pharaohs will curse you if you do."

Trenglove looked at him. Khaemhet was pleading, his eyes full of sincerity. For the first time he didn't look like the scheming thief that Trenglove had known.

"Of course not," blurted Trenglove. "I told you, we just want to take a closer look unencumbered by the tourists."

"Don't, Mr. Howard, please do not go inside. They say the priests placed curses to protect the Pharaohs. You will die if you dare to disturb the Pharaoh."

"Yes, well, that's jolly good to know. You can be on your way, Khaemhet," said Trenglove, ripping his arm free from the man's hand.

Trenglove and Vipond climbed on top of the kneeling camels, and then got them upright. Khaemhet came up and unleashed the camels from the tree. Trenglove and Vipond started off towards the big pyramid looming like an arrow towards the heavens and twinkling stars.

"I warned you, Mr. Howard. I warned you," came Khaemhet's shouts as the camels slowly walked away, carrying Trenglove and Vipond as well as their dreams and hopes for riches of untold boundlessness.

"These damn superstitious people," spat Trenglove, "no wonder we've had to come and help them into the technical age."

Vipond looked at his friend.

"Though there might be something to it, I suppose," said Vipond, swallowing hard, not wanting to give away the spectral fear that ran up and down his spine. Trenglove looked at him and laughed.

"My good man," he said, "you must be joking."

"Naturally," said Vipond, lying.

Trenglove laughed heartily again.

"To our fortunes, Alfred, and away from this godforsaken place."

The camel is not known as a fast mammal. Not like the horse. In fact, its disposition is more ornery and it prefers to limp along at a much more leisurely place. Still, to be fair to the camels, they were dragging behind themselves a decent load and the Egyptian heat is oppressive, even at night.

"We'll keep to the left of the Great Pyramid of Giza," said Trenglove

He was smiling, in fact Vipond had noticed that his tall, thin friend had a permanent smile plastered to his face since they had climbed onto the camels and started towards the pyramids. His enthusiasm and optimism was contagious and Vipond was starting to think that they might actually find the secret chamber they were looking for.

The moon was sufficient to give them the light they wanted and needed to find their way. The traveling was easy and steady. The sand of the desert was firm in this area, and flat, and the camels begrudgingly trudged along persuaded by the occasional heel from both Vipond and Trenglove.

It was around midnight when Trenglove and Vipond rounded the Pyramid of Khafre and saw the Pyramid of Menkaure. They made their way steadily towards the north of it, where the entrance was that led them into the pyramid's interior. This is where they had entered into the bowels of Menkaure before.

Trenglove stopped the camel several feet away from the entrance, and Vipond came up and halted his camel next to him. It was quiet under the Egyptian moon. They had not seen anyone else around since they had met up with Khaemhet. They got the camels to kneel and climbed off.

Trenglove and Vipond took a long stake from the saddle and pounded it into the desert sand with mallets. The spike looked much like an armless ankh. They tied the rope from the camel's neck to the loop in the spike.

"We've been in here before," said Vipond, "I'm not sure what you're hoping to find."

"I know we've been in here before, but there is one area that I recall from our last excursion that might have held a secret passageway."

"I don't remember seeing anything to suggest that at all," said Vipond.

"The upper chamber. I'm sure there must be a hidden door there."

"But we looked, and Sanehet swore to us that there was nothing at the end of the upper chamber. He had said everyone had looked before."

Trenglove nodded tersely, while he unpacked his kerosene lantern and lit it.

"I know what he said, Art, I was there too. I want to have a look myself without any persuasion from the damn guide. Are you coming or are you going to sit out here and pout?"

Vipond grumbled something under his breath and got his lantern out and lit it. They walked over to the rickety stairs that had been placed on the north side. This was the only entrance that anyone was aware of to get into the pyramid, and the entrance was about twelve feet off the ground.

Trenglove climbed up first, followed by Vipond. Trenglove ducked into the entrance passageway. It was completely dark, but holding his lantern in front of him gave a slippery and eerie yellow light that moved like a spectra as Trenglove trod down the slight decline of about twenty-five degrees.

Trenglove was bent forward at the waist as the entrance passageway was a stingy four feet tall. The going was easier for Vipond's shorter height, but it was single file all the way until they reached the paneled chamber where Trenglove could stand upright.

This chamber had several false doors that Trenglove did his best to open without any success.

"Walker told me that it was a false door that would lead to riches," said Trenglove, talking to himself.

Vipond had looked around carefully, but he too had been unable to open any of the false doors.

"I'm not doubting what he told you, but wouldn't it be too obvious to have this false door right here in the very first chamber. Surely it would have been found out by now if that was the case?"

Trenglove nodded.

"I should have paid closer attention, though the old man's memory wasn't as clear as I'd hoped. He said something about the bigger of the three pyramids. He said it was in Menkaure on the south. But Menkaure is the smaller of the three pyramids."

"Yes, well when you spoke with Walker, it was well over fifty years earlier when he was actually here wasn't he?"

Trenglove turned to look at his friend and the lantern distorted his features into grotesque shadows.

"But he seemed so certain."

Vipond nodded.

"All right then. Fifty or sixty years is a long time to remember everything with detail. Perhaps he meant to say that the secret chamber was in the smaller of the three pyramids. That has to be, because he mentioned it was in Menkaure several times, right?"

Trenglove nodded.

"And let's pretend he meant that this secret chamber was attached at the south end, well, we're heading south, so perhaps we need only continue on. We've tried these false doors before, and they didn't work. Honestly, I think it would just be too easy if it was right here, right at the beginning."

Trenglove stroked his unshaven chin and then nodded.

"You make sense, Art. Let's carry on."

Trenglove continued south through the passageway hunched over, until they emerged into the large antechamber which was rectangular as compared to the paneled chamber's square shape. The shortest length of the antechamber was also longer than the longest side of the paneled chamber. Trenglove and Vipond climbed up into the upper passageway which doubled back just above the passageway they had used to first enter into the antechamber.

Almost a third of the way back towards the paneled room, the upper passageway rose at approximately twenty-five degrees, heading towards the entrance. Trenglove and Vipond, both hunched over, with Trenglove leading climbed this upper passageway as they had done before. Below them would be the paneled chamber, and the passageway continued on for several feet, until it abruptly came to an end.

Trenglove stopped with Vipond behind him. There was barely enough room for the two of them to stand hunched over, side by side. It was quite uncomfortable.

"Hold my lantern," said Trenglove, "so I can get a better look of what's going on up here."

"Nothing's going on up there," answered Vipond, only slightly exasperated.

"Just hold the bloody lanterns so I can see what's going on," said Trenglove, clearly losing his cool.

Vipond kneeled down and held onto the lanterns as Trenglove reached up and in front of him, trying to explore the end of this passageway. It ended almost abruptly, though there was what appeared to be a shelf which was horizontal to the ground. Trenglove climbed up into it, and lying down he searched deeply into the end of it, but he couldn't see very well.

He wormed his way out and turned around to Vipond.

"Hand me my lantern."

Vipond gave him the lantern and Trenglove crawled back into the furthest end of this wedge. There was nothing there, not even very much pink granite which had adorned the walls of most of the rest of the interior of this pyramid.

Trenglove crawled back out on his hands and knees. He stopped at the end of this shelf and stood up. Vipond was just below him. Trenglove could stand tall here as in front of him was another open chunk that was cut like a square at an almost forty-five degree angle to the passageway that sloped downwards from where he stood.

Trenglove took his lantern and held it up high. He could reach inside almost all of this additional excavated end of the passageway, but there was nothing there. He held his lantern up and moved it from side to side. Nothing seemed to give any hope that there was a secret passageway from this angle. Worse than that, if there was, he wasn't sure how they would get into it. The wall was smooth and gave not hint of any cracks or fissures. Trenglove cursed under his breath.

"Nothing there?" asked Vipond.

Trenglove didn't look at him.

"Bloody hell, where can it be?" he asked to no one in particular.

"Why don't we head down into the burial chamber and see if there aren't any clues in there?"

"Very well."

Trenglove took his lantern and bowed down as he squeezed past Vipond and headed back down towards the antechamber. They walked the rest of the way in silence. Inside the antechamber, Trenglove led them down a narrow corridor that was in the center of the chamber and led quickly to a horizontal hallway off the right of which was a smaller room, that Walker had called the cellar.

Trenglove walked right past and on into the main burial chamber which was the largest chamber of all. It was about twenty feet long by eight feet wide and reached ten feet high. Trenglove stood and stretched out his hands. The room was empty except for a small platform upon which, it was said, held the sarcophagus that Richard Vyse had supposedly found, which later sank in the Mediterranean.

Trenglove paced up and down, stopping every few feet to touch the wall and run his fingertips up and down it. He moved his lantern around and looked up at the ceiling. The walls and ceiling were of pink granite, smooth as cottage cheese, and slight mottled like it. But there was no indication of secret doors to secret chambers.

Vipond helped in the search, and spent a great deal of time kneeling and touching the granite platform. He felt for any telltale signs of cracks or openings. It was against the long side of the wall, but nothing seemed to indicate a secret passageway at all.

"What did Walker say about where this secret passageway would be?" asked Vipond.

"Something about under the sleeping pharaoh the guards stood watch. Something like that," said Trenglove.

"That's it," said Vipond, "I think I've got it. This must be where the treasure lies."

"Where?" asked Trenglove, looking at him with an arched eyebrow.

"Here, under here," said Vipond, stamping his foot upon the granite platform. "This is where the sarcophagus of the pharaoh was, was it not?"

Trenglove nodded.

"Apparently."

"Well, help me slide this granite down there. Perhaps the secret passageway to the chamber is just under here."

Trenglove smiled and walked over to where Vipond was.

"Sometimes I'm glad I brought you along, Art," he said.

At the far end of this burial chamber, away from the entrance they had come from, was a small platform that took up the width of the chamber. It was a few feet from the platform that had previously held the sarcophagus.

Trenglove and Vipond braced their feet against this end platform and with both their hands they pushed against the platform they were trying to move. It didn't budge.

"All right," said Trenglove, "let's be smart about this. Let's try and push it on three. I'll count. One, two, three."

They both dug in and pushed with all their might for several seconds. The platform wouldn't budge.

"Maybe it's just too heavy," offered Vipond.

"Maybe you just weren't correct," suggested Trenglove, snarkily.

Vipond tried to push again, but Trenglove didn't help him.

"Okay smart aleck, you tell me where this bloody chamber is then," said Vipond, also now losing his cool.

Trenglove looked around the room once more. He knew he had checked out every last nook and cranny. There was nothing there. What had he overlooked? What had he missed?

"The last place we haven't looked is in the cellar," said Trenglove. "I want us to take a look in there."

Trenglove strode out of the burial chamber and back into the passageway and then he turned left into the cellar. Vipond took off after him. It was one of the smaller rooms. It appeared to be a little over half the length of the burial chamber and a little over half the width. There were six niches cut into this cellar, and they were not quite wide enough to fit a man without having to turn slightly. Four niches ran equally spaced along the length and two niches were equally spaced at the far end.

"We've already looked in here," said Vipond.

He didn't like the darkness and the small spaces inside the chambers and passageways. He wasn't exactly claustrophobic, but he was finding that the more often he went into the bowels of the pyramid, the more he realized how much he preferred the outdoors. The somewhat dank and musty smell was not something that he found particularly pleasing either.

"I know we've looked in here already," said Trenglove, "but that was with the annoying, nosy, and always in your way Sanehet. I want to look without any distractions... including you."

Vipond stood, hunched over at the entrance to the cellar while Trenglove, also hunched over, took his time peering into each niche and gently caressing the walls as if he were somewhere private with a beautiful woman. He was looking for any telltale signs that might offer a clue as to something hidden just behind the walls. He found none. He cursed and slapped his hand against the inside of one of the far niches.

Trenglove walked back towards Vipond, still hunched over, holding his lantern in his hand fully extended down towards the side of his knee. It made him look very much like Quasimodo. He brushed past Vipond rudely.

"Maybe you were right," he sneered, "maybe Walker did lie to me."

Vipond followed Trenglove out of the cellar and along the hallway and then up the corridor back into the antechamber. Without stopping, Trenglove continued down the hallway towards the paneled chamber, his lantern swaying up and down by his side, causing his shadow to leap past him and then retreat behind him like an annoying schoolboy. Vipond kept up.

Trenglove entered the paneled chamber and exited it just as quickly as he entered. He walked as fast as he could, while hunched over, up the remaining incline of the last passageway until he made it out onto the platform right in front of the pyramid. He clambered down the stairs, and as he got to the ground he kicked at the sand and cursed again. He wanted to throw his lantern up against the damned pyramid and burn it to the ground. He knew it wouldn't only be a waste of a lantern but foolish as well. Stone didn't burn, but he really wanted it to.

Vipond came down the stairs and stood off to the side. If he knew one thing, it was to let Trenglove blow off some steam before suggesting any sort of alternatives.

"I'll kill him, I swear I'll kill him for lying to me," spat Trenglove.

Vipond knew exactly who he was talking about. He wouldn't mind killing the lying bastard himself, though he realized they were taking a gamble. Vipond walked back towards the camels which were on the northeast side of the pyramid. He walked past them, lost in thought and then turned towards the south. There was nothing else out there except for some crumbling pyramids. Three small ones. The tallest one perhaps half the height of the Pyramid of Menkaure. The distance between the three small pyramids was only seventy feet or so.

Vipond walked back towards the camels and looked out over the mortuary temple, a scrabble of crumbled walls and stones, long ago pilfered, and much of its beauty now lost to antiquity. He turned his attention to Trenglove who took one last kick at the sand before starting to walk back towards the camels with his head bowed.

Trenglove didn't say anything to his companion, he just climbed the camel and brought the beast up from kneeling. He looked down at Vipond with disappointment and anger all over his face like a mask of pain.

"All right," he said, his voice soft and somber as if he were sharing a secret, "I'll admit it. You were right and I was wrong. Walker was a liar and a scoundrel. I guess there is no secret chamber here. So let's get going. We're finished."

Trenglove stared down at the Egyptian sand. He had liked this place up until now. It had carried his dreams in the mirages and the hot baked sand. Now like a ghost it had whisked away his hopes and dreams and ground them into nothing against the granite of the pyramids. He pulled out a fresh white handkerchief and mopped his brow. Vipond looked up at him from his own camel and shook his head sadly. He had never known Trenglove to be a quitter, let alone a doubter. That was his job. But here he was, about to turn his back on millions.

"What are you waiting for, I said we're leaving," said Trenglove, his voice getting a littler angrier.

"I'm disappointed. I am really, and truly, very disappointed in you, Howard."

That caught Trenglove off guard. He pulled his head back and frowned at Vipond.

"You of all people. I never would have thought that you'd give up so easily."

"Now listen here," said Trenglove. "We've been over the chambers and passageways with a fine toothed comb and we've come up empty. You've seen it yourself. There is nothing inside that bloody pyramid. What are we supposed to do? Really, Art, there is nothing there. If there was, then why the hell didn't you say anything when we were inside."

Trenglove was exasperated. He looked down at Vipond and shook his head.

"There's nothing there, Art. Nothing. It's time we faced the truth of the matter, which you've been trying to tell me for days now."

"I agree, Howard. There is nothing inside the Menkaure's pyramid. You're right. If there was a secret chamber we would have found it. I agree with you, there is nothing to be found. At least not by the north entrance."

Vipond nodded towards the entrance they had just come out of.

"But what if there is another way into the pyramid?"

"There isn't another entrance to the pyramid. Everybody knows that."

"I know," said Vipond, walking up closer to Trenglove, and put his hand up on the rump of the camel. "But I've been thinking about something you said Walker told you."

"And what's that?"

Vipond had piqued Trenglove's curiosity now. Trenglove was a man whose curiosity was easily piqued and that's mostly how he had found himself on these wild adventures.

"You told me that Walker had said something about the entrance being in the bigger of the three pyramids."

"Yes, but we've already discussed this, the Pyramid of Menkaure is the smaller of them," said Trenglove.

"Right," said Vipond nodding, "but he also mentioned the entrance being on the south."

"He was confused. The Pyramid of Menkaure is the southernmost pyramid, that's probably what he meant. He said it was the biggest, and it's not. As you rightly pointed out, it was over fifty years ago when he was here last. The first and last time I might point out."

"But he wouldn't let you write any of this down would he?" asked Vipond.

"No, he didn't want the information getting into the wrong hands."

"That's a pity, because we both know how unreliable your memory is."

"Yes, well, I wasn't sure I believed him at the time until I did my own research."

"I'm not blaming you," said Vipond, "I'm just saying, maybe what you remember him saying, which is likely not all of it, is actually accurate."

"And how do you come to that conclusion?" asked Trenglove.

"Get off your camel. I want to show you something."

Trenglove brought the camel to kneeling and climbed off it. He followed Vipond who started walking towards the northeast corner of the pyramid where he stopped and faced southwest.

"All right," said Trenglove, when he was standing next to Vipond. "I don't see anything. This place is mostly barren."

"You're looking too far away," said Vipond.

He pointed his finger at the closest pyramid of the three that ran from west to east, the largest of them a true pyramid, the other two were terraced pyramids.

"The biggest of the three pyramids on the south side of the Pyramid of Menkaure."

Trenglove followed Vipond's hand pointing at the closest true pyramid. It was centered in the middle of the Pyramid of Menkaure.

"By Jove, Art, I think you're right. The biggest of the three pyramids."

"Maybe we've been looking at the wrong place all this time," said Vipond.

Trenglove nodded his head thoughtfully.

"Perhaps your enthusiasm is contagious, Howard, but what if, just maybe, there's a secret passageway from that pyramid to Menkaure's?"

Trenglove put his index finger and thumb of his right hand around his chin and thought for a moment. Then he pulled out his pocket watch. He adjusted it until he could read the dial in the moonlight.

"It's just gone half past midnight," he said. "At four we have to meet our carriage if we have any hope of getting anything to the boat on time."

Vipond nodded.

"Then we best go exploring," he said.

"Right," said Trenglove. "You grab a spade and rope and I'll grab a pickaxe and rope, just in case."

The two of them started off back towards the camels and found the gear in the boxes that they needed. They checked the fuel in their lanterns and found that they had more than enough until morning, though they'd be long gone by then.

"We've never been inside this pyramid," said Trenglove, "we'll be learning as we go."

Vipond nodded. As they rounded the corner of the Pyramid of Menkaure Vipond noticed an entrance on the north side of the closest third pyramid, just a foot or two above ground level. Trenglove nodded.

"If I recall correctly, some had thought that this is the pyramid of Khamerernebty, Menkaure's wife."

Vipond nodded.

"Apparently. But perhaps it was just a myth. Perhaps this pyramid is actually nothing more than a secret passageway for accessing the riches that we'll find in the Pyramid of Menkaure."

"Time will tell," said Trenglove. "We'll find out soon enough."

Trenglove climbed up into entrance way of this pyramid. It was of a similar height but tighter on the width. Only one man could fit in at a time. Vipond climbed up behind him. The tightness of this passageway made Vipond even more uncomfortable than he had been before.

The corridor dipped downwards at a similar angle as the entrance passageway inside Menkaure's pyramid had dipped downwards. Eventually after about fifty feet they came into a burial chamber. It had been ransacked. There was nothing in it except for broken pieces of ceramic, some ratty matting and burned and charred wood. It was small and square with about eight foot long lengths. The height was about six feet, not quite enough for Trenglove to stand fully erect inside it.

The two of them surveyed the area for a while, traveling up and down each side. There was no indication of secret doorways or passageways, though at the far end, it appeared as if the wall there was made of a separate large stone piece. Trenglove took his pickaxe off his back and tapped at the stone wall. It sounded thick, there was no sense that it was hollow on the other side. He turned to look at Vipond.

"This appears to be the only suggestion that there might be something on the other side."

Vipond came up and had a look at the corners where the far wall joined the side walls. He nodded.

"It's definitely a separate wall," he said. "Though the workmanship is incredible. You can't fit a finger between the joints."

"But if it is wall, how the hell do we get through it. It sounds incredibly thick. You'd need dynamite just to make a dent in it."

"And that would bring the whole pyramid down around you."

Trenglove nodded. He held his lantern up and around. The ceiling was right above him, and he still had to duck his head down slightly in order not to bump his head.

There was a smaller and thinner granite platform that might have held another sarcophagus on it at one time that was on the right wall as you entered the chamber.

"Perhaps we can move that slab of stone. Maybe the way past that wall is under it," offered Vipond.

"Worth a try," said Trenglove, "I see no other options."

They both moved round to the entrance side and sat down. Vipond removed the spade from his back and sat it next to the pickaxe. There was about two feet between the far wall and the platform slab. The slab itself was about four feet long, leaving two feet on the far end for it to move if indeed it could move.

Trenglove and Vipond braced their backs against the wall and put the heels of their feet against the slab.

"On my count," said Trenglove. "On three. One, two, three."

They both pushed with all their strength and the slab moved more easily than they thought it would. After about a foot, the slab stopped. They tried again to push as hard as they could, but it wouldn't budge. Vipond got up and walked around the other side of the slab and noticed that it was caught by the bedrock that had been carved up into a wedge to stop the slab from moving further.

"We won't be able to push it further," he said. "Looks like the bedrock here has been cut in a manner to act as a stop for the slab."

Trenglove looked at his side, and there was a similar stop carved out of the granite.

"Same here," he said. "But this is hardly enough space for us to fit through."

Vipond came over and they held their lanterns so that they could see into the small one foot opening, which was two feet wide. Peering inside, it looked to be no deeper than two feet. But there was what appeared to be a granite cog with two small levers attached to it.

"You put your feet on that one," said Trenglove, "and I'll put my feet on this one and let's see what it'll do."

It was as good an idea as any, so Vipond got back down and they braced themselves against the wall again and pushed as hard as they could on the levers. They moved ever so slowly away from them. It took incredible strength to push these levers each inch. After a few minutes they had to take a break.

"Well, at least they're moving," said Vipond, breathing heavily as a trickle of sweat rolled down his cheek. He wiped it away with this shirt sleeve.

"Yes, but nothing's bloody well happening yet."

"Maybe we have to push it the whole way before anything happens."

Trenglove grunted.

"Then let's get it over and done with to see if we're going home into the pyramid," he said.

They got repositioned and pushed hard against the levers again. At the very last moment, when they felt they were out of breath, as sweat trickled down the sides of their faces, and their legs were about to give out, shaking from the exertion, the levers clicked into their last place.

Trenglove and Vipond leaned back against the wall, their chests heaving with the exertion. Trenglove reached into his front pocket and took out his handkerchief. He wiped his face, and then looked over at Vipond.

"Well," he said, trying to get a handle on his breath. "That was for naught."

And just as he said it, a loud sound, stone scraping upon stone, brought their attention to the far wall which began to move. It only took several seconds and then it stopped again. Trenglove and Vipond watched, slack jawed. The far wall had moved, showing an opening of no more than two feet that seemed to lead into another passageway.

Trenglove got up and Vipond followed him. He picked up his lantern and went over to the far wall.

"Good grief man, it seems that Walker might have been right after all."

Trenglove put his hand through the opening and looked down the rest of the passageway.

"What can you see?" asked Vipond.

"A short passageway, it's tight, like the first one we came through, and it appears to jog right about six feet up."

Vipond slapped his friend on the back, and laughed out loud.

"We might yet find those riches after all," he said.

Trenglove walked into the hallway, blading his body slightly to get through the opening.

"What about the tools?" shouted Vipond after him.

"I want to find the chamber first, then we can determine what tools we need. Leave them there and follow me."

Vipond went back and picked up his lantern and followed Trenglove down the narrow hallway that continued on a decline of about twenty-five degrees.

Vipond looked back at the wall that had moved and he noticed that it seemed to be circular, riding in a track of some sort. He didn't know how they did it, and he didn't particularly care, just so long as it stayed open for their return. Vipond turned back, and as he did he saw Trenglove, hunched over, disappeared right, which would have him heading west. This hallway continued downward at the same angle of decline.

"We've got to be underground by now, surely," said Vipond.

"I'd say we're likely fifteen feet, if not more underground at this point," came back the answer from Trenglove.

That didn't bolster Vipond's confidence. The only thing that kept him going was the imagery of riches beyond his wildest imagination. Trenglove disappeared right again, now heading north, and as Vipond came round the corner it still headed downward at a steady angle.

After about fifteen feet it leveled out horizontally.

"How deep do you think we are now?" asked Vipond, the telltale sign of nervousness hollowing out his voice.

"What do you care? The deeper we are the more secure we are. Probably at least twenty feet though."

They carried on hunched over along this level and small passageway for what must have been a hundred and thirty feet or so, when the passage they were in took a left at about a forty-five degree angle, heading northwest. It was at this point that the passage started at an incline of about twenty-five degrees.

"Ha!" exclaimed Trenglove, "we must be inside the Pyramid of Menkaure now."

"How can you be so sure?" asked Vipond, hopefully.

"I'm not, but I've been counting our steps and we must have walked over a hundred feet, maybe as much as a hundred and fifty, that would put us well within the pyramid. Additionally, why would this passageway start angling up if it weren't inside Menkaure's pyramid?"

"Yes, I suppose you're right," mumbled Vipond.

The air was dank and musty in here, with a smell of moss and rotting wood and mulch, which seemed odd as they were surrounded by stone. They continued up this incline for about a hundred and thirty feet when it turned at a ninety degree angle to the right heading northeast. The angle remained the same. They continued on in silence for another fifty feet before another right ninety degree turn had them heading southwest at the same constant incline.

"I'm getting dizzy," said Vipond, trying to make light of what was making him nervous. They had to be well into the Pyramid of Menkaure by now, and well above ground.

They continued in this direction for seventy-five feet when the passage jogged right at ninety degrees, heading northwest for about thirty feet and then it jogged right one last time, keeping the incline consistent for the last fifty feet where it opened up into a large chamber that had to be fifteen feet by ten feet with eight feet ceilings.

The chamber was ornate with brightly colored paintings and Egyptian hieroglyphs all over the wall. A large sarcophagus lay lengthwise to Trenglove's left as he stepped into the chamber. Two granite sculptures stood on either side of the sarcophagus in the image of Horus, and they carried spears. Vipond smiled at Trenglove.

"I think this is what Walker meant when he mentioned two guards that would stand by the sarcophagus. The hidden chamber must be under him," said Vipond, pointing at the sarcophagus.

"Agreed," said Trenglove, still surveying the chamber.

The chamber held wooden shelves at the opposite end from where the sarcophagus was, and upon these shelves were everyday items such as combs, tools, bowls and now dried food. The bowls were simple and made of copper or wood. There was nothing of great value in this chamber.

"All right. You see if you can't dislodge that guard and I'll push this one out the way," said Trenglove.

Vipond walked around to the far side of the sarcophagus and pushed on the Horus sculpture. It didn't take immense strength to topple it over, and it crashed down onto then stone floor raising dust and making a loud thundering sound. One of the arms broke off, the one carrying the spear and the beak broke off as well.

"That was loud," said Vipond somewhat guiltily.

"I suppose that's one way of doing it," said Trenglove struggling to wobble and move his Horus out of the way. He gave up and just push it over as Vipond had done. It picked up more dust and made a great crash. Trenglove and Vipond waved their hands in front of their faces to dissipate the dust. They both coughed, the air inside wasn't thick and the dust wasn't helping them breathe.

Trenglove's Horus broke both his arms and beak as he lay there looking up at Trenglove admonishingly.

"Let's try pushing this coffin off the platform from your side," said Trenglove.

He walked around to where Vipond was standing.

"I think the correct term is sarcophagus," offered Vipond.

"I don't care about the correct term, I want at the gold and jewels."

They stood up onto the platform and pushed, but the sarcophagus just wouldn't budge. They tried a few more times before giving up.

The dust had settled and Vipond hung his head in defeat. He noticed something odd. There were tracks on each side of the sarcophagus that ran for a few feet towards the end of the platform. It looked as though the sarcophagus might have been put in place on rollers.

"I think we're pushing from the wrong end," he said to Trenglove. "Look at his tracks, I bet we're supposed to push from your end."

Trenglove slapped his friend on the shoulder.

"Good heavens you're right again, Art," he said. "Once again, I am delighted to have you along."

"Then perhaps we can renegotiate my percentage. I'll keep fifty percent and you can pay Walker out of our fifty percent."

Vipond grinned at him.

"I didn't say I was that delighted."

They moved round to what was the head's end of the sarcophagus and started pushing. For a surprisingly heavy granite sarcophagus it moved easily. It was indeed on some sort of rolling mechanism. They pushed it slowly but steadily as far as they could. It came to a stop about four feet from where they had started.

Below them was a four foot by three foot wide opening that held a staircase built out of granite that went down about twenty feet. Trenglove went over and picked up his lantern and brought it back. He laid down by the opening and dangled his arm into the opening with the lantern.

"By God, Art, we've found it!" he exclaimed.

The room below was full of gold vessels, chalices, bowls and all sorts of artifacts and sculptures. The gold shimmered and jewels twinkled red and green from the lantern light. Leith Walker had not lied. There was enough jewelry and gold in that room to make all three of them millionaires many times over.

Four

Frances and Florence took the elevator down to the main floor. They were both dressed simply but elegantly. They each had on a long summer dress with patterned flowers. Frances' flowers were yellow and Florence's were pink. The large dining room at The Palace Hotel was across the large foyer from the reception desk. It was just about six in the evening when Frances and Florence stood by the maître d'hôtel's desk, and waited for him to return from showing other guests to their tables.

The maître d' returned with quick and short steps and smiled at them with a closed mouth. He had over his left forearm a white cloth napkin, and he was dressed in a black tuxedo. His thinning black hair was combed backwards across his head with the help of pomade. He wore a bushy but well manicured black mustache. His skin was much paler than many other Egyptians, and in fact he might have been mistaken for a European under other circumstances.

"Welcome, ladies," he said, as if they were his first and only guests. "I am Paser and I will be your maître d' for the evening. If you need anything at all, please do not hesitate to call upon me. Just the two of you?"

Frances nodded.

"Please follow me," said Paser, as he swept the dining room with his right arm before walking towards the far side of the room. At a set of large bay windows he stopped behind the far chair of what was a two chair setting. Paser pulled the chair out and helped slide it in as Frances sat down. With perfect timing, he managed to get behind the opposite chair just as Florence was sitting down. He then stood in front of the table between the two of them.

"Ammon will be your waiter for this evening. Our special tonight is poached haddock in a lemon and white wine sauce accompanied by garlic buttered mashed potatoes and pan seared asparagus."

"Sounds wonderful," said Frances.

Florence nodded, and Paser bowed and then left just as quickly as he had after seating the couple before them. Frances had a wonderful view of the entire dining room. She surveyed the room and found it mostly empty.

In the middle of the room sat the larger couple she had seen earlier in the day from the boat. A couple of tables from them and closer to Frances and Florence were the military man and his companion. They were not talking to one another at the moment, but the larger couple were in animated but hushed conversation.

There was a line of people starting to gather by the entrance to the dining room. Paser was not perturbed by this. He had come to intimately know the ebb and flow of customers as they came for lunch and dinner throughout the week. It would be busy for him until about six thirty at which time the torrent, if you could even call it that, of customers would trickle to stragglers.

Paser had worked for this hotel for twenty-five years, and he took pride in his position as maître d'. He knew everything about service and dining. He had started after all as the dishwasher and worked his way up through busboy, waiter, head waiter and then finally to maître d', the highest honor, and the position he had held for five years now.

Paser was extremely slow to anger and anxiety. Serving had been his passion, and he had come to excel at it with an almost military perfection.

Frances watched him show a lone gentleman to his seat at a table just behind Florence. He was a tall, and slender man with a gaunt face that was clean shaven. He wore a brown suit with a matching fedora, which he took off and placed in the chair opposite. He faced Frances but took no interest in her. He appeared to be in his early sixties though the heavy bruised bags under his eyes made him look much older.

Frances watched him as he unfolded his napkin and placed it in his lap. He steepled his fingers in front of him and rested his chin on top of them. He closed his eyes and drifted off into deep thought. Out of the corner of her eye, Frances noticed movement and looked over to find a waiter standing at the edge of the table dressed in black pants and a black shirt with a white apron around his waist. He was smiling broadly at her.

"Good evening, ladies," he said, "my name is Ammon and I'll be your waiter for this evening."

Ammon handed them each a leather-bound menu.

"Good evening, Ammon," said Frances.

Ammon smiled at her and then turned and smiled at Florence as she greeted him by his first name.

"I'm sure Paser told you about our special this evening?" he asked.

Frances and Florence nodded.

"It is exceptionally good. If you can't decide on anything else, I don't believe you'll go wrong with the haddock."

Ammon looked at them for a moment. He was a slim man of average height with black shiny hair that was parted on the left. It was kept short around his dark brown face and his eyebrows met like two black worms kissing at the bridge of his nose. His face made him look younger than his mid-thirties, primarily because it was fatter than the rest of him. He had a large mole in the middle of his left cheek.

"While the two of you are deciding on dinner, may I get any drinks for you?"

"I think I might like to try the Pinot Grigio," said Frances.

"An excellent choice," answered Ammon, beaming at her.

"In that case," said Florence, "I'll have a glass too."

"Why don't we make it a half liter then," said Frances, looking at her friend. Florence nodded, and Frances looked up at Ammon and nodded at him.

"A half liter of Pinot Grigio then," replied Ammon, and with that he walked off.

The restaurant was starting to fill up slowly but steadily. Paser was getting his exercise in his clipped and regimented walk.

Another couple was seated behind the tall man with the fedora. The older woman looked like she could be the grandmother of the younger one. There was at least thirty, but perhaps even forty or more years between them. Her place was set for a left handed person. The older woman had a severe face etched with more lines and wrinkles than one would expect. Her lips were razor thin and her eyes seemed constantly wet as if they were floating in a puddle. Her hair was dyed poorly and tinted red.

The young woman didn't look at the older woman much except to address her directly, and that wasn't often. They spoke in soft whispers when they spoke at all which wasn't often. The older woman kept looking around as if she was expecting company but it never came.

The younger woman was a waif, she was slim and plain featured and wore clothing more suited for someone of her grandmother's age. Her hair was mousy brown and straight and fell around her face in a pageboy. She was almost a younger carbon copy of the older woman. She had the same thin lips and wet eyes. Frances didn't pay much attention to the two of them, they had a way of merging into the background. Quite unremarkable and unnoticeable.

She did notice the larger man who had previously sat down with the larger woman get up and come over to the young woman and her grandmother. He nodded at them and apologized for intruding.

"I hope you won't mind if I say that you remind me of someone," said the large man to the older woman. She didn't smile at him, but held his gaze.

"You look like someone I used to know."

"What's your name?" asked the grandmother.

"Albert, Albert Warrant."

The grandmother shook her head.

"Sorry," she said, "but that doesn't ring a bell."

"What's your name if you don't mind me being so forward?"

"Really," said the grandmother, "that is quite rude of you, I don't know you at all."

"I do apologize," he said and got ready to turn around.

"It's Mrs. Orpha Bendled," she said and offered him her hand with a small smile. He shook her hand, and bowed at the both of them.

"Sorry again for intruding. I must be mistaken," he said.

"That's quite all right," said Orpha, and the large man named Albert returned to his table and his dinner companion.

"The restaurant is getting quite busy," said Frances.

"Is it?" said Florence, turning to look around. "So it is, and I think we have the best seat in the house."

Florence turned back around to look at her friend, and then she looked outside through the windows of the dining room.

There was a modest patio in front with some tables and chairs and umbrellas, but for some reason it was not being used tonight. Frances kept an eye on Paser, he was intriguing to her. He was very particular and regimented in everything he did. He had just finished showing another single gentleman to his table at the opposite diagonal end to where Frances and Florence sat. He was of average height with black wavy hair and clean shaven. He seemed quite pleasant, he smiled easily and showed straight white teeth. He had a strong jaw and good looks. He wore blue pants and pale blue shirt with the sleeves rolled up just below the elbows. His pants were held up by dark blue suspenders. Frances could almost hear him when he spoke, his voice was loud and carried well.

Another man who had been seated a few minutes before this handsome man looked over at him with clear revulsion on his face. He was tall and slender but with a small pregnant belly. He had the ashen face of a smoker and deep lines from his nose to the corners of his mouth that turned his mouth down. His nose was large and beaked and he had a high forehead with a mess of curly brown hair. He took a long white cigarette out of a gold cigarette case and lit it with a matching gold lighter. He looked over at the handsome man with contempt, but the handsome man was studying the menu and didn't notice. He blew smoke absentmindedly out through his nose and then placed the cigarette in the ashtray and with great exaggeration he put the napkin on his lap. He then looked towards window where the man with the fedora sat. He nodded at the other man, but Frances didn't see if the man with the fedora nodded back.

Ammon came by with two glasses and the carafe of wine. He poured some for Lady Marmalade which she swirled, sniffed and tasted. It was to her liking so Ammon poured them each a half glass. Frances raised her glass to her friend.

"To good friends, good food, good wine and shared joys," she said.

Florence raised her glass and they clinked together.

"Thank you Fran, this is such a treat. To us, may we continue to enjoy each other's company for years to come."

"Cheers," said Frances, and they both sipped the wine from their glasses.

"Hmm, that is good. Perfect choice," said Florence.

"What do you think you'll have to eat?" asked Frances.

Florence looked down at the menu which contained a variety of meats including duck, chicken, seafood and beef.

"I like the sounds of the haddock Paser mentioned. I think I'll stick with that," she said.

Frances nodded.

"Me too."

Ammon returned after delivering drinks to some other patrons.

"Do you know what you'd like?" he asked, looking at Frances.

"I think I'll go with the haddock that you and Paser mentioned."

Ammon smiled at her and wrote her order down on his pad of paper with his short pencil.

"And for you?"

He looked at Florence.

"The same. The haddock sounds wonderful," said Florence.

Ammon smiled at her.

"You won't be disappointed," he said.

After he had made another mark on his pad, he picked up the menus and left them.

"So," said Frances, "tomorrow we have an early start at eight in the morning. Thankfully the bus leaves right outside our hotel so we don't have far to go."

"How long do you estimate the bus ride will be to Cairo?"

"I think the brochure suggested it would be about three hours. We have lunch in Cairo at around eleven thirty if I recall, and then at one o'clock we leave by bus again for the pyramids."

"Sounds marvelous," said Florence. "I can't wait. Did I tell you that I had just recently bought an Argus camera so that I can take some pictures of this trip to refer back to?"

Frances shook her head.

"Oh yes, and I think I really like it. It seems quite simple to use. I've already taken a few pictures of my garden and flowers. I can't wait to see how they turn out."

"Sounds wonderful. You must show it to me when we get back up to the room."

Florence nodded.

"You won't believe how small it is," she said. "Technology nowadays is simply astounding. It's only the size of a small brick if you can believe it."

"You don't say," said Frances. "Was it expensive?"

"Not too bad. A bit of a splurge but I think it will be well worth it."

"I'd love to take a look at the pictures once you've had them processed. Perhaps I'll come up to Puddle's End for Christmas. Do you think you'll have them done by then?"

"Oh, I should certainly hope so. I'd love to have you round for Christmas, if Declan wouldn't mind?"

Frances smiled at her friend.

"No, I don't think he'd mind at all. I think he and Everard wouldn't mind some time alone for a change, instead of having me hovering around them every moment of every day."

Frances laughed out loud, as did Florence.

"Well, then that's what we'll do," said Florence.

"Lovely. I hope you brought enough film then."

"I believe so. I have three rolls with me."

"That should be enough. One hundred and eight pictures divide by the four weeks we're here is what? You were better at mathematics than I was," said Frances.

Florence looked off and up towards the ceiling as she tried to do the division.

"Um, that's twenty-seven pictures per week, or... just under four per day. That doesn't seem like very much on a daily basis does it?"

"Oh, I don't know, Flo. It should be enough, we'll just have to be choosy. Though I'm sure there will be days when not many pictures are needed."

Florence nodded, but inside she was wondering if she should have brought an extra roll or two. Perhaps one roll per week would have been better, but there was nothing she could do about it now. As Frances said, she'd have to be choosy.

"Now I don't want you pouting the whole trip through Egypt, Mahulda," said the older, severe looking woman.

She was looking sternly at the young woman in front of her. Mahulda looked up tentatively at her.

"But I don't think it's a good idea, what we're doing here," she answered.

"We can talk about that later," said the older woman, "we are here to have a good time and to take a look around Egypt and the pyramids. That's the end of it."

The young woman sighed and looked out the window.

"Listen, young lady," said the older woman tersely, "if you really want us to get into trouble then you should continue to look and behave upset. Honestly, my dear, we are on a holiday and you should act the part. We don't need to draw any further suspicion to ourselves now do we?"

Mahulda looked at the older woman.

"I suppose you're right grandmother, but this whole thing just makes me a little nervous."

"I know it does, but nerves will not help us now. We need to carry on with the rest of the trip, and you'll see, it will all work out in the end."

Mahulda nodded, and they stopped talking for a while. Florence noticed that Frances seemed a bit distracted.

"What is it?" she asked.

Frances looked away from the older woman and her granddaughter and smiled at Florence.

"Sorry, Flo," she said. "I can't help but to be curious about all the other guests here. It appears that young woman behind you is here with her grandmother. I can't help but to wonder why she isn't here with her parents or husband or fiancé."

"Oh dear, Fran, you aren't suspecting them of something are you?"

Frances chuckled and shook her head.

"No, I'm just curious that's all. I wonder what brings them here. Much like everyone else. Especially the three single men who seem to be eating alone."

"Maybe they're waiting for their wives."

Frances shook her head.

"No, I don't think so. They've all ordered. I'd think they'd rather wait for their wives if they weren't eating alone."

"Then perhaps they just happen to be businessmen here on business."

Frances nodded.

"I think that's probably it."

"Well, I imagine some of them who are here might be going to Cairo tomorrow and you can ask them then, why they were eating alone or what their reason for being here is."

Florence grinned at Frances. Frances slapped her playfully on the wrist.

"You're silly, Flo, I'm just being curious that's all. People interest me."

"Because you think they're up to something nefarious," teased Florence.

Frances chuckled again.

"You know me too well. No, that's not what I'm always thinking. But having helped with dozens of murder cases, I guess I've just become more observant and curious about people and their motives."

"Can't their motives just be something as simple as being in Alexandria for a holiday."

"Yes, they can, Flo, yes they can."

Ammon came by and placed a white plate in front of both Frances and Florence. The Haddock was fresh and steaming and the lemon wafted to their noses and incited their gastric juices. The mashed potatoes smelled of garlic and warmth and the asparagus was a shockingly bright green. Ammon took the carafe and refilled their wine glasses, emptying the carafe in the process.

"Please enjoy your meal," he said. "Is their anything else I can get for you?"

There was nothing else they needed, so Ammon left, carrying the empty carafe with him. He and the other waiters were in and out of the kitchen carrying plates of food for the diners. The dining room was about two thirds full. Frances took the pepper and salt shakers and dusted her food with them. Florence did the same. She took a bite of the haddock.

"Absolutely delicious," she said.

"Should be," said Frances, "I think I heard that it's fresh every day."

They ate in silence for a while, each to their own meal, enjoying the full and subtle flavors. Taking a moment to have a sip of wine to help things down.

The gaunt man behind Florence received his steak. It was a large rare steak that was accompanied by a baked potato topped with sour cream and chives. There was also a clumping of green beans next to the potato. Frances watched as he pushed the potato and green beans to the far side of his plate, and cut into his steak. From what she could tell, it looked like the steak had a pepper sauce upon it.

Frances and Florence made quick work of their meal. The haddock had been deboned, but Florence still found one in it that she set aside. They both ate every last morsel on their plates. At the end of the meal Frances wiped her mouth with her napkin and placed it back on her lap.

"I can't believe I managed to eat it all," she said.

"Me too, though I must confess that I was quite famished by the time it arrived."

Frances nodded.

"I was too, actually."

Frances watched the gaunt man finish with this steak. He had eaten it all, except for the layer of fat on the outside of one end. Like a surgeon he had excised that part, and it lay limp on his plate like a piece of rubber. He delicately and carefully pulled free one of the green beans. He cut it in two and ate each piece cautiously, taking his time, as if it were the first time he had ever tried something like that.

He placed his knife and fork on the plate like kissing cousins and moved it away from him. Frances found him a very curious specimen. He had eaten all the meat and had eaten one green bean. A gesture that had appeared difficult to him. The potato he had not touched. He sipped from a glass of water that was in front of him. He had not ordered anything harder.

Ammon came by and took Frances' and Florence's plates. He asked how their meal had been and they answered with delight. He went over to the gaunt man and inquired if everything had been acceptable. Ammon looked quite disheartened seeing so much of the food still left behind.

"It was fine, thank you," said the gaunt man in a phlegmy voice. "I'll take a coffee with cream and sugar."

Frances could tell he was American by the accent she heard.

"What about a coffee?" she asked Florence.

"Why not," said Florence. "I've heard many exclaim how good Egyptian coffee is. I think we should try it."

Frances put up her hand just as Ammon was about to leave the gaunt man's table. She caught his eye.

"Yes, madam," Ammon asked.

"We'll take two coffees too, if you don't mind."

"Of course," he said, bowing slightly while still holding onto the three plates. "Cream and sugar for you?"

"Yes please," said Frances.

Ammon bowed himself away and headed towards the kitchen. Frances leaned in towards Florence.

"That American behind you," she said in a low voice, "only ate his meat, and nothing else."

"Really?"

Frances nodded her head.

"How do you know he's American?"

"From his accent, when he asked Ammon for coffee."

"I see. Perhaps that's how he keeps so slender then," said Florence half jokingly, "by not eating his vegetables."

Frances grinned at her.

"Or rather, that's how he keeps so unhealthy," she said. "He looks sick."

Frances looked up at him again. He had steepled his hands and was resting his chin on them with his eyes closed. He looked tired and sad, but perhaps that was just the natural expression to his face.

Ammon came back with a tray carrying three coffee mugs. He placed two down, one in front of Florence and one in front of Frances. He put a small jug of cream down and a bowl of sugar which contained a sugar spoon. On each of the saucers upon which their coffee mugs sat was a silver spoon.

"Thank you, Ammon," said Frances.

"Would you like to look at the dessert menu?" he asked.

Frances shook her head and looked over at Florence. Florence shook hers too.

"No thank you," she said.

Ammon went over to the gaunt man and placed cream, sugar and coffee in front of him. He asked if he wanted the dessert menu to which the gaunt man said no.

Mahulda and her grandmother were just finishing up when Ammon went to their table and picked up their plates. Ammon asked them if they'd like anything else. For a moment Frances thought that the young woman might have liked a dessert, but her grandmother was quick to dismiss Ammon and they got up from the table and left. Mahulda trailing the older woman by a few feet, her head hung low and dejected.

The gaunt man reached into his inside jacket pocket and took out a silver tin containing cigarettes. He pulled one out and put it in his mouth where it dangled precariously while he fished for his lighter, leaning back and stretching his left leg in front of him as his hand reached inside the trouser pocket.

He got what he needed and lit his cigarette. He inhaled deeply, and close his eyes. He blew the smoke out slowly through his nose, then he opened his eyes again and placed the lighter on top of his cigarette case. He poured cream into his coffee and two heaping spoonfuls of sugar. He stirred the coffee for a long time. He tasted it, and finding it not quite up to snuff, he added another quarter spoon of sugar. He stirred again for a long time and then tasted it. The beginnings of a smile curled his lips and he inhaled again on his cigarette, closing his eyes.

Florence had finished with the cream and sugar so Frances added both to her coffee. She took a sip. It was rich and dark and robust in flavor.

"For not being a regular coffee drinker," she said to Florence, "I must say that this is particularly good coffee."

Florence nodded.

"Full of flavor," she said. "I can see myself enjoying more cups of this while we're in Egypt."

Frances nodded and smiled.

"Strong enough to put hair on your chest, as Eric liked to say."

Florence laughed out loud.

"I really hope not."

"Metaphorically speaking," said Frances.

"Of course," said Florence.

Five

It was just before eight in the morning when Frances and Florence were seated in a soft cream colored couch in the main lobby of the hotel. The fountain was quietly spraying and splashing water some distance behind them. Florence was fiddling with her camera in its camera bag.

"May I have a look at it?" asked Frances.

"Certainly," said Florence.

She took the Argus out of its bag and put it on her lap. It had a leather strap attached to each side that went around your neck. On this occasion it sat relaxed on her legs.

"It's a rangefinder camera," said Florence.

"I see," said Frances, "I'm not sure what that means."

"Basically," said Florence, "as the salesman explained it to me, the rangefinder uses two images of what you're trying to take a picture of, and you use this dial to bring the two images into focus so that they become one. When they are one image, you know you're in focus so you can take the picture."

Florence pointed to the vertical dial on the front, upper right corner of the camera.

"Try it out," said Florence, handing the camera to Frances. "You look through the viewfinder there on the left and turn the dial until both images become one."

Frances took the camera and put it up to her right eye. She pointed the camera outside, through the large windows and across the street at an outdoor cafe that was filled with Egyptians. She turned the focusing dial until the images became sharp and singular.

"I do say, that is simply marvelous. One could get used to this. I might even pick it up myself as a hobby," she said.

Frances handed the camera back to Florence who put it away back in its bag.

"That is simply astonishing," she said. "The wonder of modern technology. I can't believe how small and light it is."

"I know, and it wasn't all that expensive either. Not like they were ten or more years ago."

"You simply must share those pictures with me when you get them developed."

"If they're any good, I will," said Florence.

"Nonsense, I'm sure they'll be terrific. Practice makes perfect."

Florence chuckled and they sat back into the couch. Outside, a large bus drove up to the main entrance. Frances looked around. She noticed that everyone she had noticed from dinner last night was present. She turned to Florence.

"Do you remember these people from last night?"

Florence looked around for a moment.

"I remember that older woman there with her granddaughter," said Florence nodding towards the couple who were seated in individual chairs with a table between them. They were both reading. The older woman was reading a magazine and Mahulda was reading a novel which Florence couldn't make out. "I also remember that tall, thin chap, who you mentioned only ate his meat last night and not his vegetables." Florence chuckled. "As for the others, I can't say I remember them distinctly."

Frances leaned in towards her friend.

"I remember them all. If not from dinner last night, then from the boat ride over here."

Florence smiled at her friend and nodded.

"You are exceptionally observant, Fran. I have no fear that we will get lost anywhere."

Frances smiled. The tall, thin man was smoking a cigarette and standing facing the windows and looking outside at the bus. The bus driver, a fat and older Egyptian man with thinning hair, climbed out of the bus. Following him was a tall, slim Caucasian man with a deep tan. He looked in his element. He wore khaki shorts and a matching khaki short sleeved shirt buttoned up to his neck except for the top button. He looked fresh and unperturbed by the morning warmth. He had a bushy mustache and rugged features with dark brown curly hair that was kept short. He strode into the hotel with an air of authority, leaving the driver standing by the rear of the bus, smoking the last of his cigarette.

The deeply tanned man walked up to the grouping of tourists. They were all gathered loosely towards the front of the lobby. This young chap, perhaps in his mid-thirties, stood and looked around at all of them for a long moment. As he did so, those on the outskirts started in towards him. He smiled broadly and already he seemed immensely likable.

"Ladies and gentleman," he said, in an English accent with a deep baritone warmth to it. "Welcome to Thoth Tours. I will be your guide for the next four weeks. My name is Perry Fowler. Your driver who will take us to Giza this morning and to the boat this evening is Darius."

Fowler pointed outside to the fat Egyptian standing at the rear of the bus. As he did so, the Egyptian flicked his spent cigarette towards a flower bed off to his right.

"Our estimated ETA to Giza and the pyramids will be between eleven thirty and twelve this afternoon. We will set up an outdoor area within walking distance of the pyramid where you'll have a chance for light repast while I share some interesting tidbits with you about ancient Egypt, the Pharaohs, the pyramids and the mythology surrounding them."

Fowler looked around and grinned at them each in turn. Frances couldn't help but smile back at him. His warmth and enthusiasm was infectious.

"All right," he continued. "I'll come around and take a look at your tickets, and then you can take your bags out to the bus where Darius will pack them away for you. If you need help with your baggage, please let me know when I come to you, and I'll help you with them."

Fowler walked up to the tall thin man who had by now put out his cigarette in a waist tall ashtray. Despite the gaunt man's lack of friendliness, Fowler still offered him his hand and shook it vigorously. He smiled at him broadly.

"Mr. Samuel Newton," said Fowler, "welcome to Thoth Tours and to Egypt. Do you have any baggage?"

Newton pointed to one medium sized suitcase that was off to one side. On top of it was his brown fedora.

"Very well, please make your way to the bus where Darius will help you with it. We are delighted to have you with us."

Newton didn't say anything. After Fowler had moved on, he rubbed his face and squashed the heels of his hands into his eyes. He took them away and blinked tightly. Then he picked up his suitcase and with long strides, and without looking at anyone he made his way outside.

Fowler made his way to the next couple who were closest to him. Frances remembered these two from the boat the day before. He looked military and very crisp in his uniform. Today however, he was dressed in khaki pants and a cream colored shirt.

"Lady Abigail Pompress and Captain Timothy Wainscott, a very warm welcome to both of you," said Fowler, taking their tickets and looking at them.

"It's Lady Pompress," said the attractive woman. "Abigail to my friends, and Mr. Fowler you are not my friend."

Her voice was haughty and crisp. Frances saw Captain Wainscott wince as she spoke so dismissively to Fowler. Fowler looked up at her and smiled even more broadly. He seemed not in the least bit put out.

"My sincerest, and humblest apologies, Lady Pompress," he said, "it is not often we are blessed with the company of nobility."

She nodded at him and then tossed her head up to the side. Across her elbow was a handbag and white parasol that was closed. Capt. Wainscott extended his hand to Fowler and shook it warmly.

"I'm really looking forward to hearing all about the pyramids from you. Please call me Tim."

"I will do, Tim, and you may call me Perry. I hope you have a marvelous time with us. My Lady."

Fowler nodded, handed back their tickets and moved on to the next passenger closest to him.

"You're an imbecile," said Lady Pompress to Capt. Wainscott. "These people are our servants not our friends."

Lady Pompress stormed off towards the exit as Capt. Wainscott shook his head ever so slightly. He looked around him and took the two suitcases out to the bus, then he came back and grabbed the third and last. He looked around and caught Frances' eye. She smiled to him and he smiled back before walking back out. Frances noticed Lady Pompress give him a stern lecture, about which she couldn't hear but she was certain she knew what it was about. Capt. Wainscott protested at which point Lady Pompress turned her back to him as Darius loaded their baggage.

"Mr. Nigel Durmott," said Fowler, shaking a man's hand vigorously.

Durmott was one of the men who had sat alone eating dinner last night. He was average height and good looking with a square jaw. He had a pleasant manner with black curly hair. He eagerly shook Fowler's hand and his voice carried when he spoke.

"Mr. Fowler, I am delighted to be here. I have heard that you know your Egyptian history like no one else. I am very eager to hear all about it. Though it looks like you might have your work cut out for you."

Durmott laughed heartily just then, as Fowler continued to smile at him.

"What a horrid woman," added Durmott.

"I have dealt with worse, Mr. Durmott, trust me."

"Without reservation," said Durmott, "as long as you'll call me Nigel."

"Only if you'll return the favor," said Fowler.

"Agreed."

Fowler moved on to the next guest who was another single man. Durmott picked up his single suitcase and headed out towards the exit. Fowler was just about to extend his hand to this tall, thin man with a plump belly, when the older woman, Mahulda's grandmother stepped up. She was visibly upset.

"Excuse me, Perry," she said, in a high pitched annoying tone. "But surely you should be helping the ladies first."

And with that she looked at Frances and Florence and gave them a curt nod and a severe smile. Fowler looked over at the single gentleman, and he gestured with his hand towards the older woman.

"Ladies first," he said, and he didn't sound particularly upset.

The older woman turned towards him and nodded ever so slightly and gave him a pinched smile so small you might have thought it was currency of which she had little. Mahulda was clearly embarrassed trying to hide behind her novel in the chair she had been in.

"Mahulda, dear," said the older woman in a voice that was shriek but which likely wasn't meant as such. "Come on, dear."

Mahulda got up and walked briskly over to her grandmother bringing with her the tickets, which she handed to Fowler. Fowler smiled at her warmly, and he looked at the tickets.

"Mrs. Orpha Bendled," he said, looking at the older woman, "and you must be Mrs. Bendled's daughter, Miss Mahulda Montague."

Fowler smiled at Mahulda.

"Don't get smart with me, young man," she said to Fowler, "I am Mahulda's grandmother."

"By George, you don't say," said Fowler, keeping a straight face, "you look much younger."

Orpha practically tore the tickets from him and stormed past.

"Get the bags, Mahulda, quickly," shrieked Orpha, and this time she meant it.

Fowler tried to stifle a chuckle but he didn't manage it very well. The tall, thin man in front of him took a few steps closer, smiling at the spectacle.

"That's two difficult women you'll be dealing with," he said, handing Fowler his ticket.

"That matches my record, Mr. Maurice Gabberdeen," said Fowler.

"Good luck with that," said Gabberdeen, no longer smiling. He took the ticket from Fowler and picked up his suitcase and walked out.

Fowler walked up to the fat couple that Frances had seen getting off the boat. They looked similarly enough that Frances wouldn't be surprised if they turned out to be siblings.

The ever indefatigable Fowler walked up to them and the man stood up and handed him their tickets. Fowler smiled warmly at them.

"Mr. Albert Warrant and Mrs. Abigail Beckles, we are delighted to have you with us. If there is anything you need, I hope you won't hesitate to call up on me."

Warrant stood up and shook Fowler's hand.

"We will, Mr. Fowler, we will. Thank you."

Fowler walked over to Lady Marmalade and Florence. They both stood up and shook his hand. They each in turn handed him their tickets.

"Lady Marmalade and Mrs. Florence Hudnall. I must say, this is quite a treat. Never before have I had the pleasure of showing two Ladies around Egypt at the same time."

He smiled at them broadly.

"Please, Mr. Fowler," said Lady Marmalade, "please call me Frances."

"Only if you'll call me Perry."

"I shall," she said.

"Do you need help with your baggage this morning?" he asked.

"No thank you, Perry. We travel light, there isn't much in them," said Frances.

"Very well," he said, "I hope you do enjoy your trip with Thoth Tours. As always, if there is anything I can do to help, please let me know."

"That's very kind," said Florence.

Fowler bowed himself towards the door as Frances and Florence followed after him. They lined up behind Warrant and Beckles as Darius was putting Gabberdeen's suitcase away.

Gabberdeen was climbing into the bus behind Montague and Bendled.

Darius took Beckles' suitcase and as he did, the lid slipped open and he lost control of it and it slipped to the ground. Part of its contents spilled out. Amongst clothes, Frances saw a few items of jewelry. They looked expensive and old. There was also a gold bowl and a gold statue that looked like an ankh, but Frances couldn't be sure.

Beckles hurriedly righted her suitcase and quickly put the contents back in. She looked mortified. She turned around, and her face was redder than it usually was.

"Oh dear," she said, "I guess that's what you get when you buy cheap. We've already done a bit of shopping as you can tell."

Frances smiled at her kindly for her embarrassment. Warrant came up and helped her stuff her clothes and other items back into the bag.

"I thought you told me you had secured it," she said, in frustrated whispers.

"I had," he replied quietly.

"Now everyone knows," she says.

"They don't. They hardly saw anything."

Albert spent extra time ensuring that the latch was secure this time. Darius went to take the suitcase from him when Albert had put it on its base.

"No thank you. I think I'll take care of that myself," said Albert.

He put the suitcase into the back of the bus and then he did the same with his own. The two of them scurried into the bus, still quite embarrassed by the whole scene.

Darius tentatively went to take Frances' and Florence's suitcases and they allowed him to. They walked up the stairs and onto the bus. It was a luxurious bus, with thick padded seats with ample room. The two of them sat together on the left hand side of the bus which gave them a great view out the front window.

Darius climbed back into the bus and a few moments later Perry Fowler climbed up too. It was about eight fifteen. He looked around and counted the heads on the bus.

"We are missing someone, but alas we were scheduled to depart at eight and we're already behind schedule."

Fowler looked around one last time, and as he did so, he saw a young man crash through the exit doors of the hotel. He was somewhat disheveled. You could tell he had rushed to get changed. His shirt was untucked and his hair was a mess. He looked to be in his early twenties, of average height with a large scar down his left cheek. He was carrying a rucksack on his right shoulder that bounced with every step he took.

"Ah ha, looks like our straggler has arrived," said Fowler getting back off the bus. Darius started to get up and follow him out. "I've got it," said Fowler, and Darius sat back down.

Outside, Frances watched Fowler and the young man talk for a moment. The young chap showed his ticket and they both walked around to the back of the bus. When they returned, the young man didn't have his rucksack anymore. He climbed into the bus and as he walked past Frances she noticed how blue his eyes were in his round face. He had a pleasant boyish face, despite the scar, and he grinned nervously as he walked to his seat somewhere in the back. Fowler climbed in after him and stood in the middle of the aisle at the front.

"Now we have everyone," he said. "Your latest companion on this journey is Mr. Simon Gragg."

Everyone gave Simon a round of applause. Darius started up the bus and they slowly drove out of the hotel's driveway, heading towards Cairo.

"Just a couple of items to be aware of as we head towards Cairo. We are a small group on a small bus, so I ask that you refrain from smoking. We have some who are in poor health and some with asthma. Having said that, we will be stopping every hour or so to stretch our legs, have a cigarette or use the toilets. As we drive towards Cairo, I'll be drawing your attention to some sights that you might find interesting. But for the next several minutes, please sit back and enjoy the ride. I'll be coming round with some brochures if you don't already have any."

Six

Including the three stops for stretching the legs and smoking, the bus that Lady Marmalade and the others were on, arrived at the outskirts of Giza at just before noon. The timing was impeccable.

Darius drove the bus up a dusty road that led towards the pyramids. The Great Pyramid of Giza loomed large in front of them like at giant brown prism. The ambience in the bus was electric, the giant pyramid was no more than two hundred feet from them.

Darius took a left hand turn and traveled for a few hundred more feet until he came to a stop. He stopped under a canopy that had been erected as a carport for the bus. At least that's what it looked like.

"Ladies and gentleman," said Fowler, "behold the pyramids of Egypt. We'll be enjoying a light repast for the next hour, after which we'll be able to explore the pyramids and other ancient sights that are here at Giza. During lunch I'll be offering some information about what you can expect here as well as some of the options for your exploration later this afternoon after lunch. Please make your way to the outdoor canopy to my left and take a seat wherever you like."

Fowler walked off the bus as Darius opened up the door. Frances and Florence were the first to walk off, followed quickly by Captain Wainscott and Lady Pompress, and then the others.

"How marvelous, simply marvelous," said Florence as they exited past a smiling Fowler. "I suppose to you it's old hat?"

Fowler kept his smile on his tanned face.

"Not at all, quite the contrary. With each new guest I bring out here, I see it anew through their eyes."

Florence smiled as she and Frances walked towards the canopy underneath which stood the chairs and tables. Florence looked off to her right and stared at the brown pyramids under a Persian blue sky.

"I want to start taking some pictures already," she said to Frances, smiling and feeling almost giddy as if it were the first day of school. Florence headed back to the bus and waited until everyone had disembarked when Darius came round and opened up the rear of the bus. He took her suitcase out and she opened it and took out her camera. Then she closed up her luggage and Darius put it back in the bus. She walked back to Frances.

"It is a most majestic and awe inspiring sight. I'm so glad we're here," said Frances.

Florence nodded and as they made their way to the tables and chairs she kept looking to her right at the pyramids. Frances and Florence took a seat at the farthermost table. There were four tables all in a row to fit four people each. The white canopy was open to all four sides and the view, as they sat facing the pyramids, was taken up mostly by the Great Pyramid of Giza, though they could see a sliver of the Pyramid of Khafre and to the left of it, a small sliver of the Pyramid of Menkaure.

The chairs that Frances and Florence sat on were comfortable. They were wooden chairs painted white with cushions tied to the seat and backrest. They also had wooden armrests. The tables were covered with white tablecloths and this all stood upon a wonderfully intricate Persian rug. There was very little wind in the area, and the immediate vicinity was not very sandy in any event, but rather hard dirt.

Frances and Florence sat next to each other facing southwest. That left two chairs opposite them which wouldn't offer a view of the pyramids as they faced northeast. These seats were the last to fill up. Albert Warrant and Abigail Beckles took them. Everyone introduced themselves to each other as they sat down.

"What brings you to Egypt?" asked Frances.

Albert looked over at Abigail. She didn't say anything so he spoke first.

"We've always been interested in Egypt, ever since we were young children, weren't we, Abby?"

He looked over at her and smiled. She glanced at him before looking at Frances and Florence.

"Oh yes, very much so," she said.

Abigail was dressed in a pale pink dress with short sleeves. She had brought a light yellow umbrella which she hooked to the back of her chair. Albert was in tan knee length shorts and on his feet he had walking shoes. Most of the ladies wore flat tennis shoes, including Frances and Florence. Abigail and Albert seemed quite charming and happy.

"Are the two of you married?" asked Florence, not quite getting a bead on their relationship.

Albert laughed good naturally.

"Oh, good Lord no," he said. "We're actually siblings."

"I see," said Florence. "Now that you mention it, I can actually see the resemblance."

"Yes, almost everyone asks if we're related," said Abigail.

"Well, I never wish to assume."

"That's kind of you," said Albert. "After all, what if we were married and everyone assumed we're related. That might seem a little offensive, wouldn't it?"

"Perhaps," said Florence. "I suppose it depends on tone of the messenger."

"Yes, I suppose," said Albert, looking down.

Everyone had by now seated themselves at a table of their choosing. Lady Pompress, Captain Timothy Wainscott, Orpha Bendled and her granddaughter Mahulda Montague were all seated at the table to Frances' right. Lady Pompress who sat facing the pyramids on the far right of that table had the four single men at the next table on her right. The fourth table was unoccupied.

Orpha, appearing to Frances to be a bit of a busybody inquired with Fowler if Thoth Tours usually got more tourists considering their was an empty table. Perry Fowler said they usually did. In fact they usually had at least twice the number during the peak season. Though on this particular occasion four people had cancelled at the last minute.

"Oh my," said Orpha. "How rude. Do you know why?"

Fowler indulged her with a smile.

"Madam," said Fowler, "Thoth Tours does not make it a practice to pry into our customers' private lives. We also make it very easy to cancel, which is why we are one of the favored tour providers in the area."

That seemed to put an end to Orpha's inquiry for the time being. Each table had their own waiter. All the waiters were dressed smartly in white trousers and white button down shirts that were long sleeved. A warm but ever so slight breeze nuzzled around Frances' ankles as their waiter brought around a small plate of cold tabouli. The cool dish was a welcome start to the meal. Although it wasn't hot, it was getting quite warm in the middle of the day out there on the plains of Giza in front of the magnificent pyramids.

The waiter was a young man, perhaps as young as early twenties. He had blindingly white teeth and pitch black hair that was neatly combed to one side. He was clean shaven, with high cheekbones and a square jaw. His brown eyes were large and bright. He was handsome, something that Abigail immediately noticed. She smiled at him the whole time he was at their table serving everyone their appetizers. It was so obvious that at one point Albert had to nudge her with his elbow to bring her back to some semblance of social decency. Abigail looked over at Frances.

"I've never had the privilege of dining with a real Lady," she said, and she smiled broadly, this time only for Frances. She wasn't a young woman. Middle aged, but she had a naiveté about the world that Frances found charming, though she wasn't particularly pleased about her fawning over her title.

"Think nothing of it," said Frances between forkfuls of tabouli.

"I've always been intrigued by the peerage," said Abigail, getting more animated. "I have a hard time understanding it all."

Frances looked up at her and smiled kindly.

"Don't worry about it, it's quite the puzzle that many of us can sometimes get confused over."

"As I understand it," continued Abigail, "there are a variety of Ladies and Lords are there not?"

Albert looked at his sister sternly.

"I don't think Lady Marmalade wants to talk about it."

Embarrassedly, Abigail put her head down and played with her tabouli on the plate. Albert had clearly sucked the winds right out of her sails.

"It's all right, dear," said Frances, patting Abigail's left hand which was curled around her plate of tabouli. "I'll try and give you a brief rundown if you'd like."

"Oh, would you?" asked Abigail, "that would be ever so kind."

She looked up at Frances with a big smile and effervescent optimism popped like champagne bubbles as she spoke. Frances took another bite of tabouli and washed it down with a sip from her water.

"We'll stick to peerage which is somewhat easier to understand than royalty, and you don't want me talking about royalty because it will take too long and I don't seem to understand the nuances of it myself. I think that's because it can and has been made up off the cuff throughout the ages as the Queen or King had seen fit."

Abigail and Albert laughed. Florence smiled too. She had heard this explained to her before, and she found Frances' explanation easy to understand and simple. Though she hadn't found need to use the correct address in a long time. Frances had insisted upon it. She and Eric were not ones for much pomp and circumstance, somewhat to the chagrin of their peers.

"The peerage is made up of ranks, and that is why you're quite correct that you'll find a variety of Ladies and Lords with different ranks. In order of ranking, the peerage is made up of Dukes and their wives Duchesses, then next in rank are Marquesses and Marchionesses, then Earls and Countesses, then Viscounts and Viscountesses, and lastly Barons and Baronesses. Does that make sense so far?"

Abigail nodded excitedly, her face creased in the biggest smile she could muster.

"Would it be imprudent of me to ask where in the peerage you sit?"

"Abby!" exclaimed Albert, "that's improper."

Abigail blushed.

"Sorry, I'm just very interested that's all."

"Not to worry dear, it would be considered imprudent but I don't mind telling. But first we need to fill in the backgrounds."

Abigail nodded.

"You don't have to tell me if you don't want to. I hope you'll forgive me, like I said, I've never had the pleasure of dining with a real Lady."

"It's all right, dear. The wives of all peers except for the wives of Dukes are called Lady."

"I see, what are the wives of Dukes called?" asked Abigail.

"You'd address her as Your Grace the first time and then after that as Madam. I would address her as Duchess Teakettle, if that was her husband's title and then as Madam after that."

Abigail chuckled.

"There isn't really a Duchess Teakettle, is there?"

Frances smiled at her.

"I hope not, that would be most unfortunate."

Abigail shook her head.

"So knowing that, this brings us to your question. If I am a Lady, then what is my formal title? Do you have any idea?"

Abigail wanted to impress Lady Marmalade so she blurted out, "Marchioness?"

Frances smiled at her.

"Strictly speaking you're right, but I don't go by that title or I'd be known as Lady Sandown."

"I'm confused," said Abigail with a furrowed brow. "If you are a Marchioness, then why don't you go by that title?"

"The short answer is because my husband didn't want to. You see, my husband, Eric, wasn't particularly impressed or flattered by the social class system that is, thankfully, disappearing in England today, so he chose to use his lowest title. You see my dear," said Frances, "if you're a Marquess for example, then you will usually have earned titles from all the lower ranks."

"I see," said Abigail, but she was still clearly confused.

"I'll use myself as an example. My husband is The Most Honorable, The Marquess of Sandown. He is also The Right Honorable, The Earl of Wollinghamshire. Moving down the ranks he is also The Right Honorable, The Viscount Volmaren, and lastly he is also The Right Honorable, Lord Marmalade. That is his barony title."

"Interesting, so your husband chose to use his lowest title and so you had to follow?"

"Quite correct, however, I agree with my late husband's philosophy on this. Furthermore, I insist that you call me Frances."

"I'll try," said Abigail. "This is so thrilling."

"I have a question," said Florence.

Frances looked over at her and nodded.

"If that is the case, then why is your son Declan addressed as Lord Declan whenever I've been over to visit?"

"You mean by Alfred and Ginny?"

Florence nodded.

"Well, because we're informal, and that's what we prefer."

Frances turned to Abigail and Albert.

"My dear friend brings up an interesting point though, and something that I should clarify. You see, my son, at least when my husband was around could only use the next highest title which my husband was not using. So if Eric was using his barony title, then Declan, who is my only son, and also my eldest child, would be addressed as Mr. Branham."

"Why Mr. Branham and not Mr. Marmalade?" asked Abigail.

"Well, this is where it gets a bit complicated. Most times, the titles of Barons and Viscounts are related to their surnames, all titles above Viscounts, that is to say for Earls, Marquesses and Dukes the titles are not related to their surnames. In our particular case, all our titles are unrelated to my husband's surname which is Branham."

"So your married name then would be Frances Branham?" asked Abigail.

Frances nodded.

"Yes, but it is never used. When I sign my name it is always Frances Sandown."

Abigail cocked her neck at an odd angle, and knitted her eyebrows together.

"Forgive me, my Lady, um, Frances," said Abigail, "but why not Frances Marmalade?"

"I know, I am confusing things a bit, aren't I It's only confusing because unlike most peers, we've decided to use our lowest title, at least informally. However, in formal occasions we adhere to proper etiquette. So when we're amongst our peers, I'm known as Lady Sandown, or when formally introduced as The Most Honorable, The Dowager Marchioness of Sandown."

"Why the addition of Dowager? I'm afraid I'm not familiar with that?"

"That's added when my husband died."

"Oh," said Abigail, somewhat embarrassed. "I'm very sorry."

"That's all right my dear, it was several years ago now. I am making things a bit more complicated than they need to be. I'm generally called Lady Sandown when in formal company. However, because my eldest son is now known as Lord Sandown, if he were to marry, then his wife would become Lady Sandown and I would be referred to as Frances, Lady Marmalade."

"I see," said Abigail, beginning to appreciate the nuances of peerage.

"Am I boring you, dear?" asked Frances.

"Oh no, good heavens no," said Abigail, shaking her head vigorously. "It's all fascinating, but there's quite a bit to it."

"There is, but you'll get accustomed to it. In short, I am really Lady Sandown, Eric and I made things a little more complicated by trying to make them more equal and just. My husband would have been known as Lord Sandown, and then my eldest son, who would be the heir apparent, would take the next available title which would make him the Earl of Wollinghamshire and he would be addressed as Lord Wollinghamshire. My daughter would simply be known as Lady Amelia. Amelia is her first name. All other children of mine would be known either as Lord or Lady and then their first name. It is also common that they'd be known as Lord or Lady then their first name and then surname. So my daughter Amelia, often goes by Lady Amelia Branham. Does that help?"

Abigail nodded her head.

"It helps immensely, I think I'm starting to understand it now. But your husband is now dead, so why do you keep using your lowest title?"

"I only use it in informal situations, and primarily because that's what I've been used to for so long. It also reminds me of my late husband and our family is well known for the jam marmalade. For all those reasons, I just haven't bothered changing it."

"That's fascinating," said Abigail. "Thank you so much for sharing that with me."

"You're welcome," said Frances, getting back to eating her tabouli.

Abigail leaned in and glanced over at the table next to her.

"Do you know how Lady Pompress got her title at all?" she asked in a hushed voice.

Frances nodded and finished chewing her food.

"I do. She married Mr. Stanley Pompress who was knighted for his work during the Second World War, and who sadly died too early."

"When was that?" asked Abigail.

"Please forgive my sister," said Albert, "she's very curious."

"Not at all," said Frances. "Stanley died late last year if I recall correctly."

"That's scandalous," said Abigail, "that she's traipsing around the world with someone so soon."

"Some would suggest that," said Frances, finishing the rest of her tabouli.

Frances glanced at the menu card that she pulled out from under her bowl that once held tabouli. The next dish up was the main course. It consisted of lamb kebabs with ful medames on the side as well as sliced and cold eggs with a garnish of baba ghanoush and pita.

Frances knew baba ghanoush as she'd had it before, but ful medames was something she hadn't heard of. She hadn't recalled eating anything like it before on her earlier trips to Egypt. But she enjoyed surprises, the good kind, and usually food was always a good surprise. Her palate was comfortable with new tastes and experiences.

"Have you ever had ful medames before?" she asked Florence.

Florence shook her head, so she looked over at Albert and Abigail. They shook their heads too.

"The only thing that I know on this menu is the lamb. That tabouli was nice, but I'd never had it before," said Albert.

Abigail nodded in agreement. Fowler stepped up in front of the four tables, in the middle of them and faced them all.

"I've had some questions about the meal," he said. "Good questions."

Light laughter erupted from the tables.

"As best as we can, we are trying to give you an authentic experience here in Egypt. The meal you'll be enjoying today is Egyptian. However, there will be the comforts of English food once we're on the cruise. That first dish you enjoyed was called tabouli. It is an Egyptian salad made of bulgur as well as parsley and mint, which you could probably tell with onions and garlic, tomatoes and lemon for flavor. Did you like it?"

Fowler looked around at the crowd and grinned at them. Just about all of those seated nodded except for Lady Pompress who had pushed her plate aside after taking one taste. She sat at an angle in her chair, fanning herself with a fan that she had taken out of her bag. She was clearly not impressed. Fowler wisely ignored her.

"Next up is a lamb kebab. This is tender seasoned lamb on a skewer. You'll love it. It's accompanied with ful medames which are mashed and seasoned fava beans seasoned with parsley, onions, lemon juice, olive oil and garlic. It is delicious."

Fowler looked down at the menu card which he held in his hand.

"Eggs you know about."

He looked up and grinned at the crowd, there was soft laughter as encouragement.

"Baba ghanoush is a dish of mashed grilled eggplant seasoned with garlic, onion, olive oil, lemon juice etcetera. Are you starting to see the theme?"

He looked up at them with a raised eyebrow to more soft chuckles.

"The baba ghanoush can be eaten on its own, but I encourage you to tear off the bits of pita, which is a flat bread and use that to scoop it up and eat it. I love all this food, in fact, if you don't like it, I'll be coming round for the leftovers."

More chuckles.

"Your waiters will be coming round now with the main dish. Please let your waiters know what type of wine you'll be having. There is a nicely chilled Riesling at hand, or if you prefer red, we have a full bodied Pinot Noir. Either wine has been chosen to go perfectly with the dish."

As Fowler finished, the waiters came by, and dropped of ample plates of food. Just looking at it, Frances knew it would be too much for her in one go. It did smell warm and delicious. The olive oil, lemon and garlic were the first aromas that wafted up from the food.

Everyone at Lady Marmalade's table chose Riesling after Frances asked first. The waiters came back with the delightfully chilled white wine. Looking around, there were only two men who chose the Pinot Noir. That was Samuel Newton and Nigel Durmott sitting at the far table.

Everybody started on their food. Frances picked at everything. She found it all quite delicious. As they started to eat, Fowler stepped up in front of the group again.

"Please don't mind me. Continue eating at your leisure. I'll just be going over some of the itinerary for this afternoon, as well as offering some insights into the pyramids and other artifacts that are viewable here."

Frances looked up and took a sip of wine, enjoying the view of the pyramids from where she sat.

"That Great Pyramid of Giza or Khufu, also known as Cheops is the largest pyramid in the world. It is however, only one of what some believe to be over one hundred pyramids in Egypt. Interestingly, the Great Pyramid of Giza, which you see practically right in front of us," said Fowler, as he turned and drew his arms away from his body to encompass the pyramid, "is not only the oldest of the Seven Wonders of the World, but it is also the only one of these wonders that has survived."

Fowler paused to give his audience time to take it all in. There were raised eyebrows and nodding heads, and upturned mouths.

"Amongst the twelve of you, can we name the other six wonders?"

Fowler looked around from face to face and table to table. He came to Frances' table last. Frances knew all the Seven Wonders, but she didn't want to be a braggart about it, so she gently nudged Florence. Florence looked at her.

"But you know them all," she said quietly.

"And you know them all too," said Frances.

"Not anymore I don't."

"Mrs. Hudnall, do you know one of them?" asked Fowler, looking at her steadily with a kind face.

"I do know one," she said.

"Good," said Fowler, "would you mind getting us started then?"

"The Hanging Gardens of Babylon."

"Quite correct," said Fowler, nodding and smiling at her. He then looked over at the next table. "That is one point for the A Team. Would the B Team like to name one?"

"I didn't know this was a competition," said Lady Pompress, somewhat frustrated.

"Just a friendly competition to get us going," said Fowler unperturbed.

Lady Pompress whispered in Captain Wainscott's ear.

"Yes I know, but why don't you say it."

She whispered something else in his ear.

"Very well," said Wainscott, visibly upset. Then he tried to put on a brave smile. "B Team would like to offer the Statue of Zeus at Olympia."

"Well done, B Team. Ladies and gentleman," said Fowler. "We have a tie for first place with both the A Team and B Team in the lead with one point. Can C Team make it a three way tie?"

Fowler looked over at the third table with the four single men at it. The three men except for Samuel Newton looked around at each other, shrugging their shoulders. Newton took the cigarette he was smoking out of his mouth.

"The Lighthouse of Alexandria," he said, in a deep but quite voice.

"Well played gentleman. We now have a three way tie. There are three remaining wonders of the world left. C Team?"

Fowler was met with blank stares, so he turned to the B Team.

"B Team?"

Mahulda whispered into her grandmother's ear.

"The Temple of Artemis," said Orpha, smiling confidently.

"That is correct. Do you know any of the other two?" asked Fowler.

Orpha looked at her granddaughter but Mahulda shook her head. Lady Pompress said something to Captain Wainscott.

"I don't know any of the others," he said quite frustrated.

Fowler turned to Lady Marmalade's table.

"A Team," he said as dramatically as possible. "B Team is in the lead. If you know the remaining two wonders you could clinch the win. If not, the best you can do is tie."

"And what do we get if we win?" asked Florence cheekily.

"My undying gratitude for finishing the game so we can get on with the rest of the program."

He grinned at her.

"Well?" he asked.

"The Mausoleum at Halicarnassus and the Colossus of Rhodes," said Frances.

"God bless you," said Fowler cheekily. "Those are indeed the Seven Wonders of the World. The Great Pyramid of Giza, the Hanging Gardens of Babylon, the Temple of Artemis, Statue of Zeus at Olympia, Mausoleum at Halicarnassus, the Colossus of Rhodes and finally the Lighthouse of Alexandria. The first one, which stands before you like a champion, is the only one remaining in our modern era."

Everyone got back to their food. Frances had only managed about a third of her plate at this point. It was delicious, but it was filling, the tabouli hadn't helped and there was still one of her favorites coming up. For dessert they were being offered basbousa, a sweet cake made from semolina and soaked in a simple syrup that often included orange water or rose water, topped with nuts and sometimes coconut.

"The Great Pyramid of Giza was built for the pharaoh Khufu as a tomb for keeping his decaying remains. Astonishing to think that up to one hundred thousand men would have labored for twenty years to build what is essentially a coffin. Though quite a magnificent coffin if I might say so myself."

Fowler turned to look at the pyramid for a moment, to give emphasis to his words. He then turned back to the four tables.

"It is believed to have been finished around 2560BC, and it remained the tallest manmade structure until the Lincoln Cathedral was completed, in 1311 I believe."

"Will we find Khufu's mummy in there?" asked Simon Gragg, hoping to send shivers up the spines of the women present.

"I'm afraid not," said Fowler. "The sarcophagus is there, it weighs almost four tons, but the cover of the sarcophagus is missing as is the body of Khufu, if indeed he was even buried there. Most think he must have been, but there are others and legends that back them up that suggest that he might not have ever been buried there."

"That's a shame," said Gragg.

"Perhaps, though legend has it, that anyone found pilfering anything from the pyramids of Egypt will be felled in time. It has been said that the pharaohs had their priests cast horrible spells around the chambers to protect the mummified bodies of the pharaohs, and we've heard of some archaeologists falling ill and dying after disturbing the inner chambers.

"Poppycock," said Maurice.

Fowler looked at him with a raised eyebrow.

"Perhaps. Nevertheless, it is illegal to remove anything from the pyramids and from this area in general, and I'll ask you to not do so."

Fowler looked sternly at everyone present as they finished up their meal.

"Once you've had a chance to finish eating and let it settle, we'll tour the Great Pyramid of Giza. After that we'll take a look inside the Pyramid of Khafre which is the middle sized pyramid and then we'll finish up with a look into the Pyramid of Menkaure, the smallest pyramid here. After we've finished with those three pyramids it should bring us to around three p.m. You'll have the last hour to hour and a half, until four thirty to tour the rest of the complex by yourself, or join me as I show you around the Great Sphinx and the other areas around her including the necropolis that contains other such artifacts such as mortuary temples and the Queens' pyramids. Do you have any questions?"

"What sort of an egomaniac was this Khufu fellow to spend so much time, perhaps money and manpower on his own pyramid over twenty years?" asked Florence.

Fowler chuckled.

"I think you're quite right. I think he was quite the egomaniac. Though in seriousness, we don't know much about his life, though the Greek historian Herodotus didn't have anything nice to say about him. He called him an heretic and a cruel and vindictive tyrant. According to Herodotus, Khufu, who the Greeks knew as Cheops even sent his daughter into prostitution to help pay for his pyramid. We think he ruled for anywhere between twenty-five and thirty-five years, followed by his brother Khafre. Herodotus has a similar feeling for Khafre as he did for Khufu."

"I see," said Florence. "That takes a bit of the shine off of the myth."

"It certainly does," said Fowler. "These men, at least by some accounts, were not benevolent rulers, but rather seemed more like egotistical maniacs. I always like to keep that in mind when I'm looking in awe at the majesty of these ancient monuments. Pause for a moment to think not of Khufu, who might well have been a tyrant, but the tens of thousands of men who labored for years. How many of them probably died in the building of this monument to one man's ego?"

Fowler looked around as the mood under that white canopy turned somber for a moment.

"But we must still enjoy it, to be sure, we can enjoy the accomplishment of men with very little in the way of technology."

The waiters came by and cleared the plates. Frances had only managed to eat half of it. Florence being a little bigger than she left but a third. It wasn't long before the waiters came out with the basbousa, and Fowler continued talking in his deep baritone, offering gems of history mixed with mythology.

Seven

The lunch had been marvelous and the day was getting warmer. The group following Fowler in his safari hat and khakis was easy to spot, there were six white and off white colored umbrellas amongst them. One for each of the women in the group. Two of the waiters were still with them, carrying large bottles of water around their shoulders and refilling paper cups for the group of tourists as needed.

Fowler had guided them through the Great Pyramid of Giza as well as the Pyramid of Khafre. Coming out into the bright warm sunlight as they did, Frances welcomed the wall of warm air. The interiors of the pyramids were cool, but that was not to say they were cold, rather much cooler than the outside temperature. When they had left lunch and headed towards the Great Pyramid, Frances had noticed a thermometer near by that had put the temperature at almost twenty-nine degrees centigrade. Not that she was an expert at determining temperatures but heading deep into the Great Pyramid she would have been surprised if it were more than twenty degrees.

Fowler gathered them close. They were situated at the southeast corner of the Pyramid of Khafre, not far from the boat pits. Fowler looked at his watch. It was just past two thirty.

"We're making good time," he said. "This last pyramid here," and he turned more towards the south and pointed with this right hand to the Pyramid of Menkaure, "is the last of the three pyramids we'll be looking at while here in Giza."

Lady Pompress stood at the back of the group and ordered Captain Wainscott to get her some water, which he dutifully did.

"These three pyramids," continued Fowler, "from the Great Pyramid of Giza to the Pyramid of Khafre and now to the Pyramid of Menkaure, are all related. Khufu or Cheops as the Greeks knew him, was the father of Khafre who was the father of Menkaure. What we're really talking about here then, is a dynasty. A dynasty of pharaohs from the same family who obviously thought quite highly of themselves."

Polite laughter erupted from the crowd. Samuel wiped at his forehead and took off his fedora and waved it as his face. Frances wasn't sure why he was wearing a fedora, it was too hot out here for a hat like that, even if it did keep the sun out of your eyes.

The other men all wore safari hats which were a much better idea. Although they were all in light shirts, Samuel didn't seem to be enjoying the temperature as much as the other men. Even Simon with his pale complexion seemed to not mind the heat.

At twenty-nine, the temperature was pushing at Lady Marmalade's comfort level. She enjoyed the heat, but even she had to confess that getting into the thirties was too much for even her to bear.

"I don't want to keep you out here long," said Fowler. "It's getting quite warm, but there is a fascinating story about this Pyramid of Menkaure. Legend has it that there was separate network of chambers that aren't accessible from the main pyramid. It is believed that these chambers actually held the sarcophagus of Menkaure, as well as treasures that would be the envy of even our King George."

"I thought the sarcophagus of Menkaure was sunk in the Mediterranean?" asked Nigel.

"Quite right," said Fowler, flashing his big smile. "That is indeed the official story. On October the 13th, 1838, the ship Beatrice sank on its way to Great Britain, allegedly carrying the sarcophagus of Menkaure. However, there was told a story about a secret passageway that led into the Pyramid of Menkaure from this closest queen's pyramid to us. That true pyramid you see here."

Fowler turned to his right slightly and pointed at the easternmost pyramid, and the largest of the three of these small queen pyramids.

"If you followed that passageway which led underground and back into the Menkaure's pyramid, you would come to his burial chamber. Under his sarcophagus was a room filled with jewels, gold and other valuables the likes of which had never been seen."

"Sounds like more poppycock," said Maurice, waving his right arm around which contained a cigarette between his fingers. "Just like these curses that these pharaohs put on anyone who disturbs their chamber. It's all mythology because people haven't figured out how to answer the unknowns through science."

"Perhaps," said Fowler, "I'll let you be the judge of that. When we're finished with Menkaure's pyramid, you are more than welcome to go take a look for yourself. The secret passageway is now open to the public."

Lady Pompress looked at Captain Wainscott and smiled. Abigail smiled at Albert and he nodded at her, but with less enthusiasm than she.

"I've heard the story," said Simon. "Some say you might even find a trinket or two left over if you look closely."

"I'm afraid not. After the secret passageway was discovered in 1898, the remaining valuables were taken and stored safely in museums around the world. There's nothing of value in there anymore."

"You mean that somebody actually found this passageway to these secret chambers and took all the valuables from them?" asked Florence.

"That's what we think, yes. It appears that they, and unfortunately, the culprits appear to have been British, managed to pilfer a large amount of the valuables. Though how much can't be determined, though we do know that several statues, vessels and gold coins were sold up until 1899 when it all stopped suddenly. And these valuables from those that have been identified match those that remained in Menkaure's pyramid so we know they were taken from there."

"Why did they stop selling these valuables at that point?" asked Florence, quite intrigued by the mystery.

"We're not certain, though there appears to be two thoughts on that matter. The first is that perhaps they had already sold most of what they had stolen, and the second is that international attention was brought to the theft and Scotland Yard was notified to keep an eye out for any unusual commercial activity regarding these sorts of goods. I like to think it was a bit of both."

Florence looked at Frances and smiled.

"How thrilling," she said. "A mystery of theft, right here at the pyramids of Giza."

"I know," said Frances, "I've heard about it before. If you're interested, I might tell you about who the stories seem to suggest did it?"

"Oh, do tell."

"I will, in time."

"Let's be off, ladies and gentleman," said Fowler, "it's quite hot here out in the Egyptian sun, perhaps a cool respite inside Menkaure's coffin might be in order."

Fowler grinned at them but was met with mostly grim faces. The group was getting hot and tired. He started off and the straggle followed slowly behind him. Out of the corner of her eye, Frances saw Lady Pompress fall to the ground, her umbrella rolling away around her head.

"Wait!" exclaimed Captain Wainscott, bending down to aid Lady Pompress.

They all gathered around her to see what they could do to help.

"Give her room," said Fowler, kneeling down beside her across from Captain Wainscott.

"Does she have any conditions?" asked Fowler, looking at Captain Wainscott.

"Well, I think it might be her blood sugars, she's a diabetic, though I worry she might have taken a little too much sleeping aid last night."

"Does she have any insulin in her bag?"

"Yes, but I wouldn't give it to her until we can find out what the problem is," said Wainscott.

"Fair enough. Can you give her some shade," said Fowler looking at Abigail. Abigail walked in closer and angled her umbrella over Lady Pompress so that she was in shade. Fowler took out his clean white handkerchief, he gave it to one of the waiters.

"Wet it with water," he said.

The young man did so and handed it back to Fowler dripping wet. Fowler squeezed a bit of the water out and lay it upon Lady Pompress' forehead. She started to stir, and her eyes fluttered.

"What happened?" Fowler asked.

"I don't know. We turned to follow you and as we did, she just collapsed."

"The heat has gotten to her," said Fowler. "You're going to have to keep her cool and give her lots of water to drink."

Lady Pompress looked up at everyone with a squint.

"Why am I on the ground," she demanded to know.

"It appears you fainted my dear," said Wainscott.

He started to help her up with Fowler. They had her back standing and she put the back of her hand to her head.

"How are you feeling?" asked Wainscott.

"Lightheaded," she said.

"I think you should take her back to the canopy and let her sit down. I think she should stay out of the sun for the rest of the day," said Fowler.

Fowler looked around.

"Would anyone mind volunteering to help Captain Wainscott take care of Lady Pompress."

No one stepped forward.

"I'm afraid we'll have to cancel the rest of the afternoon then, and get her seen to in Cairo."

"I'll take care of her," said Frances.

"No, Fran, this is our first time here," said Florence.

Frances put her free hand on Florence's forearm and smiled at her.

"It's your first time here. You're forgetting that I've been here before, I've seen it all, but you go along and have fun."

"Are you sure?"

"I'm adamant."

"Thank you, Frances," said Fowler.

"Not at all," she said.

Frances took a hold of Lady Pompress' hand and Captain Wainscott tried to help her with her other hand.

"Leave me alone!" she said, "Just carry my umbrella."

"Is it your diabetes, darling?" asked Captain Wainscott.

"It most certainly isn't. We just finished eating, it can't possibly be."

"Perhaps you took too much sleep aid last night."

"Perhaps you speak too much," she said to him rudely. "I just need to rest."

The three of them walked slowly back to the canopy with the Captain a couple of steps behind, safely out of the way of Lady Pompress' wrath. Fowler watched the three of them off, just to make sure everyone was okay. He stood with his fists on his hips and his neck cocked slightly to the left.

"All right," he said, "let's be off to explore Menkaure's pyramid. Now, as I was saying, we won't be able to see the secret chamber from inside the main pyramid. But for those of you who wish to explore the queen's pyramid by yourselves, you'll easily find the hidden entrance inside it, because it is no longer hidden, and it will take you underground and back into the Pyramid of Menkaure..."

Fowler and the other nine, walked slowly towards the Pyramid of Menkaure. Fowler chatting the whole way, offering little tidbits of fact interspersed with the more tasty morsels of fiction.

Captain Wainscott pulled a chair around to the nearside of the table and helped Lady Pompress into it. He pulled another chair around for her feet which she put up onto the cushion. He pulled a third chair around for Lady Marmalade.

"Thank you, Captain," she said.

He smiled at her, and then went for a fourth chair which he brought around for himself. He was seated facing Lady Pompress on her right side. He offered her a glass of water that one of the waiters had brought. Lady Pompress drank deeply.

Frances' chair was angled towards Lady Pompress, though she still had a good view of the pyramids. She watched as the small creatures, the size of ants, who were her fellow travelers got eaten by the small maw at the bottom of the Menkaure's pyramid. It was hard to tell, but it appeared to her that Fowler was the first one in.

"You know, my dear," said Frances, looking at Lady Pompress, "if there's one thing I've learned in my travels all over the Orient that one must drink lots of fluid to combat the heat."

Lady Pompress didn't smile at Frances but she looked at her steadily.

"Yes, well, this is my first time here in Egypt. I was not quite expecting such heat at this time of year. Though I suppose my Timmy is used to it, having served in Africa during the war. Aren't you, Timmy?"

Captain Wainscott leaned in and his face was flushed.

"I would prefer it if you called me Tim or Timothy."

"Oh nonsense, Timmy, it is just a term of endearment."

Frances felt embarrassed for him, but he didn't argue any further. He looked at Frances and smiled self consciously.

"I don't think we've been properly introduced," said Captain Wainscott standing up and walking over to shake Lady Marmalade's hand. "I'm Captain Timothy Wainscott."

"How do you do," said Frances. "I'm Frances Marmalade."

Captain Wainscott looked at her for a moment quizzically.

"Not THE Lady Frances Marmalade," he asked with delight.

Frances smiled at him and nodded.

"Yes, I'm afraid, the very same."

"I am such a fan," he said. "I've followed..."

"Oh really, Timmy," interjected Lady Pompress, "you're embarrassing yourself, she's just another lady, that's all."

Wainscott turned and looked at Lady Pompress. He was still smiling.

"Oh no, my dear, Lady Marmalade is quite the renowned sleuth."

He turned back to Frances.

"You aren't expecting any trouble out here are you, my Lady?" he asked.

"Oh, I certainly hope not. I'm here as we all are, on holiday. But please, Captain, call me Frances."

Captain Wainscott nodded enthusiastically.

"Timmy, would you mind fanning me. I'm awfully hot," said Lady Pompress.

"Certainly, my dear."

Wainscott went back to his seat and sat down and started fanning Lady Pompress.

"Don't forget to drink plenty of water, dear," said Frances.

Lady Pompress didn't take any notice of Frances, she smiled tightly at Captain Wainscott.

"I don't know why you're fawning over her, she doesn't seem like much," said Lady Pompress, as quietly as she dared. Frances could still hear her.

"Frances, Lady Marmalade, has actually solved some of the most high profile cases in London. Do you remember that one where the Prime Minister's brother was murdered? Frances solved it."

"Well, I helped the police as best I could," said Frances, smiling at him.

"Nonsense, I spoke to one of the chaps at Scotland Yard and he said they couldn't have done it without your help."

Frances didn't say anything.

"That's all quite fascinating, Timmy," said Lady Pompress, "but I'm tired and not feeling well. Would you mind tending to me if it's not too much to ask?"

Her voice was cold and calculated, and it shut Captain Wainscott up.

"Tell me how you and Abigail happened to chose Egypt for a visit?" asked Frances good naturedly.

Lady Pompress turned to look at Frances quite quickly with a severe look on her face and knitted eyebrows.

"I am Lady Pompress if you don't mind using it. I've earned it honestly," she said with a hiss.

Frances thought she hadn't earned anything honestly in her life.

"My dear Abigail, I am not your equal, and I'll not use the title that came by your husband honestly."

Lady Pompress turned her head away with a flick. She was quite put out. Both Lady Marmalade and Captain Wainscott ignored her.

"We just recently got engaged, and I thought it would be a wonderful idea for us to come out to Egypt for a look at some of the antiquities. Abigail wanted especially to see the pyramids. Next year, once we're married, we'll probably spend our honeymoon in the south of France. I'm willing to spare no expense to make my darling Abigail happy."

He smiled broadly at Frances, obviously quite proud of his engagement and pending nuptials. Poor boy, thought Frances.

"How delightful," is what she said instead.

Lady Marmalade didn't have any qualms with the fact that Lady Pompress was now engaged again, after only nine or ten months since her husband, Sir Stanley died. No, that didn't bother her in the least bit, different people mourn differently. What did bother her was how difficult and self centered the woman seemed to be. She just had a way of rubbing Lady Marmalade the wrong way.

"So how do you like it so far?" Frances asked Wainscott.

"Simply marvelous. As Abigail mentioned, I had spent some time in North Africa during the war, so I'm quite familiar with the environment and the desert heat. I quite like it actually. I hope it'll be all right for Abigail."

He looked at her with genuine concern. She looked back at him with hard eyes.

"Keep fanning, Timmy, if you don't mind," she said, as he had taken a break while conversing with Lady Marmalade.

"I'm sure once we're on the boat, the breeze and the cool air from the Nile will be much to Abigail's liking."

Frances noticed Lady Pompress frown when she mentioned her name. Frances almost couldn't help stifle a smile at the smallness of this woman's inner confidence.

"I take it you've been here before," asked Captain Wainscott. "To Egypt I mean."

He was trying to fan Lady Pompress as quickly as he could. But Frances could tell it was tiring him out.

"Yes, I have been to Egypt a few times before. Mostly with my late husband. I haven't been back for at least ten years. But my dear friend, Florence Hudnall, has always held a special interest for Egypt since we were school friends. I thought it would be nice to bring her out to see it for herself."

"How very kind of you," said Captain Wainscott.

Frances smiled.

"Though I'm thoroughly enjoying it myself. It's nice to be away from the busyness of the city. Away from murders and mayhem."

Frances laughed, and Captain Wainscott did too, until he was given a look by Lady Pompress.

"I haven't been all over Egypt either. I'm rather looking forward to seeing some of the other spots I've never been before like Luxor or Aswan for that matter, and I'm looking forward to seeing the dam at Aswan. Ever since it was almost overtopped last year, I've wanted to take a look at it before they build the high dam."

"I can't say I'm particularly enamored with Egypt at the moment to be honest," said Lady Pompress.

Frances smiled at her kindly.

"I can understand," she said. "But give it a chance. I think you'll like it once we're on the boat and sailing down the cooler Nile with the breeze and the luxury."

"Perhaps," said Lady Pompress from pinched lips, "though I'm not sure we'll do any more sightseeing, Timmy and I."

Frances looked from Lady Pompress to Captain Wainscott. He looked thoroughly dejected, though he didn't say anything.

"You might change your mind once you're feeling better," said Frances.

"I never change my mind once it's made up," she said sharply.

Frances smiled at her and looked away towards the pyramids. She could see the group slowly emerging from the small mouth of the Pyramid of Menkaure. She was on the far south edge of the canopy which gave her just enough of a view to see that much of Menkaure's pyramid. Fowler emerged first with his safari hat. Florence was out right behind him. Frances could tell, because she was a tall woman, and it was her height that one could easily use to identify her.

They made their way slowly, Florence and Fowler talking and laughing about something or other. Abigail and Albert were on the other side of Fowler, actively participating in the conversation. The rest of the group straggled behind. When they were within earshot, Frances waved at her friend, and she waved back.

"Would you please not stop fanning me, Timmy, honestly," said an exasperated, but otherwise quite healthy Lady Pompress.

Captain Wainscott started fanning again, but this time his heart wasn't in it. The group of tourists led by Fowler entered the canopy and Florence came up to Frances.

"Can I get you a chair, Flo?" asked Frances.

"No, I'm quite all right," she said.

In the meantime, Captain Wainscott carried a chair and placed it next to Florence for her to sit on.

"Why, thank you, kind sir," she said. "I'm Florence Hudnall, Frances' friend."

She shook his hand before sitting down.

"Captain Timothy Wainscott," he said. "Frances has told us about you. Your first time in Egypt is it?"

"Yes, and I'm having the absolute time of my life."

"Timmy, I'm quite parched," said Lady Pompress, "can you get me some water."

Captain Wainscott left Frances and Florence to tend to his fiancée. He picked up the glass of water that was well within Lady Pompress' reach and handed it to her. He sat back down and slowly started fanning her.

"We're here to try and enjoy ourselves," she said to him in a hushed voice. "Not for you to make friends and leave me all to myself. Honestly, Timmy, this is not looking good for our future."

"I'm sorry, dear," he said quietly, "I wasn't thinking."

Fowler looked at his watch, and then he looked up at the group of tourists, most of whom were enjoying a glass of water.

"I make it three thirty, which means we have an hour before we need to leave. I'll be showing a tour of the Great Sphinx if anyone is interested. Alternatively you are free to tour the Giza pyramid complex at your leisure. However, I do ask that you return by four fifteen at the latest. We need to leave here at four thirty."

Fowler looked around at the group. He took a sip of water from the small canteen that he kept attached to his belt and then replaced it.

"If you'd like to join me, please gather in the southeast corner."

That was directly behind where Frances and Florence were seated.

"Would you like to tour the Sphinx?" asked Frances.

"Oh yes," she said.

The two of them got up and walked over to the southeast corner where they were met with Simon. Fowler came over and joined them.

"Are you up for a short walkabout, dear?" asked Captain Wainscott, hopefully. "I'd love to take a look at the Sphinx."

"NO!" exclaimed Lady Pompress, a little louder than she had probably wanted, "I'm not well. I just fainted not long ago and I'm still recovering. Have you no sympathy?"

Captain Wainscott turned a little red.

"Would you mind if I take a little look then? I won't be long. You've got fresh water here and I can have one of the waiters fan you if you'd like."

"Timothy! Good God, have you lost your mind? I don't want one of these Arabs fanning me. Have you lost your mind? If you expect to become my husband you will stay with me. What sort of a man leaves his fragile, sick fiancée in an unknown country without any care and consideration."

"Sorry, dear," he said, with his head bowed low, "I just thought you looked well enough."

"I might look well, but I certainly do not feel well," she said.

"Yes, dear."

Frances smiled sadly towards Captain Wainscott. Though he was a grown man capable of making his own decisions, and if those decisions brought him great unhappiness, then that was his own doing.

"Well," said Fowler, smiling and looking around at everyone under the canopy, "I suppose it's just us three then. Shall we?"

Frances, Florence and Simon nodded their heads.

They started off south towards the Great Sphinx.

"This is the eastern cemetery here that you see in front of the queens' pyramids."

Fowler arced his left hand over the many tombs and mastabas that littered their view to the west.

"These tombs or mastabas are burial places for the lesser royals and family members of Khufu or Cheops. As you can see, the mastaba is a rectangular flat roofed tomb with slopping stepped sides. They generally predate the pyramids as a form of burial, though these ones are thought to have been built around the same time as the pyramids were being built."

Simon nodded his head.

"Who were the sorts of family members to be buried here?" he asked.

"That's a good question. We haven't fully identified everyone who was buried here but we have uncovered the identity of many. For example, this largest mastaba right here in front was made for Prince Ankhhaf. Ankhhaf was the vizier to Khafre..."

"Vizier?" asked Simon.

"Yes, sort of a chief political advisor and overseer of the construction of the complex. Ankhhaf was the son of Sneferu also known as Soris. He was also the younger half brother to Khufu. They shared the same father but different mothers. He was obviously quite influential as can be attested to by the size of his mastaba."

"How do you remember all of this?" asked Florence, as they continued to walk towards the Sphinx.

Fowler turned to look at Florence and he smiled at her. Both she and Frances carried umbrellas above their heads which greatly reduced the heat. Behind them followed a waiter with a jug of water in his one hand and paper cups in his other.

"Just time," answered Fowler, "that's all. I've been doing this for five years now. I think it helps that I enjoy it."

Under the canopy, Abigail and Albert approached the bus. Darius was seated on a small wooden stool smoking a cigarette. He stood up as they came by.

"We need to get at our luggage, please," said Albert.

"Yes, sir," said Darius. He put his cigarette in the glass ashtray by his feet and went round to the back of the bus where the opened up the luggage compartment.

"Would you like for me to get it?" asked Darius.

"No, thank you," said Albert.

Albert reached into the compartment and grabbed his bag and then his sister's. He pulled them out and stood them up on the dry compacted dirt floor. He took each one in turn and put it on the far side of the bus. He and Abigail went round and opened up the luggage. Darius watched them out of the corner of his eye.

"Some privacy, please," said Albert to Darius quite sternly.

Darius walked around to the near side of the bus and waited for them. Albert and Abigail wrapped up some of the jewelry, including the ankh and bowl and other items in clothing and stuffed them into a rucksack that Albert took out of his suitcase.

"This is not a good idea," he said to her. "These are ours and we should keep them. I don't think any good will come from giving them back."

"But we can't sell any of it, Al, and if we can't sell any of it, what good will come from owning it. We might not have taken them but they're still not ours."

"But we can't just leave them, they'll be swiped. I know a lot of people who would kill to have these in their hands."

"We'll find a way," said Abigail.

Albert sighed and shook his head. He didn't like the idea. He was certain he could find some buyers back home on the black market who would pay a decent sum, and God knows that both he and Abigail could make use of the money.

They packed away the jewels and other artifacts into the rucksack which Albert put over his back. He returned to the near side of the bus after closing and locking their luggage and placing it back into the bus.

"Thank you, Darius," said Albert, "we've finished with our luggage."

Darius got up from his stool and put his cigarette out into the ashtray. He put the ashtray on the stool.

"So I close it now?" he asked.

Albert nodded. He looked at his sister.

"I think it's probably best we go to the queen's pyramid around the west side of Khufu's pyramid just to be safe," he whispered.

"Come on, Al, nobody's going to follow us."

"You don't know that for sure. Everyone can come and go as they please. I don't trust any of the others except for Frances and her friend Florence."

"You can't honestly believe that anyone in the group has actually followed us here from London to rob us. That's preposterous."

Albert and Abigail walked around the north side of the eastern cemetery, heading towards the north side of the Great Pyramid of Giza.

"No, I don't think anyone would be that stupid, but we could be watched and they might make their way into the pyramid after they've seen us enter it. If they are watching, they'll know that we've gone into the queen's pyramid only to enter into the secret chambers of Menkaure's pyramids."

"Albert!" exclaimed Abigail, as they started to head west along the north side of the eastern cemetery towards Khufu's pyramid, "you are paranoid, aren't you?"

Albert stopped and turned to look at his sister. He was grim faced.

"Listen," he said, quite firmly, "I have my reasons all right. I didn't want to do this in the first place. We need the money, but they're yours so I'm obliged to help you. But these are extremely valuable and there are many who would kill us to get their hands on these priceless gems. So I'd rather not give them the chance. I'd also rather not let them find out where we're taking them. Which in and of itself sounds like a ridiculous idea."

"Albert, dear brother, we don't have a choice. We can't just pop into the Egyptian museum and just say, 'oh hello, we found these little items recently and thought you might like them back'. We'll be arrested and thrown into a Cairo jail. Is that what you'd like?"

Albert shook his head. His sister had a point. Abigail touched his shoulder and smiled at him.

"Look, I'm so happy that you've decided to help me with this. But even though we didn't steal them, we have no proof of that. These items are known as some of the missing items from the King's chamber. We need to act discreetly. Once we're on the boat, at the earliest convenience, we'll tell the boat captain that we saw someone enter the queen's pyramid and after they left we entered and found some missing jewels had been returned."

Albert nodded slowly and sighed.

"Very well," he said. "Let's just get this over and done with."

He looked at his watch and walked onward. From the canopy, the others watched Albert and Abigail disappear as they passed across the north face of the Great Pyramid of Giza.

"I wonder why they're taking another look at Khufu's pyramid?" asked Captain Wainscott, absentmindedly.

"They're not," said Samuel, though nobody heard him.

Nigel got up from his chair and went over to the bus where he had Darius open up the back of the bus. He extracted his suitcase and pulled out a small rucksack and a canteen. He came back to the canopy and had a waiter fill up his canteen with fresh water. He turned around and said to no one in particular, "I'm going to make the most of the rest of our time. Anyone wish to join me?"

He got no takers, and so he walked off into the eastern cemetery to explore. Samuel went over to the bus and pulled out his suitcase and took out a small hand bag that looked like a doctor's bag. Maurice joined him and looked at Samuel's bag.

"You hoping to do an autopsy on one of those mummies, are you?"

Maurice asked, keeping a lit cigarette in the corner of his mouth.

"You never know," said Samuel.

He picked up his bag and left Maurice to himself. Maurice found the American quite rude. He shrugged and pulled out his own large suitcase. Inside he took out a rucksack that was really just a canvas bag with a drawstring close on the top and two leather straps for the shoulders. He put it casually over his one shoulder and headed south towards the Sphinx.

Captain Wainscott looked up and watched the three men disappear. Samuel went off after Nigel, but whereas Nigel went directly west into the eastern cemetery, Samuel went more to the southwest area of the eastern cemetery.

"That's curious," he said, "I wonder why those gentleman all had to take their rucksacks out at this late stage of the day."

He turned around and smiled feebly at Lady Pompress. She sighed and shook her head at him.

"Why do you always have to be such a bother?" she asked exasperatedly.

"I am not," he said, quite defensively, "I haven't bothered anyone. I'm just curios, that's all."

He brushed his mustache flat with his thumb and index finger of his right hand.

"You are so. You are such a nosey busy body. No wonder you haven't got any friends."

"I do have friends, dear. It's just difficult to see them now that most of them have families."

That wasn't exactly the truth. The main problem was that none of his friends liked Lady Pompress and she hardly let him out of her sight. But he didn't mind, he was certain that once they were married he would regain his position as the man of the manor so to speak, and he'd have access to her money which would him quite a bit. It had cost him a small fortune in trying to court her, and he had accumulated more debt now than he could ever manage repaying without the assistance of her wealth.

"Aren't you curious why they've all taken rucksacks?" he said, standing and looking down at her.

"No, I'm not. And really, Timmy, you brought a rucksack yourself. Why don't you take it out then if it'll make you feel any better," she said.

"I would if you'd let me go and have a bit of a look and see."

"You're welcome to do as you please, but remember, Timothy, there are consequences to every action, and as my fiancé, I expect better."

"Very well," he said, sighing as he sat back down.

He watched the two men for a while longer, until he lost them behind some larger mastabas. He turned towards Lady Pompress and started to fan her half-heartedly. He looked down towards the Sphinx. Maurice was quite behind Fowler, Frances, Florence and Simon. The four of them were standing on the north side of the Sphinx and Fowler was talking and gesticulating about something or other.

Maurice finally caught up with them, but passed them to the east by several feet. Frances saw him walk past without acknowledging them as he started off towards the Valley Temple of Menkaure, slightly south and west from the Sphinx.

"This Great Sphinx of Giza," continued Fowler, resting his right hand below the head, "is the largest monolith statue in the world. It was also believed to have been built during the time when the Pyramid of Khafre was being built."

"I think I'll take a picture of the Sphinx," said Florence.

"Why don't you let me take a picture of you with it," said Frances.

"That would be wonderful."

Florence positioned herself on the north side under the head.

"Would you join me please, Perry?" asked Florence.

"Certainly."

He stood next to her and clasped his hands behind his back.

Frances looked at the protruding lower jaw, the prognathism of the profile was odd, and she wondered about it but didn't ask. She focused in on them and took the picture and then handed the camera back to Florence.

Fowler continued with his talk.

"Many have wondered what happened to the nose of the Sphinx," said Fowler. "Clearly there was a nose on it at one point. Do any of you have any idea about what might have happened to it?"

Fowler looked around at the three of them. Florence shrugged.

"It came off due to erosion," said Simon.

"That's a fair and reasonable suggestion, but I'm afraid it's not true. Frances?"

"I'm afraid I'm at an unfair advantage. Having been here before, I do know, but I know you'll tell it much better."

She smiled at him and he nodded his head at her.

"It is believed that a Muslim by the name of Muhammad Sa'im al-Dahr found peasants offering up gifts to the Sphinx in the hope that their harvest would be more bountiful. Muhammad was outraged by this and took chisels and rods to the nose and broke it off."

"Good Lord!" exclaimed Florence.

"Quite," said Fowler. "Though justice was served. He was hanged for the vandalism."

119

"That seems like harsh punishment."

"To us. Though this occurred back in the early fourteenth century. At least this is what an Arab historian writing in the fifteenth century suggested happened. Others have blamed the British, of course. We're often to blame for many things, whether or not we did them, seems irrelevant."

"And which version do you give more credence to, Perry?" asked Frances.

"I find the Arab historian's version most compelling. You see there were drawings by a Danish naval captain by the name of Frederic Louis Norden who drew the Sphinx in the mid eighteenth century, and his drawings show no nose. The British weren't in Egypt until the late nineteenth century, which gives us a rather good alibi, I believe."

He smiled at Frances and she nodded in return. They walked around to the south side of the Sphinx and stood towards its rear. Frances looked west towards the Pyramid of Menkaure. She saw what looked like Albert and Abigail walking towards the entrance to the eastern most queen's pyramid behind Menkaure's. They were crossing in front of Menkaure's funerary temple.

Lady Marmalade couldn't be certain it was them, they were after all about a half a mile away, but the air was clear and she recognized them from their clothes and Abigail's parasol.

"Most of the Sphinx, until the late nineteenth century was under a lot of sand that had covered it over the past four, almost five thousand years," said Fowler. "Sand covered it almost to the height of its rump, and almost up to its neck. In fact, it wasn't until about ten years ago that the Sphinx had been fully excavated thanks to the French Egyptologist Émile Baraize."

Frances saw Maurice lingering by the tomb of Queen Khentkawes, about eight hundred feet away from her in a southwesterly direction. She thought it quite curious as he was just walking around the tomb not really paying attention to what he was looking at. It appeared to Frances that he kept glancing over towards the Pyramid of Menkaure.

"Are there any chambers inside the Sphinx?" asked Simon.

"There were," said Fowler. "Émile found a passageway at the rear of the Sphinx, right over here." Fowler walked behind the Sphinx and the three of them followed him. He pointed squarely at the middle of the Sphinx's rear. "You might even see that the rear at the bottom here, looks different. That's because Émile took a look in the passageway and finding nothing decided to seal it up."

Fowler walked around the north side of the Sphinx and stood halfway between the front and rear paws.

"Émile also found a second passageway here," he said, pointing at another area that looked smoother than the rest. "He also found this passageway led nowhere and so he sealed it up."

"Sounds to me like he might have been trying to hide something. Otherwise, why seal up the passageways so that others can't explore them?" asked Simon.

"You ask good questions, Mr. Gragg. You should consider becoming an Egyptologist."

That made Simon beam with pride, and as he smiled it crinkled the scar on the left side of his face. It made him look ruggedly handsome, smiling like that.

"You might be onto something with that line of thought," continued Fowler. "Émile said he closed up the passages for safety as he found the Sphinx to be in poor shape. However, others believe that Émile was hiding something. They think that the passageways lead to hidden subterranean chambers. The great psychic, Edgar Cayce, believed that the passageways hide the Hall of Records."

"And what exactly are those?" asked Simon.

"The Hall of Records is believed by Cayce to be contained below the Sphinx and house the only records of the lost civilization of Atlantis which were brought to Egypt by the last Atlantean survivors."

Simon grinned.

"That sounds more like it."

"It does indeed sound quite a bit more interesting," added Florence, looking at Frances. "Doesn't it?"

Frances looked back at her friend. She had just seen Nigel and Samuel wondering around independently by the boat pits on the south side of the funerary temple of Khafre.

"What was that, Flo?" she asked.

"I was just saying how interesting this conspiracy about the Hall of Records having been sealed off inside the Sphinx is."

"Oh yes, quite curious," said Frances.

"Well, ladies and gentleman, this concludes your tour of the Sphinx. I make it just after four, so you have the next fifteen to twenty minutes to do any last minute exploration you might like," said Fowler.

"I think I'll take a quick look into the secret chambers of Menkaure's Pyramid. See if I can't find any spoils," said Simon grinning.

"You might want to hurry," said Fowler. "You don't have a lot of time."

"Will do," said Simon, walking off towards the pyramid.

"Ladies?" asked Fowler.

"I think I'll just spend some time out here for a bit. It's such a wonderful day," said Frances. "I'll be back in time to leave."

"I'll keep her company, and make sure she doesn't get into any trouble."

Fowler nodded his head and then walked off north towards the canopy.

Eight

"Are you all right, Fran?" asked Florence.

Frances looked at her with a furrowed brow.

"Quite all right, Flo," said Frances, "why do you ask?"

"You seem distracted."

"Yes, I suppose I am."

"What about."

Frances turned to face the Pyramid of Menkaure. As she did so she saw Albert and Abigail exit the queen's pyramid and head west.

"That's Albert and Abigail," she said.

Florence turned to look and shielded her eyes from the sun.

"Why yes, I think you're right."

"It's curious, Flo, they snuck into the queen's pyramid and now they're sneaking out. It's as if they don't want to be seen."

"How can you tell?"

"Well, they're taking the long way back to the canopy. It would be much easier for them to walk diagonally northeast towards our meeting place, than to head west around the pyramids."

"I see what you mean."

"Further, there are now four men heading to the very same place that Albert and Abigail just exited."

"Who?"

Frances pointed to Simon who was the closest to them. Then she pointed to Maurice.

"Simon and Maurice are over there. Then if you look straight ahead," and Frances pointed towards the Pyramid of Khafre, "you'll see Nigel and Samuel."

"They're heading towards the Pyramid of Menkaure," said Florence.

"No, I don't think so, Flo," said Frances, "I think they're heading towards the queen's pyramid on the south side of Menkaure's pyramid."

"You can't be sure... can you?" asked Florence.

They both watched the four men, as Albert and Abigail disappeared from sight.

"Let's wait and see," said Frances.

They watched and waited. And indeed, the four men made their way to the queen's pyramid independently, separated by minutes from each other.

"I don't think we're going to be leaving on time," said Frances.

"What do you suppose they want with the queen's pyramid?" asked Florence.

"Let's walk back to the canopy. I could use some water," said Frances, as she turned and the two of them started off towards the meeting area. "I'm not quite sure. They could possibly be looking for hidden treasure."

"But the treasure has either been stolen or placed in museums," said Florence.

"That's correct. But do you remember when we were leaving this morning from the hotel, and Abigail's suitcase fell and opened?"

Florence nodded.

"She seemed quite embarrassed by it."

"Well, I think she was embarrassed because of the jewelry that fell out."

"That's nothing to be embarrassed by if it were her own valuables."

"What do you mean?"

"Well, I believe that the jewelry, the ankh and the bowl were items that had been previously stolen from Menkaure's pyramid."

"How do you know?" asked Florence.

"I've studied the theft before, and I've seen pictures of the remaining jewels that were recovered from pyramid as well as those recovered after they had been sold by the thieves."

"Do you know who the thieves are?"

"I think I do, though they were never charged, as the valuables were never found. They had hid them well, and wouldn't give out the location to the police. They swore they were innocent."

"So what is the importance of this stolen jewelry?"

"Well, I have a theory. I can't prove it, but you know me, I like to think about these things. I asked myself, why would Abigail bring jewelry with her on a cruise in Egypt."

"She said she'd picked up some mementos," offered Florence, knowing that she couldn't have, but wanting to hear Frances' take on it.

"That's right, except that she came over on the boat with us from Greece. She couldn't have bought any of those sorts of trinkets from Alexandria. In any event, I feel fairly confident that they're not just tourist souvenirs, that they're the real stolen jewels. So, if we accept that, then why bring them here to Egypt."

They continued walking leisurely towards the canopy.

"Perhaps she was hoping to sell them to someone here who understood their value."

Frances looked up at her for a moment.

"Perhaps, though I'm certain she'd get more money for those items in Europe or England. No, I think she brought them here perhaps to return them to their rightful place."

"Really?" asked Florence.

Frances nodded.

"Do you have a better explanation?"

"No, but it seems quite far fetched. I mean, do you think she's just going to leave it in the king's burial chamber?"

"Possibly."

"But that's open, and apparently it could be found by anyone else venturing in."

"You have a good point, Flo, but that's what I think she might have done, however naïvely it might seem. She couldn't go to the museum to drop them off. There would be too many questions asked. Perhaps she was going to inform the authorities in due time before it could be stolen a second time."

"You do have quite the active imagination," said Florence.

"It can't be helped," said Frances, smiling at her friend. "I've had to unearth the truth of so many murders, I suppose that's the way my mind works."

"Well," said Florence, taking Frances by the elbow, "I hope that nothing that nefarious is underfoot. I really hope we can just look forward to a wonderful, uneventful cruise down the Nile."

"Oh yes, I'm sure we will. It is however, admirable that she's gone to put back what isn't hers."

"You could always ask her about it," said Florence.

Frances stopped and looked at her friend.

"I don't think I shall, Flo. I don't want to stir any hornets' nests, and make the rest of the journey uncomfortable. No harm has been done, and I'm not here to investigate a theft from fifty years ago, especially when the thieves are probably dead and certainly not here."

Florence smiled, and they walked the rest of the way to join those who were waiting under the canopy. When they got there, Frances and Florence took a glass of fresh water that a waiter offered them. They sat back down in the chairs they had been in before they left.

"Did you see that couple who were sitting with you at lunch?" asked Captain Wainscott.

"You mean Albert and Abigail?" asked Frances.

"I think so, I didn't get their names."

"Yes it was Albert and Abigail."

"I said to that other chap, I think his name is Samuel, if I overheard correctly, that I wondered why they were going back to see Khufu's pyramid. He said they weren't."

"What else did he say?" asked Frances.

"Nothing, he went to the bus and took out a physician's bag from his suitcase and then he headed off over there," said Wainscott, pointing towards the eastern cemetery.

"I see," said Frances, "and you're sure it was a physician's bag?"

"Well, the bag, yes. Though I have no idea if he's a doctor or not."

"I saw Albert and Abigail venturing towards the Pyramid of Menkaure," said Frances, taking a sip of water.

"Don't you find that odd? I mean, why would they take the long way?" asked Captain Wainscott. "I told Lady Pompress that I thought it curious but she didn't think anything of it."

"It's not that I thought nothing of it, Timmy, it's just that it isn't any of our business," said Lady Pompress.

Captain Wainscott looked at her and then back at Frances eagerly.

"You're right, Captain, it is quite curious that they took the long way there. Why do you think that is?" asked Frances.

"Good heavens, me? I have no idea. Perhaps they didn't want to be seen."

"Yes, but why?" asked Frances.

"Perhaps they were hoping to find some hidden treasure inside the secret chambers of the Pyramid of Menkaure."

"But they've all been stolen or moved, Timmy," said Lady Pompress.

"Right," said Wainscott, putting his hand through his hair.

"Maybe they just wanted some time alone, and didn't want anyone following them," said Lady Pompress.

"How are you feeling, dear?" asked Frances, looking at Lady Pompress.

Lady Pompress looked over at Frances without a smile.

"Fine," she said.

"I just can't help thinking that there is some sort of mystery underfoot," said Wainscott, looking at Frances. "It would be so thrilling to see you working a case. You would let me help you, wouldn't you?"

"Well, I certainly hope that nothing untoward is going on. Florence and I are really just looking forward to a relaxing vacation."

"Aren't we all," said Lady Pompress coolly, and Frances wasn't all that sure what she meant by the comment.

Captain Wainscott smoothed his mustache and looked around out towards the pyramids for a while. Then he turned back to Frances and Florence.

"I wonder where the others went?" he asked.

"Simon told us he was going off to see the Pyramid of Menkaure to see if he could find any hidden treasure."

Wainscott nodded.

"And the others?"

Frances looked out towards the Pyramid of Menkaure. It was far away, but she couldn't make out any of their forms.

"Hard to say, but I have a feeling that they've all headed to that pyramid too."

"Why on earth?"

Frances smiled at him. He seemed like a naïve, if good natured, young man.

"Perhaps they're all looking for buried treasure, just like Simon."

Wainscott smiled.

"Though that seems odd. Didn't Perry tell us that what hadn't been stolen had been taken safely to museums?"

"He did. But there is no understanding the effervescent hope the heart holds dear in both love and riches," said Frances.

"Have you ever found the secret chambers?" asked Captain Wainscott.

Frances nodded.

"Many years ago, when I was here before, my husband and I toured the whole area thoroughly. The secret chambers are not hard to find. They have been kept open now that they're empty."

"And were they truly empty of valuables?" asked Captain Wainscott, as wide-eyed as a doe-eyed schoolboy with his first crush.

"It appeared truly empty. Not even the sarcophagus was there. But then again, I wasn't hunting for jewelry."

"Of course not," said Lady Pompress, under her breath "you had no need for more riches."

Frances turned and looked at her.

"I beg your pardon."

Lady Pompress turned and offered Frances a false smile.

"I said, I didn't suppose you were here looking for riches."

"Don't mind Abby," said Wainscott, leaning in towards Frances, "I think she's just a little bit under the weather from the heat."

Lady Pompress shot him daggers.

"Don't presume to speak for me, Timothy," she said, coldly. "I feel much better."

"Well, that's jolly good," he said.

She remained silent. Fowler looked at his watch, it was four fifteen, everyone was supposed to be meeting here at this particular time. He looked out over the Giza pyramid complex. He surveyed it steadily but he couldn't find anyone. He strode off towards the bus, and shared a few words with Darius who was sitting on the stool as if he had not moved, smoking a cigarette. Fowler walked up into the bus and reappeared moments later with a pair of binoculars.

He came back under the canopy and looked around the complex with the binoculars. There was no sign of them. He decided he would give them until four twenty and then he'd go looking for them.

"It is terribly inconsiderate of the others," said Lady Pompress, looking at her watch which was coming on four twenty. "Who do they honestly think they are? So selfish."

"I know, dear, I'm sure Perry will go looking for them soon if they don't show up."

"Go tell him to," said Lady Pompress.

"In a little while."

"No, I'm hungry and I'm tired of sitting here doing nothing. Go and tell him now."

"No, my dear. I will if he hasn't gone to find them by four thirty."

Lady Pompress sighed heavily and shook her head at him. Then she turned her head towards the right away from them all. So he does have a spine, though Frances, smiling ever so slightly to herself.

Fowler came up to her and Frances and Florence.

"You thought they were all heading to the Pyramid of Menkaure?" he asked. He stroked his bushy mustache, and for the first time the whole day she'd known him, Fowler was no longer smiling.

"I thought so, yes. I think they're all heading towards the queen's pyramid to explore the secret chambers."

Frances looked past Fowler as movement caught her eye. Fowler turned around. Albert and Abigail strode under the canopy. Albert was sweating. The front of his shirt was stained and he wiped at his brow with a handkerchief.

"Sorry we're late," he said, trying to put on a brave smile. "It's so easy to get lost in time exploring."

"Where were you?" asked Fowler non-combatively.

"We went for a quick look at the secret chambers inside Menkaure's pyramid. A little disappointing as there's nothing in there."

Fowler nodded. Abigail sat down and closed her umbrella. She was glowing too, and was patting her face with a handkerchief of her own.

"Did you see any of the others?" asked Fowler.

"Who?" asked Albert.

"Mr. Simon Gragg, Mr. Maurice Gabberdeen, Mr. Nigel Durmott or Mr. Samuel Newton."

Albert shook his head.

"I'm afraid not. Were they going there too?"

His voice gave off the smallest quaver of anxiety even though he tried to hide it.

"We believe that's where they were all headed."

"I see," he said, and he looked pained. He looked over at Abigail quizzically. She smiled thinly at him. He walked off towards the bus, carrying his rucksack that didn't look quite empty. Darius opened up the back, and he took out his luggage and went around to the far side of the bus. When he returned, he was carrying only his suitcase which he put back into the rear of the bus. His rucksack was gone. Presumably put back into his luggage. He sat back down next to his sister. They exchanged looks but didn't say anything.

Fowler looked at his watch. It was now after four twenty-five. He brought the binoculars back up to his eyes and scanned the complex again. He saw Simon walking towards them. He was in the far side of the eastern cemetery.

"Here comes Mr. Gragg," he said, more for his own edification than anyone else's.

They all sat or stood, in Fowler's case, and watched Simon slowly loom bigger as he made his way towards them. It was almost four thirty when he strode under the canopy, grinning widely as if he had just found salvation. He looked at his watch.

"Just on time, I believe," he said.

"We were actually hoping to leave at this time," said Fowler. "We're scheduled to meet here at four fifteen."

"My mistake," said Simon. "Terribly sorry about that."

He walked up to one of the tables and poured himself a glass of water. Fowler turned to watch him.

"Mr. Gragg," he said.

Simon turned, with the glass of water to his lips.

"Did you see Mr. Gabberdeen, Mr. Durmott or Mr. Newton at all?"

Simon shook his head and then drank the rest of the water. He took off his hat and wiped his brow with a hankie that was already quite damp.

"No, I'm afraid I didn't see anyone else."

"Were you visiting the Pyramid of Menkaure?" asked Fowler.

"No. I was actually looking at the builders' quarters on the far west side. Quite astonishing the poor accommodations they had considering the magnificence they were building."

"Didn't you tell us you were going to explore the secret chambers?" asked Fowler.

"Yes I did, Perry," said Simon, "but I changed my mind. I'm allowed to do that, aren't I?"

"Quite."

He turned around and looked out again over the complex, looking through his binoculars. Lady Pompress looked sternly at Captain Wainscott and nodded at Fowler. Captain Wainscott stood up.

"Perry," he said, as he walked up to him. "Perhaps we should send a search party?"

Fowler turned to look at him and nodded. Then he turned back to face Lady Marmalade.

"You're quite sure you saw them heading towards the Pyramid of Menkaure?"

"I am, though to be honest, Perry, I didn't see any of them enter," said Frances.

"Thank you, Frances," said Fowler, regaining his smile. He turned back to Captain Wainscott. "Would you care to join me on this search mission?"

"Certainly," said Wainscott.

"Then let's be about our business," said Fowler, and then turning to the group. "We won't be long."

"I hope this won't be a regular occurrence," said Orpha. "I didn't pay all this money just to sit around and wait on stragglers."

She looked at Fowler with a raised eyebrow and tight, thin lips. She was not pleased, though it seemed to Frances that she had not been pleased since Frances had first laid eyes upon her.

"Not if I can help it," said Fowler, maintaining his composure.

He nodded to the group and strode off with Captain Wainscott at his side. Wainscott was saying something to him as they walked off through the eastern cemetery at a brisk pace, heading right towards the Pyramid of Menkaure. It had gone past four thirty.

Simon walked over to the bus and placed his rucksack back inside his suitcase. He then returned back to the canopy and sat at the far end, closest to the bus and looked out towards the pyramids. Mahulda looked at him shyly. It was plain to see that she fancied him. He smiled at her, and she quickly looked away and stuck her nose back into her book. Frances noticed the book was titled Death Comes as the End. A mystery set in ancient Egypt and written by the great Agatha Christie. Frances had read it and enjoyed it immensely.

The sun was slowly dipping towards the western horizon. The shadows were growing longer. The sun had dipped just below the top of Khufu's pyramid, giving it a tremendous glow. Florence stood up and took out her camera and composed the shot she wanted to take.

"What a wonderful idea," said Frances.

Florence turned back and nodded.

"That's only six pictures I've taken today," she said.

"Not many," said Frances.

"No, but I think I took six good ones. Two of the Great Pyramid, one each of the pyramid of Khafre and of Menkaure. The one of the Sphinx and now this."

Simon got up and walked over to Florence.

"Would you mind if I took a look?" he asked.

"Certainly," said Florence, as she took the strap off her neck and handed him the camera.

Simon looked through it and focused the camera and scanned over the complex.

"I wish I had brought my father's," he said.

"Your father has one?" asked Florence.

"Yes, exactly like this one in fact."

"Would you let me take your picture with the pyramid in the background?" he asked, looking at both Florence and Frances.

"What a wonderful idea," said Florence.

"I like it," said Frances.

They stood up and posed at the west edge of the canopy, and the Pyramid of Khufu loomed large with a golden edge from the sun behind them. Simon took his time to get it just right and then he took the picture. He handed the camera back to Florence.

"I think it will be a good one. It is a great camera after all."

"If you'd like," offered Florence. "I don't mind taking a picture of you with the pyramid in the background. The golden yellow light is absolutely gorgeous. I'd be happy to mail it to you once I've had them developed."

"I don't know," said Simon, "that's awfully kind of you, but I don't want to impose."

"Nonsense," said Florence. "Go and stand over there while the light is still wonderful."

"Well, it would really mean something to have a keepsake of this trip."

Simon went over and stood by the edge of the canopy and Florence took his picture. He was grinning widely. It obviously meant a great deal to him. Mahulda was glancing up from her book and admiring his ruggedly handsome face with the scar on his cheek which made him look strong and daring.

"Let me get your address," said Florence, walking back to the table where Frances was seated. Simon followed her. She put her camera down on the table and pulled out her diary and a pencil from her purse. Simon gave her his address. He was living in Leeds.

"Thank you so much," said Simon. "I'll wait excitedly for the photograph when you have a moment to send it."

"I should imagine you'll receive it by December," said Florence. "I plan on getting the rolls developed as soon as we get back in early November."

Simon grinned at her again.

"That's so very kind," he said.

Florence smiled and nodded at him. Simon went back to his chair to sit down, when Maurice arrived.

"Where's Perry?" he asked.

"Gone to find you lot of stragglers," said Orpha, clearly upset.

"Oh, I see," he said. He looked down at his watch. "I suppose I am a bit late. Terribly sorry."

He started off towards the bus.

"Where were you?" asked Simon.

Maurice looked at him, and thought for a moment about whether or not he was going to answer him or not. He decided he would.

"I've just come from the western cemetery," he said. "Why do you ask?"

"Well," said Simon, grinning at him, "Perry wondered if I'd seen you, and I'd just come from the builders' quarters, so obviously I hadn't. He thought we'd both gone to Menkaure's pyramid."

"I see," said Maurice. "That's a shame. I wasn't there."

"Did you see the other chaps?" asked Orpha.

Maurice looked at her.

"No, who?"

"Perry's went looking for you of course, and Nigel and Samuel."

"Oh, the American fellow. No, I haven't seen either of them."

"It's still very inconsiderate of you, Mr. Gabberdeen, to show up so late," said Orpha.

"Yes, well, I think I'm not the last one, am I?"

Orpha didn't say anything to that. Maurice walked off towards the bus where he put his rucksack, being more of a sack, back into his suitcase. He leaned against the near side of the bus and stared at the rest of them under the canopy absentmindedly. He reached into his shirt pocket and pulled out a cigarette tin.

Then he leaned into his trouser pocket and pulled out a silver lighter and lit his cigarette. Darius watched him carefully.

Lady Pompress stood up and started pacing up and down the length of the canopy.

"This is so terribly unfair," she muttered to herself. "I've spent a small fortune for this holiday and most of the afternoon has been spent sitting around waiting for inconsiderate louts."

"I know, Lady Pompress," said Orpha, "these boors will be the end of us if we let them. I plan on giving Mr. Fowler a piece of my mind. I expect better service and better adherence to the schedule going forward."

Lady Pompress nodded.

"Quite right. I can't stand waiting around for inconsiderate clods. Men, I tell you. Absolutely uncouth and uncultured."

"You are quite correct. But we've both spent a lot of money and I'll be damned if we let them get away with it."

Lady Pompress and Orpha commiserated for a while longer. Frances stood up and looked out towards the southwest. She couldn't see Perry or Timothy, though she did hope they found the last two and brought them back quickly. She noticed a man walking towards them, coming through the eastern cemetery. It was Samuel Newton with his fedora in his one hand and his doctor's bag in the other. He was walking with purpose, taking large strides towards them, his head looking straight ahead.

He went straight past the canopy and towards the rear of the bus. Seeing Maurice there smoking a cigarette he nodded at him and Maurice nodded back. Samuel put his bag back in his suitcase and then returned to Maurice. They exchanged a few words and Maurice offered him a cigarette which he accepted. Maurice lit it and then Samuel came back and stood under the canopy, facing away from the rest of the group, towards the pyramids. He held his cigarette in one hand and his fedora in the other.

"Mr. Newton, do you mind telling us what was so important that you've kept us waiting for over half an hour?" asked Orpha, looking up at him from her chair.

Samuel turned around and looked at her. He then looked at his watch.

"Nothing," he said.

"Nothing won't do," said Orpha, with a schoolmarm's scolding. "Where were you?"

"Madam, I don't see how that's any of your business."

"You made it my business," said Orpha, getting visibly upset and flustered, "when you decided to be so disrespectfully late."

"If you must know," said Samuel, "I was over at the western cemetery viewing the Tomb of Hemon."

Samuel turned back to face the pyramids and took a deep inhalation of his cigarette. He let the smoke drift slowly from his nose.

"Then you must have seen Mr. Gabberdeen," said Lady Pompress.

Samuel turned around to face Lady Pompress, and he smiled thinly at her. He took another puff of his cigarette, and walked over to the table closest to her and picked up an ashtray in exchange for this fedora.

"No, I didn't see Maurice," he said.

He walked back to the west side of the canopy and stared out over the complex, smoking his cigarette and ignoring everyone. Orpha continued to sigh and grumble under her breath while everyone, even Lady Pompress ignored her. Mahulda continued to read Death Comes as the End, while stealing glances at an unnoticing Simon. Frances and Florence continued to sit and wait patiently.

"I wonder what's on the menu tonight," said Florence, looking at her friend.

"Are you getting hungry?" asked Frances.

"I am a bit peckish. I think all this walking around over the complex has given me quite an appetite."

"I think I see them," said Lady Pompress, sounding more excited than she had the whole day, and that wasn't saying much.

Frances and Florence stood up and walked over to the edge of the canopy where Lady Pompress was now standing. They could see three men walking north along a dusty path squashed between the Great Pyramid of Giza and the eastern cemetery. Samuel squashed out his cigarette, went back to the table where he put the ashtray down and then picked up his fedora. He didn't put it on, but he fanned it against his face. He stood by the table silently. Simon came up and stood at Lady Pompress' right, whereas Frances and Florence were to her left.

The three men turned east at the funerary temple and started towards the canopy.

"It is them," said Florence. "I think that's Nigel in the middle with his head down. He doesn't look too happy."

"I should certainly hope so," said Lady Pompress.

They waited in silence while the three men closed the distance. When they were within earshot, Lady Pompress scolded Captain Wainscott.

"What took you so long," she said, "it's after five."

"Nigel took us so long," said Wainscott, "he wasn't that easy to find."

Timothy looked over at Nigel who wouldn't look back at him. Nigel looked at the group of them sheepishly. He put on half a smile but he wasn't met with any jollity from the others.

"I'm very sorry to have kept you all waiting," he said.

"Well, we hope it was worth the trouble," said Lady Pompress, sarcastically.

"Actually it wasn't," he replied.

"Really, Mr. Fowler," said Lady Pompress, "I must strenuously urge you not to allow this sort of thing to happen again. It really sets a poor precedent for this vacation."

"I will certainly do my best," said Fowler, "but Thoth Tours doesn't leave any vacationer behind."

Perry looked around the room, and he was not smiling. A rare event that was becoming a little too common.

"If I can have everyone's attention now that we're all here," he said. He looked around and his gaze settled on Maurice. "Mr. Gabberdeen, if I can have your attention too please."

Fowler waited until Maurice slowly walked back under the canopy.

"These tours," continued Fowler, "work all the better when everyone is considerate of each other. They're more fun, and more friendships are formed. Now, the policy of Thoth Tours as I explained to Lady Pompress," he nodded at her, "is not to leave anyone behind. However, you have all put down a security deposit of one hundred pounds. As you know, if you read your travel agreement with Thoth Tours, this amount is refundable so long as you remain in fulfillment of those conditions. One of which is that you don't cause any delays, and you respect the authority of your guide, who is me. I want this to be a happy vacation for everyone. I'm easy going, and as such, I'll forgive this first indiscretion. However, please accept this as my final warning. If any of you are unable to respect your fellow vacationers and cause us to be delayed again, I'm afraid you will forfeit your security deposit. Am I clear?"

Perry looked around at the group and he was smiling again. He received a variety of nods.

"Good," said Lady Pompress. "May we go now?"

"Indeed. Please gather all of your belongings and get back onto the bus. There is a wonderful meal waiting for you on the boat, and an evening of relaxation which might be exactly what we need after a vigorous first day."

Fowler made his way to the entrance of the bus. Darius had packed away his stool and was sitting in the driver's seat. Everyone gathered their belongings and made their way onto the bus.

"Despite the delay caused by the scalawags," said Florence, "I had a thoroughly wonderful time."

Frances patted her friend's hand.

"Me too," she said, as they looked out the window taking in the awe inspiring magnificence of the Giza complex as the sun started to wobble precariously close the horizon.

Nine

Dinner which was supposed to start at six thirty upon the Queen Nefertiti, a wooden ship with sails fore and aft, had been delayed to seven p.m.

The Queen Nefertiti had been christened just two years before, and held twelve double occupancy cabins, as well as the Queen's cabin which took up the width of the aft portion of the ship. It was a traditional Nile cruise ship called a Dahabiya. This cabin had two separate rooms as well as two bathrooms, and was the cabin that Frances had booked for her and Florence.

Queen Nefertiti was only three stories tall, not counting the deck below the waterline which held the crew's cabins, the kitchen and other necessary rooms for the functioning of the ship. The rooms were located on the main deck just above the waterline, and other than the cabins it held a small room at the bow which contained a small ice maker for those who needed ice for drinks they took in their rooms. On the second deck was the library, dining room and smoking rooms. The top level offered covered lounging areas as well as the captain's cockpit at the bow and a small carpeted area for croquet at the stern.

"I think we should go for dinner," said Frances, looking at her watch. "It's seven."

Frances and Florence headed up to the second level for dinner where everyone else was just taking their seats. There were four tables that had place settings for four people, though they could have handled six if needed.

Frances and Florence took a seat opposite Orpha and Mahulda. At the table across from Florence and Frances sat Nigel, Simon, Lady Pompress and Captain Wainscott. To Frances' right sat Samuel, Maurice, Abigail and Albert. Behind them sat Perry Fowler, and another gentleman by the name of Anton Pung.

Anton Pung was another one of the tour guides they had met up with at the boat. Anton appeared to be of similar age to Perry. He was just as tall, but clean shaven. He had a mess of curly ginger hair, and his pale oval face was splattered with freckles. He was pleasant enough to look at, but his whole demeanor reminded Frances of a giraffe. Perhaps it was his long neck or long face. Perhaps it was his many freckles, either way that was what came to mind when she first set eyes on him.

Two waiters were serving the fourteen of them. Frances' and Florence's waiter was a young man named Jafari. The other waiter was named Ishaq. Jafari was a short, slim young man, dressed in white. He was a dark Egyptian with a mole below his left eye and a quick smile and quiet voice.

Jafari placed white shallow bowls of salad in front of the dinner guests. The salad was comprised of cucumbers, Kalamata olives, red onion and tomatoes. It was dressed in a light olive oil, vinegar dressing. They started in on their salads.

"I saw you reading Death Comes as the End," said Frances, looking at Mahulda. "Are you enjoying it?"

Mahulda glanced up shyly at Frances and smiled, keeping her head lowered.

"Are you enjoying it?"

"I am," she said. "It takes place in ancient Egypt."

"I know," said Frances, "I've read it. I'm a very big fan of Agatha Christie's writing."

"Me too," said Mahulda, smiling at Frances.

They continued to eat in silence for a while. Jafari came by and cleared away the dishes. A carafe of water was placed in the middle of the table and he kept everyone's glasses full.

"What brings the two of you to Egypt?" asked Frances.

Mahulda looked up at her grandmother, and Orpha nodded at her briskly.

"My grandmother brought me to Egypt, as she thinks I need to become a little more worldly."

Mahulda looked at her grandmother again. Orpha took a sip of water and looked at Frances with her wet rheumy eyes.

"Mahulda's mother died when she was four years old. I've raised her ever since. But she's a very shy girl, and I thought a trip to Africa would be something to help her come out of her shell. So far it hasn't happened."

"I'm sorry to hear that," said Frances, looking at Mahulda. Mahulda smiled a small, fragile smile, soft as butterfly wings. Frances then looked back at Orpha. "That's terribly kind of you."

Orpha offered a quick thin smile, and cocked her head ever so slightly.

"I try my best with Mahulda. It's not easy as you can imagine. My husband has been dead several years, so we've only got each other now."

"I understand," said Frances. "What happened to your father?" she asked, looking back at Mahulda.

"That's not something we like to talk about," said Orpha.

Mahulda sat looking down at her empty place setting.

"That's quite all right," said Frances.

"What about you two?" asked Orpha. "What brings the two of you to Egypt?"

Frances looked at Florence. She wanted her friend to tell the story. Florence smiled and nodded at Frances.

"I've always wanted to come to Egypt ever since I was a young girl. In fact, ever since the two of us were schoolgirl friends. I've always had a great interest in Egyptology, and my dear friend, Frances, decided to surprise me with a trip to Egypt this year. I'm overjoyed as you can imagine."

"Yes, I imagine it would be something to have someone pay your way on a vacation like this," said Orpha, looking at her granddaughter a little more sternly than was necessary.

Jafari came by with the main course. It was individual servings of beef pie with a side of green peas and corn with a square of butter melting slowly on top. It smelled warm and comforting and thick. Jafari poured Bordeaux for Frances, Florence and then Orpha. He went over to offer Mahulda some, and she looked at her grandmother who nodded curtly. Jafari poured Mahulda a glass too.

"Can I be of any further assistance?" asked Jafari, smiling.

"No, thank you," said Frances. Florence and Orpha shook their heads.

Frances watched Orpha and Mahulda carefully as she sipped on her Bordeaux. Mahulda and Orpha started on their pies. Mahulda mashed the crust into the steaming pie, and mixed it all in together. Orpha was more surgical with hers, cutting a small piece carefully with her knife and fork. She blew on it from pursed lips before popping it into her mouth.

Frances tucked into her meal. It was deliciously thick and savory. A very good beef pie. One of the best pies she had tasted in recent memory. She mixed up her peas and corn, making sure they all had kissed the melted butter. She poured some pepper and salt onto her whole meal.

"Oh my," said Florence, "this is a wonderfully rich and satisfying pie. I can't believe I'm so hungry."

"One of the best I've tasted in recent memory," said Frances.

Florence looked over at Orpha. After a small pause, Orpha noticed Florence staring at her. She took another bite of her pie.

"Not as good as some. For all the expense of this trip it really could be a lot tastier."

Frances and Florence didn't say anything to that. Mahulda seemed to be enjoying it. They ate in silence. At the next table Samuel and Maurice were talking.

"Did you find what you needed?" asked Maurice.

"No, I didn't," said Samuel, looking at his pie and taking a bite from it. "What about you?"

"No, I'm afraid not."

"What were you gentleman looking for?" asked Abigail.

"Not your concern," said Maurice, resting his fork and knife on his plate and looking at her. Samuel looked up at them with a bland expression on his face.

"Mind your business, miss," said Samuel.

"Listen, lads," said Albert, "she was just trying to be helpful."

"Yes, well, we didn't ask for help, did we?" asked Maurice.

"You insolent, ill-mannered man," said Albert. "We'll be sure to sit elsewhere," he said, looking at his sister.

"That would be greatly appreciated," said Maurice, sarcastically.

The table went silent for a while before Maurice looked over at Samuel and spoke again.

"I think it might be closer at hand."

Samuel didn't look up from eating his pie.

"It appears so. That meddling woman should really mind her manners."

Samuel finished up his pie and speared a single pea on his fork. He ate it, and then placed his fork and knife down on the plate and pushed his plate forward. He took his napkin from his lap and wiped his mouth.

Ten

It was dark at nine that evening, though far from pitch black, on the topside of the boat. The western horizon was still a navy blue, and all along the Nile embankments dotted yellow lights burned like small fires. Everyone was on the top deck, where a group of four musicians played traditional music with the singer singing in Arabic.

Florence and Frances sat on a divan under a large canopy. The music was soft on the ears and lulling in its melody. Dinner had been very satisfying and everyone was enjoying the fresh, humid air. Lamps were posted like pharaonic statues intermittently along the sides of the boat. It was enough light to read by, and Samuel was reading yesterday's copy of The Times.

As they all sat quietly in little groups, it seemed contrary to the facts, that they had just come out of the largest global war just a little over two years ago. It was if that was just a foggy dream that they were slowly burning away with the waking sun.

Frances realized how important this vacation was, not only for her, but perhaps for all of them, to get away from it all. To leave the cares and the rebuilding of England alone for even just a few weeks. It was like a breath of fresh air to a drowning man.

Maurice stood off to one side, smoking a cigarette and looking out across the western Nile. Nigel was reading a recent copy of Life magazine, haphazardly turning the pages until he found something that caught his eye where he read for a moment. He had a snifter of brandy in front of him, half finished.

Mahulda was off at the far side, sitting with Simon. It had appeared he had found the courage to talk to her. And who had once been a plain girl, had now transformed into someone with much light and intelligence to her eyes. Frances watched the two of them for some time. All she had needed was a bit of time away from her grandmother and some interest from a decent young man.

Orpha was closest to them. She was crocheting but every so often, she looked up with a scowl in their direction. But her gaze was never returned.

Albert and Abigail were sitting close to Frances and Florence, at the other corner of the divan which went out towards the inner canopy.

"Did you get them to get my warm milk ready?" asked Abigail.

Albert nodded.

"I asked for it to be left for nine thirty."

Abigail nodded.

Lady Pompress and Captain Wainscott were sitting on another divan at the other end from Frances and Florence. Timothy was smoking a Cuban cigar and enjoying a snifter of brandy. Lady Pompress was drinking a small glass of digestif which looked like it was sherry. She was leaning away from Timothy, having seated herself on the far end of their divan.

"Do you have to smoke that bloody thing?" she asked, looking at it as if it were a hideous snake that was about to bite her head off.

"It's one of my small pleasures, darling. I'll go and stand over there by Maurice if that's all right."

"I'd rather you did," she said.

Captain Wainscott got up and walked over to where Maurice was standing, finishing his cigarette.

"Do you mind if I join you?" he asked.

Maurice shook his head, and kept staring out at the far banks.

"It's hard to imagine that this place was once the richest cradle of civilization," said Maurice.

"Yes, I suppose it was majestic at one point," agreed Timothy. "Though it's still not too bad."

"Yes, well, the spoils of this place have long been stolen, and those that have them don't seem to appreciate it."

"What do you mean?" asked Timothy, looking over at Maurice with a frown on his face.

Maurice turned to look at him.

"There are enough ancient artifacts, jewels, gold, and that sort of thing to make hundreds, probably thousands of men around the world rich beyond their wildest dreams, and some of them don't appreciate that."

"I see," said Timothy. "You know where some of them are then?"

Maurice smiled at him and shook his head.

"If I did, I wouldn't be here. I'd likely be retired on some estate in the English countryside."

"I suppose you would," said Timothy, "you don't happen to know how much the spoils were worth that were stolen from Menkaure's secret chamber do you? I found that ever so fascinating that story Perry told us."

Frances noticed Samuel look up and cock his head towards Timothy and Maurice. It looked to her as if he were eavesdropping. He saw Frances looking at him. She smiled sweetly. He ignored her and pulled the paper up to cover his face from her.

"Most likely several million pounds worth, and what's more," said Maurice, "most of it has not been found."

"You don't say," said Timothy.

Maurice nodded.

"If you'll excuse me," said Maurice, "I think the drink has made my tongue a bit loose. I'll be off to bed then."

He walked round the large central canopy to the stairs which he took quite carefully. Captain Wainscott watched after him, curiously, smoking his cigar, holding his snifter in his one hand at navel level. Maurice didn't say goodnight to anyone else.

Samuel folded up the paper, and stood up. He tipped his fedora.

"It is getting late, I think. If you'll excuse me, ladies and gentlemen, I'll be on my way."

Samuel nodded and looked around the room, as he received farewells from those remaining. He too went straight to the stairs and exited the top deck. Frances took a small sip of her sherry.

"This is the good life, Flo, is it not? Sitting under God's canopy without needing a heavy coat or blanket."

Florence looked at her, and chinked her tulip shaped sherry glass with Frances'.

"I'll second that, Fran. This trip has started off marvelously."

Albert and Abigail who were sitting in the corner next to Frances and Florence grinned at them. Albert was sipping from a brandy snifter and Abigail had a small glass of sherry.

"It's wonderful to be resting under the night sky after a vigorous day of sightseeing," said Albert.

Frances smiled at them.

"Captain Wainscott tells me that you're a renowned sleuth," he said tentatively.

Frances looked over at him and smiled.

"I think the good captain exaggerates," she said.

"If I could be so bold," said Albert, "I wonder if I could ask you a question regarding that."

"Certainly."

"Do you think they'll ever find the remaining treasures of Menkaure?"

Abigail gave him a look of shock. Frances looked across the deck and out over the water.

"Unlikely," she said. "Though it all depends on the thieves I suppose. I imagine they're both dead by now, and if they were smart which I believe they were, then the spoils have likely been well hidden or dispersed. But in fairness, I'm sure some will keep cropping up for some time and many of them will be pinched by the police."

Frances looked at him.

"Why do you ask?"

"I'm just curious that's all. I found the tale of the burglary of Menkaure's pyramid utterly fascinating."

"I see."

"You said 'both' when you spoke of the thieves. So you think there is more than one?"

"I believe there were two of them."

"How do you know that?"

"I have spent some time looking at it as sort of a hobby, ever since this one chap tried to sell my husband and I a small golden statue that we bought and returned to the British Museum. They confirmed it was likely from the Pyramid of Menkaure."

"And what if these thieves wanted to return the spoils? What if they had a change of heart?"

"That's unlikely. Men of that sort, don't often go to such extreme measures to burglarize only to be moved by a twinge of remorse later. In any event, I doubt it would do them any good, they'd still be charged with the crime."

"I see," said Albert, looking down dejectedly. Abigail looked at him, but he didn't look back. He was lost in his brandy.

Orpha packed up her crocheting into her bag and went over to Mahulda and Simon.

"I think it's time for bed, Mahulda," she said in her sternest tone. "It's getting late, and Perry said we're up for an eight a.m. breakfast."

"Just a few minutes, please," she said.

Orpha stood there looking at the two of them for a while. Then she looked down at her watch.

"Very well, but don't make me come up here after ten," she said.

"Thank you, nana," said Mahulda.

Orpha put her bag in the crook of her arm, and walked diagonally through the canopy towards the stairs.

"Good night," is all she said, as she walked by.

Nigel closed his magazine, took the last mouthful of brandy from his glass and stood up. He smiled warmly at everyone.

"Seems I might as well follow everyone's lead and head off to bed myself. Been quite a vigorous day I should think.'

He nodded and walked off towards the stair and what he hoped was a comfortable bed. Lady Pompress finished off her sherry and set it down. Captain Wainscott walked over and took his seat next to her. He still had half his cigar to finish. She waved the smoke away from her face with her hand, only there wasn't any smoke in her vicinity. It was more for effect than anything else.

"Could you put that odious thing away so we can go to bed?" she said.

"I still have some brandy left. I won't be long, darling, just a few moments more if you don't mind."

"I do," said Lady Pompress, standing, "enjoy that damned weed by yourself. I'm off to bed, and don't disturb me when you come in. You know how my sleeping aid doesn't always work well."

"I'll be quiet," he said.

Lady Pompress stormed off without a lot of commotion and did not bother to say goodnight to the remaining guests. Captain Wainscott walked off to the far edge of the boat and looked out over the black, inky water of the ancient Nile. He thought about how the ancient Egyptians might have traveled upon her surface.

"I feel for that young man," said Abigail.

"Who?" asked Albert.

"Captain Wainscott, Timothy."

"Why?"

"He seems to have become involved with a very demanding woman," she said.

"That's one way of putting it."

"All relationships have their demands," said Frances, looking away from Timothy's back and meeting Abigail's eyes.

"What do you mean?"

"Well," she said. "In Captain Wainscott's case, the demands are extreme upon his patience, but in return he will have access to Lady Pompress' wealth. Those who marry for love, might have the demands of hard labor and earning their keep. Each relationship has its demands and its gifts."

"So Lady Pompress is quite rich, is she?" asked Abigail, her face showing the eager anticipation of the gossip.

"It depends who you're comparing her to," said Frances, "but by most accounts I'd say she's quite comfortable. Captain Wainscott however, paid a small fortune I'm sure, to bring her out here. On top of what is likely to be an especially expensive wedding if I know the likes of Lady Pompress. And the likes of her I am well acquainted with."

"Poor man," said Albert, "I hope he finds it worth the effort. Personally, I find the whole idea of demeaning oneself for money to be quite pointless."

Albert was looking off at Timothy who blew smoke out across the water which only came back in to curl around his neck like a loose noose.

"You've never been married then, I take it?" asked Frances.

Albert shook his head.

"Never found the right woman," he said.

"You too?" she asked, looking at Abigail.

Abigail nodded her head.

"Though in my case, it wasn't so much not finding the right woman as it was finding the right man. Though I quite fancy Captain Wainscott if he weren't taken."

They all shared a light chuckle.

"Do you know anything about the spoils of the secret chambers of Menkaure?" asked Frances, abruptly changing the subject and looking directly at Albert.

Albert coughed, or spluttered would be more accurate, and then he finished his brandy.

"Sorry, dry throat," he said. "I don't know much about the spoils that were once in the Pyramid of Menkaure, other than what Perry told us earlier. Quite fascinating. Why do you ask?"

"I was just wondering why the two of you went off secretly this afternoon?"

Frances kept a steady eye on both of them.

"Well, frankly, we've had enough of the rudeness of Samuel and Abigail, Lady Pompress, we wanted some time alone to see what we wanted to see."

"I see," said Frances, looking off at Simon and Mahulda who were getting up and walking towards them. Simon and Mahulda stopped a few feet from the group.

"I think I'll escort Mahulda to her room. I don't want her to get into trouble with her grandmother. It's almost ten. Good night."

They exchanged good nights and Florence looked at her watch. It was just past nine forty five.

"I saw a picture once," said Lady Marmalade, "of Arthur Vipond."

She stopped and looked back at Albert and then Abigail. They held her gaze briefly before looking away.

"And who is that?" asked Albert, not very convincingly.

Frances smiled at him.

"He was believed to be one of the two thieves who stole most of the valuables from the Pyramid of Menkaure. Him, along with an accomplice of his named Howard Trenglove."

"Interesting," said Albert.

"Well," continued Frances, "what's really interesting is that you look very much like him, only quite a bit heavier."

"I see," said Albert. "Well, I can assure you that I am no relation."

He said that last bit with a bit too much enthusiasm.

"Was he ever caught?" asked Albert, as Abigail looked down at her lap, trying to avoid the conversation altogether.

"No. He was brought in for questioning on one occasion, but they never found any of the valuables in either his or Trenglove's possession or apartments."

"Then perhaps they didn't do it," suggested Albert.

"Perhaps," said Frances, looking at him and smiling. "Or maybe they hid them better or dispersed them amongst family members."

"That sounds rather trusting for a pair of thieves," said Albert.

"Yes, I can see how it might."

"In any event, without amnesty, I can't see why the thieves or their family would ever return the items stolen."

"The thieves are dead," said Frances.

"Right, that even bolsters my point. Why would a cousin or brother risk jail to return items they never stole?"

"There could be a variety of reasons," said Frances, "for instance, the power of mythology is very powerful. Some have suggested that over six deaths have been directly attributable to disturbing Tutankhamen's tomb."

"Yes, well those of small minds will believe in witchcraft if given the chance," said Albert.

"I find it quite compelling," said Abigail, "I too hope that those in possession of the spoils will find a way to return them. It could be done honestly."

"And how might they do that?" asked Frances.

"Well, I suppose they could leave them by the museum or put them back in the burial chamber where they were stolen from. Perhaps while no one was looking."

Timothy turned around from the deck railing and extinguished his cigar in the closest ashtray on the closest table. He took the last swig of his brandy and placed the snifter down.

"Good night all," he said. "I'll see you in the morning."

He nodded at them all in turn as they said their good nights. Abigail smiled shyly at him.

"It would be dangerous to leave any valuables at the tombs," said Frances, looking at Abigail. "One couldn't be certain that they would be found by the proper authorities."

"Yes, I suppose so," said Abigail. "I'm just thinking that there might be ways of doing it if they didn't want to get caught."

"This is all speculation, of course," said Albert.

"Of course," replied Frances.

"I don't see anyone in their right mind giving up valuables like that. Not at times like these."

"What do you mean by 'times like these'?" asked Frances.

"Well," said Albert, "these are austere times. We're just recently out of the war, and things are difficult. If I had any sort of new found wealth I might be inclined to hang onto it. Whether that wealth was from a theft I wasn't involved in or not."

"But surely you couldn't do anything with it," said Florence, "after all, Scotland Yard and ICPC are on the look out for these sorts of trinkets."

"ICPC?"

"The International Criminal Police Commission," said Florence.

"Right. Well, as I said, I'm not a criminal so I don't know how one would go about fencing anything of the sort, I'm just saying I'd likely hang onto things of that sort."

"That's fair enough," said Florence. "Though I find the whole idea of stealing ancient artifacts ghastly."

"I understand that, my dear Flo, though we, thankfully, have never been in the depths of desperation that perhaps fuels that sort of activity," said Frances.

"Very true."

"He that is without sin among you, let him first cast a stone," said Albert.

"John chapter eight verse seven," said Frances, smiling.

Albert stood up and smiled at everyone.

"This has been an intriguing conversation," then turning to Abigail, "I'll go and make sure your milk is just how you like it."

"Thank you, Al," she said, "I'll be right behind you."

"Good night, Frances, Florence," said Albert, as he walked off.

They watched him disappear down the stairs. The musicians were just finishing up. It was just after ten according to Frances' watch. Frances took a sip of her sherry. Albert had left a finger of brandy in his snifter on the table in front of where he had just been sitting.

"I can't believe what a wonderful and warm evening it still is," said Abigail. "I quite like it."

"Me too," said Florence.

"This is a pleasant time of the year to be in Egypt," said Frances. "The summers can be too hot. Some might even find the days too hot now even, but not when you compare them to the summer days. I don't know how they do it."

"And to think they sweated in this heat to build the pyramids," said Abigail. "Taking years and years. That's pure dedication."

"And without modern technology," offered Florence.

"Right, just logs and twine and perhaps beasts of burden, but no machines, no engines, just the back breaking labor of men."

They sat in silence for a while, watching the twinkling stars, each alone to her thoughts.

"Do you really think that the curse of the pharaohs is something real?" asked Abigail.

Frances looked at her and smiled.

"No, I don't think it's real. I'm sure there's a valid scientific explanation to it, but it does make for an interesting story. Why do you ask?"

"It just seems unfair that someone who didn't do anything wrong should get punished for the wrong of others."

"Is there something you'd like to talk about, Abigail?" asked Frances, kindly.

Abigail looked at her lap and smoothed her dress over her thighs, then she looked up at Frances.

"I just think it would be a shame if, like you said, those who were given the spoils of the burglary should be punished for it if they were just trying to return them."

"Do you know something about that?" asked Frances, carefully.

Abigail didn't say anything for a while. Then she shook her head.

"No, I was just wondering. That's all. It's getting late. I should be off to bed. Good night."

Abigail stood up and smiled at them. As she walked by, Frances grabbed her hand tenderly. Abigail stopped and looked down at her.

"I can help if you need me to," she said.

"Whatever for?"

"For whatever sort of trouble you might be in," said Frances.

"Nonsense," said Abigail, trying to laugh it off. "We were just talking in theory. All I'm saying is I can understand their predicament."

Frances looked at her steadily in the eyes, and let go of Abigail's hand. Abigail walked off.

"What was that about?" asked Florence, once they were alone again.

"I'm not sure," said Frances. "But I found the whole conversation quite curious. Why would they care about the secret jewels of Menkaure if they weren't somehow involved."

"But I thought you said the thieves were long dead?"

Frances turned and looked at her friend.

"They are indeed. I believe I read that Arthur Vipond died in 1930, and Trenglove much earlier than that. I think it was 1907. But Albert's resemblance to Vipond is uncanny."

"What are you suggesting?" asked Florence.

"I don't know. Perhaps they know where the stolen artifacts are. Perhaps they're related to the late Vipond, and perhaps they've come on a scouting mission to see how they might return what has been bequeathed to them, but isn't theirs."

"Honestly Fran, that sounds quite fanciful. And what about Abigail, you didn't say she reminds you of anyone, and she's Albert's sister."

Frances nodded.

"Very true, and she doesn't remind me of Vipond at all, only Albert."

Florence laughed softly.

"Oh Fran, you can't help but see a mystery wherever you go, can you?"

"I suppose not," said Frances, looking out over the black sky, as the musicians packed up their instruments and headed down into the bowels of the boat where they would spend the night.

"Maybe you can tease a little more information from her tomorrow."

"I think she'll need a lot more sherry than she had tonight," said Frances.

"That shouldn't be too hard. She didn't have any tonight," said Florence.

Frances finished the last of her sherry and put her glass down. Ishaq was going around to all the tables and cleaning them up, putting the empty or mostly empty glasses onto his tray.

"What a wonderful night," said Florence, taking Frances' arm in hers, as they strolled towards the stairs.

"A perfect start to what I hope will be our most memorable holiday yet," said Frances.

Eleven

Lady Marmalade had been up since six in the morning. She had quickly gotten dressed and came up to the top deck to watch the sunrise over the eastern banks of the Nile. The Queen Nefertiti had anchored about three hundred feet off the western banks of Saqqara.

The day was going to be spent strolling through Saqqara which was the necropolis of the Ancient Egyptian capital city of Memphis. Frances was looking forward to it. It was a part of the country she had not visited for some time. Just about eighteen miles from Cairo it was an underappreciated tourist spot.

After spending a half hour on the top deck, Frances had gone back down to the cabin at around six thirty or so to get ready for breakfast. Breakfast had been promised to be a fine English and European breakfast. Satisfying and filling. Enough to keep the spirits up for a long day of touring through Saqqara.

Florence was up and had just come out of her bathroom. She walked into the main common area to grab the paper.

"Good morning, Fran, I didn't know you were here."

"Just got back."

"How is the weather today?"

"Absolutely marvelous. Warm and sunny, just like it was yesterday."

"I can't believe we'll be in Saqqara today," she said. "How does it look?"

"As one would expect, dry, barren and full of monuments." Florence smiled and turned to head back into her own room.

"I'm going to go and get ready," she said to Frances.

"Me too."

At eight in the morning, Frances and Florence were seated at their table in the dining are on the second level. Orpha and Mahulda were already seated but hadn't started to eat yet. In fact everyone was just sitting down to breakfast, except for Abigail. Albert had decided to join Anton and Fowler at their table.

Jafari came by and wished them a good morning.

"We have orange juice, champagne or mimosa for drinking," he said.

"Mimosa," said Orpha not waiting for anyone else to order.

"Let's live a little, Fran," said Florence, "how about mimosas?"

"Sounds wonderful to me. We'll have mimosas too," said Frances looking at Jafari.

"Just an orange juice, please," said Mahulda.

Jafari smiled, bowed and left to collect their drinks.

"I wonder where Abigail is?" asked Florence, looking over at Albert sitting with Perry and Anton. "I also wonder why he's sitting over there?"

Frances looked over at them.

"He and his sister had a bit of a row with Samuel and Maurice last night," said Frances. "Didn't you hear them?"

Florence shook her head.

"They were quite rude to her in particular, so I'm not surprised he doesn't want to sit with them."

Jafari came back around with their drinks and took their breakfast order. Bacon and a hardboiled egg with a croissant for Frances, sausage and fried eggs with a strudel for Florence.

Mahulda just wanted a hardboiled egg with a croissant and Orpha asked for scrambled eggs and sausages.

"How did the two of you sleep?" asked Frances, looking at Mahulda and Orpha.

"Like a log," said Orpha. "I found yesterday quite strenuous, and I think I shall stay on the boat today. But you can go along, my dear," she said to Mahulda kindly. "How did the two of you sleep last night?"

"Wonderfully," said Frances, "I find the gentle swaying of the boat to be quite relaxing."

"Me too," said Florence.

Jafari bought their meals back and they ate mostly in silence. Frances noticed that Samuel and Maurice didn't share a word together the whole breakfast. Anton, Perry and Albert talked softly and intermittently and Nigel and Simon had an animated conversation about the many tombs that could be found in Saqqara. Captain Wainscott and Lady Pompress barely shared a few words.

It was just after nine when Jafari took away the last plates and refilled coffee cups of those who were drinking coffee which was both Orpha and Mahulda. Perry stood up and walked into the middle of the dining room.

"It's just after nine," he said, looking at his watch. "We're scheduled to depart at ten for Saqqara. It's not mandatory that you come, but I would highly recommend it. If any of you are staying behind, I'll stay to be of service. If we're all going then I'll be along too, though today's tour will be led by Anton Pung. Any questions?"

Fowler looked around at the blank faces.

"Good. We'll meet on the second level at the stern. That's at the back of the boat."

Fowler walked off and climbed up the stairs to the top deck. Frances stood up, and went over to see Albert who was sipping on a coffee.

"Do you mind if I sit down?"

"Please, Frances," he said gesturing at the empty seat across from him. Anton got up, placed his napkin on his setting and walked off, presumably to join Perry. Florence sat down next to Frances.

"Is Abby not feeling well this morning?" asked Frances.

"I'm not sure," said Albert. "She's a heavy and a late sleeper. I thought I'd just leave her to get her beauty rest. I'm going to check in on her just after I've finished my coffee. Ishaq said that they can easily get her some toast or pastries if she likes."

"That's good to hear, I was worried about her."

"Why is that?"

"Well, she said something strange to me last night."

"And what was that?"

"She said she thought it would be unfortunate that those who were innocent of any wrongdoing would be punished for it. She was referring to the burglary of Menkaure. She said she thought it would be unfair to be punished for doing the right thing, for trying to return the spoils. Do you know anything about that?"

Albert drained the last of his coffee and shook his head.

"I'm afraid not. But you must understand, Frances," said Albert, "my sister has always been concerned about justice and she's been especially vocal about righting wrongs. If you'll excuse me, I think I'll go and wake her. I'm sure she doesn't want to miss today's tour, and she'll need the time to get ready."

Albert stood and bowed.

"Of course," said Frances, smiling weakly at him.

Albert strode away. Florence looked at Frances.

"You really do think they are involved somehow don't you?"

Frances turned and smiled at her friend, and nodded.

"I do, Flo. Not that they're bad people, quite the contrary. But I think they're perhaps hiding the fact that there's more to this vacation than they're letting on."

"Can we not let them be?" asked Florence. "You're making me nervous."

"How is that?"

"Every time you get to thinking there's a mystery underfoot you're often right, and I don't want this perfect holiday to be jinxed by some sort of mystery. If they're not hurting anyone, can you let it be, at least until the end of the trip?"

Florence smiled at her friend. Frances looked at the place where Albert had sat not minutes before. She was deep in thought. Then she turned around and looked back at her friend, and smiled.

"All right," said Frances. "You're right, we shouldn't look for trouble when he's not looking for us. Let us enjoy ourselves instead. Shall we go and collect our things for the day's tour."

Florence smiled and nodded her head. They stood up and made their way to the stairs to carry them to the main deck where their room was.

Twelve

Frances and Florence were walking down the hallway towards the end of the boat, when Albert burst out of his room, spilling like a lunatic into the hallway. He looked around, he was obviously panicked. He saw Frances and Florence walking towards him from the bow of the boat.

Albert and Abigail's cabin was on the starboard side, sandwiched between the cabins of Lady Pompress and Captain Wainscott and Orpha and Mahulda.

"Help!" he yelled, at Frances and Florence, his eyes as big as bulging eggs.

Frances and Florence hurried up to him.

"What is it Albert?" asked Frances.

"My... it's my sister..."

The words wouldn't come to him, he pointed into the cabin. Frances and Florence walked in and saw Abigail in one of the single beds. She was closest to the balcony. The balcony curtains had been drawn, and Frances could already tell that she had been dead for a little time by the color of her ashen skin.

Frances walked up to the edge of the bed and looked at Abigail. Her eyes were closed and she looked quite peaceful. She was lying on her back and her arms were folded across her stomach. By the look of the hands and the arms, she was clearly in the intimate clutches of rigor mortis.

Albert came back into the room. He was rubbing his head and weaving his hands through his hair.

"How can this be? I don't understand," he said.

Frances turned to look at him.

"Did you find her like this?"

The blankets had been torn off her and she lay at an awkward angle on her back, as if someone had tried to pull her out of bed. She was naked underneath her long white nightie.

"Yes... I mean no."

Albert was shaking his head.

"Take a breath, Albert, and tell me how you found her."

Albert took a breath and looked over at his sister and he squeezed his eyes shut. A tear rolled down his cheek. Frances took his arm and walked him to the door of his cabin.

"Tell me how you found her?" she asked.

"She was lying in her bed."

"Was she on her back like she is now, or was she on her side?"

"On her back like I found her. I went and gently shook her shoulder but she wouldn't wake up. I took off the blankets and tried to pull her out and that's when I realized she was dead. Her skin was cold, and I looked at her face, and it was waxen and dead to the touch. That's when I came running out here and saw you."

"Good, Albert, good," said Frances. "Please go and get Perry Fowler and Captain Chuma Badawi."

Albert nodded and jogged off down the hallway towards the bow. Simon came out of his room, which was on the port side, and one cabin towards the stern from Albert and Abigail's. He was dressed in khaki shorts and a tan short sleeved shirt.

"Is everything all right?" he asked, looking at Frances.

She shook her head.

"Do me a favor please, Simon. Guard the door here, we've had a murder. Ms. Abigail Beckles has been murdered. Don't let anyone in."

"Oh my, that's awful," he said, coming up to the cabin and peering in from the door.

"Just stay here, please, and don't let anyone in except for Fowler and the boat captain."

Simon nodded, and Frances went back into the room and started to look around. There were no signs of a struggle.

"Good heavens," said Florence, looking at Frances, "this is not something I was expecting."

"Me neither."

"How do you know she was murdered?"

"She's a healthy woman in her late forties or early fifties, and here she lies dead. Further, I think this might be related to the secret spoils of Menkaure. And if I'm right, then she was murdered for those spoils, or information related to them. I want us to see if there is any sign of foul play, or any hint as to how she was murdered."

Frances started looking around the room, and Florence went into the bathroom. The dresser was opposite Abigail's bed, next to the door to the cabin. Beyond that was the bathroom and moving starboard was the balcony, and stern of the balcony were two chairs and a table and then Abigail's bed, and beyond that, Albert's.

The chairs were undisturbed, and the table only held some stationery that didn't look like it had been used. Frances moved to the bed and removed the blankets and sheet, shaking them out as she did so. She put them in a pile on the floor. There was nothing on the bed or in the blankets that offered any clues.

Frances looked at Abigail's body. She pulled up her sleeves, looking for any injection marks, she did the same at her feet and looked at the back of her knees. There were no marks to indicate

she had been injected anywhere. Next to her bed was a small
side table that held a clock and a lamp. There was also a glass
that held just a skiff of milk on the bottom. Frances picked it up
and looked at it. There was something odd about it. There were
fine granules, almost silty in texture that clung to the side of the
glass from where the milk was sipped. It occurred to Lady
Marmalade that she might have been poisoned with her nightly
milk, and the person who had prepared that for her, was now the
main suspect.

Florence came out of the bathroom holding the wastebasket.
She looked over at Frances who was holding up the glass that
had earlier that evening held milk.

"I think you might find this interesting," she said.

Frances looked over at her.

"What do you have there?"

"I might have the murder weapon. In a manner of speaking."

Florence walked up to Frances and held out the wastebasket.
Frances looked into it.

"I didn't want to disturb anything until you saw it."

Frances nodded at her and reached into the wastebasket
with her hand, after putting the glass back down. She pulled out
two small blue envelopes that had the word "Somunol" on them.

"A sleeping draught?" inquired Florence.

Frances nodded.

"The sodium salt of barbiturate. Two one gram draughts.
This would be sufficient to kill Abigail, especially if she did not
take any sleeping draughts regularly."

Frances took a tissue from the dresser and wrapped the two
envelopes in it and then put them away in her handbag.

"We'll have to keep these safe until we can deliver them to
the police."

Florence nodded, and then returned the wastebasket to the
bathroom. Commotion at the cabin door attracted France's

attention. She looked up as Fowler, Pung and Badawi entered into the room. Fowler was leading them.

"Good Lord," he said, looking down at the body. He turned to Frances. "What happened?"

"Albert came in to check on his sister this morning after breakfast as she hadn't woken in time, and he knew she wanted to attend the tour."

Fowler nodded.

"He mentioned this to me."

"He found she was dead, and rushed out of the room where he bumped into Florence and I. He asked for our help and here I am."

Fowler kept looking back and forth from Frances to the dead body.

"You've never seen a dead body before?" she asked.

Fowler looked back at her and nodded.

"It's quite off putting actually."

"I'll need your help."

"Of course."

"I'll need a room to interview everyone. I'm afraid at this point, everyone and indeed anyone is a suspect. I'll also need any information you have on my fellow tourists. Their maiden names, their occupations. Anything at all that might have been filled out for this particular tour."

"Yes, of course," said Fowler.

"What about you?" asked Pung.

"What about me?"

"Well, how do we know you didn't do it?"

"A detective in the wings. That's a fair question, Anton. Though I have an alibi. I believe that Abigail was poisoned with Somunol."

"The sleeping draught?"

Frances nodded.

"In any event, everyone will attest that Florence and I were the last ones to leave the upper deck, long after Abigail and Albert had left for their cabin. We wouldn't have had a chance to slip the draught into her evening's milk."

"Why not?"

"Because it was after dinner that Abigail asked Albert about it and he had advised her that he had requested the staff to bring it to the cabin for nine thirty."

"Very well, sorry I doubted you," said Pung.

"Not at all, none of us are beyond reproach at this stage," said Frances. "Speaking of which, where were you two between nine thirty and ten last night?"

"You're asking us seriously?" inquired Fowler.

"I am indeed."

"We were playing cards in the mess hall," said Fowler.

"You and Pung?"

Pung nodded.

"Jafari was there too, until he left to deliver the milk. Ishaq came later. The two cooks were cleaning up the kitchen and the first mate was reading a book in the corner..."

Frances nodded and put up her hand.

"I'm not very interested in the staff at this point."

Frances looked at Captain Badawi.

"Captain, can you please contact the authorities and have them meet us here."

"Right away, my Lady," he said, and Captain Badawi with his round kind face and full black beard left the cabin.

"Why don't you think it was any of the staff?" asked Fowler.

"We'll get to that," said Frances, "in due time. What we need now, if you don't mind Perry, is for you to collect any of the records that you have on all of us and let me take a look at them. Then I'd like to have somewhere to interview everyone."

"Well, it won't be lunch for some time, and I'm assuming the tour is cancelled, so why not the dining room?"

Frances nodded.

"We also have to do something with the body. We can't leave it here, at least not once rigor starts to dissipate. Which cabins have baths in them?"

"Just yours, I'm afraid," said Fowler.

"The smell is going to be awful if we don't keep the body cool," said Frances. "Does this boat have an ice maker, other than the small one on the main deck?"

"Yes, but it's also not a very big one."

"It will have to do. We need to move Abigail's body and put her in the bathtub and keep it nestled in ice, until the authorities can take her."

"I see."

"Would the two of you mind moving her into my bath?"

Fowler looked over at the dead body and swallowed.

"I suppose not."

He looked over at Pung, who had also turned slightly white.

"We'll cover her in a sheet and you'll hardly know it's her."

"Very well, let's get it over with," said Fowler.

Fowler and Pung made a move towards the bed.

"Just one other thing before you do, Perry. I imagine there are a few empty rooms here. Florence and I will need a room each, and I imagine that Albert will not be able to use this room any longer."

Fowler thought for a moment and nodded his head.

"There should be five vacant rooms," he said. "I'll double check and we'll get that sorted out."

Frances nodded.

"Good, we can move her now."

Fowler and Pung went towards the bed and Frances and Florence exited the cabin. The remaining guests were all huddled around Simon, murmuring and whispering to each other.

"I'm a doctor," said Samuel, stepping up to Frances and Florence.

"Dr. Newton then," said Frances. Newton nodded. "I think it's a bit late for a doctor. Abigail has been murdered."

"Are you sure?" asked Samuel.

"You're welcome to take a look at the body yourself. I wouldn't mind your expertise in helping determine if there was any other foul play involved."

Samuel nodded. Pung and Fowler slowly came out of the cabin, and Simon and Frances and Florence pushed the guests back further towards the bow of the boat. Fowler and Pung awkwardly wrestled with the stiff body to get it out and around the entryway and into the hall. They then moved her sternward towards Lady Marmalade's cabin.

"Flo, do you want to open it for them," said Frances.

Florence nodded and slid past the side of Fowler and Pung and opened up the cabin door for them. Samuel went back into this cabin, which was just in front of the gathered guests and on the port side. He came out moments later with a doctor's bag and walked off towards Lady Marmalade's cabin.

"What's going on?" asked Captain Wainscott.

"Yes, let us know," said Maurice.

Frances put up her hand to quiet the group.

"As I said, it appears as if Abigail has been murdered. As such, the authorities have been contacted and the day's activities have been cancelled. I'm going to have to ask all of you for your full cooperation. I'll be investigating until the authorities arrive and I'll be asking questions of all of you."

"Why you?" asked Maurice.

"She's a famous sleuth," said Captain Wainscott to him, "she's often helped Scotland Yard on some of their more difficult cases."

"Is that so?" said Maurice.

"It is quite correct."

"Good Lord," said Lady Pompress. "Are you saying that there is a murderer amongst us."

Frances nodded.

"I'm afraid so," she said, "but we will uncover this mystery."

"I think it's her brother," said Lady Pompress, "he seemed quite upset with his sister."

Frances put up her hand again to quell the whispers.

"Please, let us not start any wild accusations. If you have any information that might be of help I want to hear of it. But please, let us not put the cart before the horse."

Thirteen

Frances was sitting behind one of the dining tables. In the middle was Fowler and to his left was Florence. Pung was sitting slightly behind Frances and off to her right. For about the last hour, they had been going through all the records that Thoth Tours had managed to collect on all their guests. Frances was ready to start interviewing the others.

Captain Badawi came in and walked up to the table. He did not look as happy as his usual disposition suggested.

"My Lady," he said. "I have received a telegram back from the police in Cairo."

"Good," said Frances. "Will they be here by this afternoon?"

They were approximately eighteen, maybe more, miles from Cairo. A motorized police boat shouldn't take longer than a few hours to reach them.

"I'm afraid not," said Badawi, crinkling his face into a sad smile. Frances admired the dedication and commitment he had to his beard. It likely took him longer to groom each day than his hair. It was also clearly colored a wet, shiny black onyx. Badawi cleared his throat.

"There is a terrible simoom coming across from Jordan that will be hitting Cairo in about one hour," he said, looking at his watch.

"I thought they usually only occur during the spring and summer."

Badawi nodded sadly.

"Usually," he said. "But the weather, she does what she wants. I'm afraid I have no further information at this time. They have asked us to contact them this evening when they'll have a better idea of when they might be able to send a police boat."

Frances nodded.

"Thank you, Captain," she said.

The simoom was a hot dusty wind that blew in from the Sahara in the west or as far east as Syria. It created excessive heat, with temperatures regularly reaching above fifty centigrade, and dust and was translated as 'poison wind'. The only small mercy was that they were usually of short duration. Most often less than a half hour. Though Frances wasn't going to bank on it.

Badawi left the dining room and Frances turned to Fowler.

"We'll need to keep the body packed in ice."

"I've already mentioned it to them. If the ice maker holds out."

Frances nodded.

"Who do you want to talk to first?" he asked.

Frances looked at the stack of papers in front of her. The top one was of Dr. Samuel Newton.

"Let's talk to the doctor first," she said. "I'd also like to hear if he found anything else related to Abigail's murder that might be of help.

"Very well," said Fowler.

Frances had noticed that Perry hadn't been smiling as much as he usually did. Not ever since he saw Abigail's dead body this morning.

Pung got up and went up to the top deck, where all the guests had been asked to gather. He came down not long after with

Samuel Newton following him. Samuel's eyes were even more heavily bagged and smudged almost a purple black. He looked like hell. Like the grim reaper had just warmed him up and put the barest amount of life back into him. His face was ashen and his thin body looked frail. He was no longer wearing his fedora, and his thin straight brown hair, parted in the middle, was showing gray at the roots. It was in desperate need of a touch up.

Samuel took a seat across from Frances, Fowler and Florence. He reached into his shirt pocket and pulled out a cigarette case. He offered it around but no one accepted. He fished out a lighter from his pants and lit his cigarette. Florence got up and brought an ashtray back from one of the other tables. She placed it in front of him and he nodded at her.

"Thank you for joining us," said Frances.

"Don't see how I had a choice," he said.

He was leaning back in his chair, his brown eyes, cold and hard like agate. He held Frances' gaze steadily as if they were tied to each other's foreheads by invisible twine.

"I wanted to ask you if you found anything unusual about the state of Abigail's dead body."

"I took a look, but I found nothing unusual. In fact, I'd suggest that she died naturally in her sleep. There were no signs of foul play."

"Perhaps that is as the murderer wanted it."

"What gave you the impression she was murdered?" Samuel asked.

"These," said Frances and she took out the two small blue envelopes from her handbag and put them in the middle of the table. Samuel looked at them, and nodded.

"That ought to be enough to do it."

"That's what I thought."

"And how was it administered?" he asked.

"I believe it was in her evening milk last night."

Samuel nodded.

"That would mask any taste."

Frances looked back down at the papers in front of her.

"It says here, you're from New York."

Samuel nodded.

"You have a practice there?"

"I do."

"But you've decided to take a holiday to Egypt. That seems quite the excursion when there are so many holiday spots closer to you."

"What's your point?"

"What brings you to Egypt specifically?"

"A curiosity, like us all I'm sure. I'm trying to retire, but I can never get away for long enough. I have a young lad working at my office while I'm away. If all goes well I'll likely sell it to him."

"Tell me, Doctor, do you have any sleeping draughts in the bag you bought with you?"

"I have these very kind," he said, stabbing at the blue envelopes in the middle of the table.

"I see, and you usually carry them around with you?"

"I do. I sometimes take them myself, I've been an insomniac for years."

"Are all of yours accounted for, Doctor?"

"I believe so, though I haven't looked closely."

"I'd greatly appreciate it if you would make a record of all drugs you have with you, so that we can be certain that no more go missing."

"Certainly."

Samuel took a puff on his cigarette and knocked out the ash into the ashtray. He blew the smoke up towards the ceiling.

"Can you tell me what you were doing yesterday afternoon with your bag at the boat pits south of the funerary temple of Khafre?" asked Frances.

Samuel put the cigarette to his mouth and inhaled deeply. He took his time exhaling, all the while keeping his eyes steadily on Frances'. He smiled, which was unusual for him.

"I thought I saw someone in distress out there. Turned out I was wrong."

"So you decided to explore while still holding onto your bag?"

Samuel shrugged.

"Why not? I thought it too warm to come back and return my bag and then head out again."

"I also saw you heading towards the Pyramid of Menkaure at shortly after four."

"You don't miss much do you?"

"Well, it just seemed curious. Everybody was heading towards the Pyramid of Menkaure just after Abigail and Albert had exited it via the queen's pyramid."

"Maybe we were looking for stolen treasure."

"I think you were."

Samuel looked at Frances and Frances held his gaze. They stared at one another for a while.

"I'm not joking," said Frances.

"I was," he said.

"But you were headed towards the Pyramid of Menkaure, were you not?"

"I was. Like I said before, I have a great interest in the pyramids and Egypt. I wanted to see as much as I could. So I headed out with my bag, thinking someone needed my help. I thought I saw someone swoon in the heat. Turns out they were just resting against a mastaba. So I then decided to explore the eastern cemetery and from there I made my way towards the pyramid like you said. From there I took the western route back to look at the Tomb of Hemon and the western cemetery."

"I find the tomb quite fascinating. What did you think of the reliefs of Hemon on his tomb? Considering he was the chief architect I found it quite surprising that he was shown so emaciated."

"Quite surprising indeed."

Frances smiled at him. He didn't smile back.

"Last night, Doctor, where did you go when you left the top deck just after nine thirty."

"I went to bed. As I've said before, I have terrible insomnia and I wanted to try and get some sleep during the night. The earlier I can turn down the lights the better."

"Did you see anyone went you went below decks to your cabin? Anyone at all?"

"No."

"Not even Maurice? You left moments after him."

"Well, yes, I did see him, but I didn't speak to him. I saw him enter his cabin as I came down the stairs to the hallway."

"I didn't ask you if you spoke to him."

"But you were going to."

"Did you murder Ms. Abigail Beckles, Doctor?"

Samuel laughed aloud, a forced laugh that didn't last long. Then he took the last puff on his cigarette and put it out.

"No, I didn't. Why would I?"

"Because you wanted to find out where the spoils were that she was carrying. You wanted to search the room."

Samuel looked away off to his left. For the first time he didn't hold Lady Marmalade's gaze.

"I didn't do it. Now if that'll be all, I'll go and itemize my drugs for you."

Samuel stood up and Frances watched him walk out of the dining room.

"He's lying," she said.

"How do you know?" asked Florence.

Frances looked at Fowler and he smiled at her.

"Because the reliefs of Hemon on his tomb do not show an emaciated figure, but rather someone quite plump."

"I see," said Florence.

"Which means, my dear Flo, that he never visited the Tomb of Hemon, and it brings into question his whole story. I don't for a moment think that he took his bag to help a fellow tourist."

"Then what do you think it was for."

"Well, Perry told me something quite interesting this morning that he hadn't thought important until we found Abigail's dead body."

"What was that?" asked Florence.

Frances looked at Perry. Perry looked from Frances to Florence.

"Darius, our driver, said he overheard Albert and Abigail arguing yesterday afternoon before they headed off towards the north side of the Great Pyramid of Giza."

"Fascinating. What were they arguing about?" asked Florence.

"Darius couldn't say for certain, but he said it had something to do with putting it back, and Albert arguing that they needed the money."

"I see," said Florence, looking at Frances.

"I believe, that as naïve as Abigail was, I think she had some of the missing items from Menkaure's pyramid and she was going to put them back. Albert wanted to keep them."

"Interesting," said Florence. "That puts Albert in a bad spot. Do you think he could have killed her?"

"Quite possibly, though there are the other four men who went into the pyramid after Albert and Abigail came out. What if Abigail had a change of heart and decided that they did indeed need the money and decided not to return the missing items. Then Maurice, Samuel, Nigel, and maybe even Simon head into the pyramid looking for it but discover that it hasn't been left behind."

"So they come looking for it, thinking that Abigail must still have it with her," said Florence.

Frances nodded her head.

"So one of them might have come into her room looking for the item or items and then decided to kill her so that she would not find out they had stolen it."

"That sounds like a very plausible explanation," said Fowler.

"But who could have poisoned her other than Doctor Newton?" asked Florence.

"That's what we have to find out. Perhaps it was Doctor Newton or perhaps it was someone who knew that Doctor Newton kept Somunol in his bag."

"Hmm," said Florence. "So we still haven't narrowed it down?"

"Not yet," said Frances.

Fourteen

Orpha walked into the dining room following Anton. She walked slowly as old people do, shuffling her feet. Frances pegged her at seventy or thereabouts, the oldest person on the tour. Anton held the chair out for her and helped her into it, then he returned to sit back down behind Frances.

Orpha's wet eyes looked sad. Like gray stones under a clear puddle after the rain. Her thin lips were pulled down and her face was lined. She had on makeup and her tinted red hair was neatly done in short curls.

"This is just awful," she said, clutching her handbag in her lap with thin bony hands that reminded Fowler of chicken claws. Frances smiled at her.

"It is a terrible incident that has happened here. You understand that we need to ask everyone questions, including you."

"Why me? Can't you see that I'm old and feeble. How could I have possibly have done something so heinous?"

Orpha looked at them sternly as if just being asked about the murder was an affront to her dignity.

"Mrs. Bendled," said Fowler, "we're not saying we suspect you, but Lady Marmalade does need to do her investigation."

"Why her? She's not a constable or inspector."

"That is true, Orpha," said Frances, "but I am the most qualified person here, and I'm just conducting a rudimentary inquiry until the police arrive. I hope you won't mind?"

"If you insist," said Orpha. "When will the police be coming anyway."

"Unfortunately a simoom is traveling through Cairo in the next little while..."

"A what?"

"A hot dry, dusty desert wind, and the Cairo authorities aren't able to send anyone out until afterwards. Could be as early as this evening, though if my familiarity with these sorts of events stands correct, I'd likely say it'll be tomorrow sometime."

"I see."

"Orpha," said Frances, "you rested under the canopy after Fowler finished the tour yesterday with the whole group and before he took Florence, Simon and me to see the Sphinx, is that correct?"

"It is."

Orpha held onto her handbag as if it were a skittish kitty that was trying to get free.

"And you didn't leave at all for the rest of the afternoon?"

"No, I didn't."

"And somebody else can corroborate this?" asked Frances.

Orpha frowned at Frances and pursed her lips, she was feeling highly indignant.

"You know very well I was there the whole afternoon as you saw me."

"I saw you until I left for the final tour with Perry here where he took us to have a look at the Sphinx."

Fowler kept looking at Orpha and nodded in agreement with what Frances had said. He felt sorry for the old bid. She wasn't a pleasant woman but she was old and perhaps she did honestly find this whole matter quite disagreeable.

"Yes, I remember now. My memory isn't what it used to be. I stayed the whole time under the canopy while everyone else left. Not everyone of course, that nice Captain Wainscott stayed, as did his horrible fiancée Lady Pompress, and of course, I was with my granddaughter Mahulda."

"That's what I thought Orpha, we just want to keep our timeline in order."

Orpha nodded and tried to smile weakly, but it seemed her mouth was not used to smiling and it looked unpleasant on her.

"If I might ask," said Frances. "What brings you to Egypt for a holiday?"

"Mahulda has always been fascinated by the pharaohs and Queen Nefertiti especially and we've never had a holiday before, just the two of us. And when I saw the name of the boat, I thought this would be marvelous for her."

Fowler smiled and nodded at her. A very generous holiday for her granddaughter indeed.

"So you've never heard of the secret chamber of Menkaure and the great robbery that emptied out the kings chamber?"

"Oh no, not at all. I don't tend to pay much attention to superstition."

"It's not superstition Orpha, there really was a robbery of the pyramid and many precious and valuable artifacts were stolen."

"Yes, well I know that now. I just thought it sounded quite fanciful at first. I mean you hear all these absurd things like the curse of the pharaohs. Soon someone will be telling us that Abigail was a victim of that curse."

"No one is suggesting that, Orpha. Abigail's death is quite certainly at the hand of a murderer."

"Oh dear," said Orpha, "how was she killed?"

"With sleeping draughts."

Orpha nodded.

"Which brings me to the most important question. Do you take sleeping draughts at all?"

Orpha shook her head.

"Are you suggesting I killed her?"

Orpha scowled and pursed her lips.

"I am only asking if you take sleeping draughts to help you sleep."

"No, I do not. Really, this is becoming preposterous."

"Then you wouldn't mind us taking a look for them in your room?" asked Frances.

Fowler looked at Frances with a frown. He thought she was being a bit hard on the old bid, but he didn't say anything.

"Is nothing sacred?" said Orpha, looking at Fowler. "Is this how Thoth Tours conducts itself? You go spying on the private matters of old ladies?"

Fowler shook his head.

"My dear Mrs. Bendled, I assure you, Thoth Tours takes the privacy of its guests very seriously. But you do understand that there has been a murder on this boat that needs to be investigated. It would be ever so helpful in confirming your innocence."

Orpha huffed for a moment.

"I don't know why I should be inconvenienced just so that you can cross me off your list. I am insulted and appalled by this kangaroo court."

"Orpha, this is not a court of any kind, merely a preliminary and cursory inquiry into the events preceding Abigail Beckles' death. Are you saying that you will not allow us to look into your cabin to confirm you do not take any sleeping draughts?"

Frances looked at her for a while and held Orpha's gaze until Orpha broke it and looked down at her hands clutching her handbag.

"You can look if you must, if it will help end this trial of my honor quicker."

She put her handbag on the table and thrust it towards them.

"Might as well go snooping around in my handbag then too."

"That won't be necessary at the moment," said Frances.

Orpha took her handbag and put it back on her lap. Her lips were pinched and she was quite upset at this whole matter and the veiled accusations.

"May I go then, if you're not going to throw me into gaol."

"There is no gaol on the boat," said Fowler trying to be helpful, "and we don't suspect you, we're just trying to clear the air and get our ducks in order."

Orpha looked up to the left and shook her head very slightly. She had never been so embarrassed in all her life.

"Just one more question, if you don't mind," said Frances.

"You went to bed by yourself at around nine forty five or so..."

Orpha closed her eyes slowly and shrugged her shoulders.

"Forgive me for not jotting down the time I went to bed. I didn't know that was a crime now, too."

"You were the third person to head downstairs to bed, after Maurice and then Simon."

"If you say so. I don't recall."

"That's not important," said Frances. "I was just wondering if you noticed anything unusual once you got down to the main deck? Did you see anyone or see anything that seemed out of place?"

Orpha looked off to the right for a moment.

"Well, I don't know if it's important or not. Maybe it isn't."

"Anything might help us," said Fowler.

"Well, the door to Maurice's cabin was open just a bit and I could hear Maurice speaking to another man, must have been Samuel, the American."

"Could you hear what they were saying?" asked Frances.

"Not very well, but I heard the American say something to the effect of 'well where is it' and then Maurice said something I couldn't hear and Samuel said something about his life depending on it."

"Anything else?"

Orpha shook her head.

"No, I think they must have heard me in the hallway as someone came up and closed the cabin door to Maurice's room."

"Nothing else comes to mind?"

"No."

Frances smiled at Orpha.

"Thank you Orpha, sorry this was hard on you, but you've been quite helpful."

Orpha pinched a smile at the three of them across from her and stood up.

"Will that be all?"

Frances nodded.

"Yes, thank you."

Orpha shuffled herself out and headed downstairs to her cabin. She was still quite rattled and mortified by the humiliation of the whole event. After she had left, Fowler turned and looked at Frances.

"Don't you think you were a little hard on her?"

Florence nodded.

"I think you were a bit tough, Fran."

"Perhaps, but she's not an easy woman to like and she wasn't very helpful at first."

"But she's old. She must be seventy at least. Maybe she has just been frightened by this whole incident. I mean it is quite traumatizing. Imagine being a seventy year old woman and being questioned about a murder that you didn't commit in a way that makes you look like a suspect."

"Fair enough, Flo," said Frances. "But everyone is a suspect until we've cleared them."

"Well, she's been cleared now, I imagine."

Fifteen

Lunch had been served up on the top deck, so that Frances could keep her papers all together and not have to worry about moving them. She and Florence had eaten in the dining room at their table as they went over the first two interviews. Fowler and Pung had gone up to the top deck to mingle with the rest of the guests. Frances had asked them to keep their ears to the ground related to Abigail's murder.

They were back down in the dining room. The four of them were gathered around the table. Pung had brought his chair up close to the end of the table next to Frances. The rest of them sat at the table as they had before.

"Did you catch anything during lunch that might suggest a suspect?" asked Frances, looking at Pung and Fowler.

Pung shrugged his shoulders and shook his head.

"I didn't really hear much of any note. Orpha was going on and on about how unfair it was that you dragged an old woman through this interrogation as she put it," said Anton.

Frances nodded.

"She was complaining ceaselessly to Lady Pompress and the two of them were getting quite up in arms about it."

"What did Lady Pompress have to say about the whole matter?" asked Frances.

"She commiserated with Orpha extensively. She kept complaining about the whole trip being ruined by this murder, and how she was not going to put up with any insult to her honor. Not by anyone especially someone who didn't have the authority by law to investigate such matters."

"I assume she was speaking of me," said Frances.

"Yes, I'm quite certain she was. They went on and on, the two of them, about the indignity of this whole affair. I got tired of listening to it. I think Mahulda did too. She went off and sat with Simon as soon as she was finished eating."

"Did they share anything interesting?" asked Frances.

"Not particularly. They were both quite horrified that someone had been murdered on the boat, and on a holiday at that. Simon was trying to console here."

"Was Mahulda tearfully upset?"

"No, not tearfully, but she kept asking why someone would do that to the old woman."

Frances smiled at that. Abigail was hardly an old woman, at worst she couldn't have been more than mid-fifties.

"What did Simon have to say to that?"

"He said there were a variety of reasons to murder someone, including hatred, anger, jealousy and greed. He thought it was greed. He said it had to have something to do with the spoils of the Pyramid of Menkaure. She asked him how, and he said it was because not all the jewels had been found, so there must be some somewhere. Why not right here in Cairo."

"Interesting," said Frances.

"How would he know something like that?" asked Florence.

"That's a good question, Flo, and one I aim to ask him myself."

Frances looked over at Fowler.

"I'm afraid I can't be quite as helpful as Anton, as I didn't hear anything at all. Though I found something quite suspicious."

"What was that?" asked Frances.

"Samuel and Maurice were talking a lot, off towards the bow of the boat. Whenever I came up towards them they either stopped talking or changed the subject. It appeared to me that they were deeply unhappy by my intrusion."

"I see," said Frances, nodding thoughtfully. "And what about Nigel or Captain Wainscott?"

"Timothy had left his wife shortly after lunch. I imagine he'd had enough of her complaining along with Orpha. He went and engaged Nigel," said Fowler. "The two of them were quite intent on trying to figure out who did it."

"And who did they think it was?"

"Nigel was quite adamant that he thought it was the brother. Timothy on the other hand fancies the American for it."

"What were their reasoning?"

"Nigel said it was obviously the brother because who else would have more motive than a disgruntled sibling. Timothy asked him what the motive was, and he said he'd heard them bickering about something related to money at the hotel a couple of days ago. When pressed by Timothy, he wouldn't say anything more."

Frances nodded her head.

"And what about Timothy?"

"He seemed just as sure it was Samuel as Nigel was sure it was Albert. He thought it was too convenient for the brother to have done it, so he said it must be someone unrelated, and his suggestion was Samuel, the American."

"What reasoning did he give for that?" asked Frances.

"He said that he found it odd that there was only one American amongst all the English people on board. Nigel pressed him about that, saying that just because he was American, didn't make him a murderer. Timothy acknowledged that, but asked Nigel if he didn't find the chap to be quite odd and rude. Nigel admitted that Samuel was quite dismissive and standoffish. Timothy also mentioned how rude Samuel had been to Abigail at dinner the night before. Nigel didn't think that was enough to murder the poor woman, but Timothy was sure it was."

"Fascinating," said Frances, "we'll have to ask them ourselves."

Sixteen

Anton left to fetch Mahulda. Frances wanted to interview her right after her grandmother while Orpha's testimony was still fresh in her mind.

"I can't see how it could be that young woman or her grandmother," said Florence.

"No, but we do need to interview everyone."

"Yes, but I'm trying to figure out who would have done this."

"And who do you think did it then?"

"Well, it's hard to say. I know you think it has something to do with missing Menkaure artifacts, but we haven't seen any of those yet."

"We will soon. If they are involved then I'm sure they'll show up by the time we speak with Albert."

"That's just the thing. If he didn't want to leave the jewels behind, why not just tell his sister and take them? Why kill her?"

"Because he pretended to let her leave them but decided to swipe them at the last minute."

"But then why kill her? If she's none the wiser..."

"Perhaps she found out."

"Fair enough," said Florence. "I guess that makes Albert a prime suspect."

"It does."

"But what about Maurice and Samuel? They've been acting strangely by all accounts, and if Orpha did really hear them in Maurice's cabin last night, that means that Samuel lied to us which makes him a good suspect."

"Him or Maurice," said Frances.

Anton came back down the stairs that led into the dining room. Mahulda was behind him and looked around nervously. He held her chair for her as she sat down. Mahulda looked up at the three of them and then nervously looked back down and fiddled with her fingers in her lap.

"Don't be nervous, dear," said Frances, smiling at the young woman. Mahulda looked up and gave her a tentative smile. "We just want to ask you a few questions if you don't mind."

Mahulda nodded her head.

"Can you tell us what brought you and your grandmother to Egypt for a holiday?" asked Frances.

"Nana thought it would be a good idea. She paid for everything."

"I see," said Frances. "Does Orpha have a curiosity for ancient Egypt."

Mahulda shrugged her shoulders.

"I'm not sure. I mean I've never heard her speak about it often, if at all."

"Then why did she choose Egypt?"

"Well, I did a school paper once on Queen Nefertiti for history class when I was in lower sixth. I did very well in it as I enjoyed everything about ancient Egypt. Nana thought it was time we went for a visit. We've never been on a trip together before, so I was quite excited. It's terrible what happened to that poor woman."

"Yes it is."

"I wish I had bought a camera. Nana never told me we would be cruising down the Nile on the Queen Nefertiti boat."

Mahulda's eyes widened and twinkled as she said that. When she wasn't with her grandmother she could become quite animated.

"I'll be sure to take a picture of you in front of the boat when we dock, dear," said Florence.

"Would you really?" asked Mahulda with increased enthusiasm, smiling as broadly as she had ever done so in her life.

Florence nodded, smiling back at her.

"Oh, thank you so much. You have no idea what it means."

"How does Orpha treat you, dear? You seem quite different when she's not around?" asked Frances bringing the topic back to the subject at hand.

"Oh, she treats me well. She's quite strict though, but that's only because she wants the best for me. Things have been difficult for her too. Every since Pops died, we haven't had much money. Well, we haven't had much money ever really, but it got particularly hard when he died."

"When was that Mahulda?"

"1935."

"I see. Do you mind telling me about your mother."

"There's nothing really to tell. Nana has raised me since I was small. My mother was a prostitute, and she died in 1925. I never knew my father."

"I'm sorry."

"No need," said Mahulda, finding her tongue freely now. "Nana has been good to me. Strict, and she expects certain behavior from young ladies, but she's kept me fed and clothed, and for that I'm grateful."

Frances looked at her and smiled.

"I know a lot of people don't like her. She's difficult sometimes. I understand that, but you see, she's had a tough life, but she's got a good heart. For me, at least."

201

"I'm glad to hear that, dear," said Frances. "Now, I recall that when my good friend Florence, Perry, Simon and me left for the Sphinx, you were still at the canopy with your grandmother. Is that right?"

Mahulda nodded her head, smiling. Her plainness became quite attractive when her face lit up and she smiled. Frances could see how Simon would take notice of her.

"And did you stay there the whole time?"

Mahulda nodded again.

"Did you find anything unusual while you were there waiting?"

Mahulda scrunched her eyebrows together, cocked her head to the left and stuck her tongue into her left cheek. She thought for a moment.

"Not particularly," she said, "though as soon as Albert and his sister left with their rucksacks, everyone else started leaving too."

"Who did?"

"Nigel, the American, and Maurice."

"I see. Did they leave in that order?"

"I don't really remember. Yes, come to think of it, I think it was in that order. It was odd though. I watched Albert and Abigail pause on their way and argue. I couldn't hear what about, but they seemed upset about something before they continued."

"And which way did they go?"

"They went around towards the far side of the Great Pyramid of Giza. I didn't watch them the whole way."

"Did anything else seem unusual to you at that time?"

"No, not really, although Nana said something that was interesting."

"What was that?" asked Florence.

"She noticed that everyone had headed off with rucksacks, except the doctor of course, but he'd taken his doctor's bag with him. Nana said that nothing good could come from everyone carting rucksacks around in this heat. I asked her what she meant, and she asked me why they would be taking rucksacks with them if it weren't for digging up things or hiding something. I said it might just be for carrying a water bottle and she said if they'd wanted to carry a water bottle they'd have just carried a water bottle instead of a whole bag."

"After everyone had left then, that left you and your grandmother and Captain Wainscott and Lady Pompress, correct?"

Mahulda nodded.

"Yes, that's quite correct. Nana got quite upset with having to wait so long and she kept nattering at me while I was reading."

"That was Death Comes as the End," said Frances.

Mahulda nodded a smiled.

"You noticed. A jolly good book too. I haven't finished it yet, but I like the way it's set in ancient Egypt. Have you read it?"

"I have. Tell me about what your grandmother was upset about?"

"Well, I don't wish to speak unkindly of her, but she can be a bit impatient. She was complaining about having to sit and wait in the awful heat. Though I didn't mind it, I thought the weather was quite fine."

"She could have gone off with us and explored the Sphinx, for example," said Frances, "or the two of you could have gone off by yourselves."

"Nana said she was tired and didn't want to do any more walking. She's really quite fit. I've seen her carry a rucksack and complete the Three Peaks Challenge. Not all at once you understand, but she just became the oldest woman to summit Ben Nevis last summer."

"That is quite an accomplishment."

"Though I think she's not quite as happy in the heat."

Frances nodded.

"So there wasn't anything in particular she was upset at during your wait?"

"Not particularly. Like I said she gets impatient sometimes."

"And you didn't want to go off on a hike yourself?"

"Well yes, actually I would have liked to but I couldn't leave Nana alone, and besides, I'd never hear the end of it. This holiday has cost her an absolute fortune, and I want to make sure she has as much fun as I am. Of course when the other men didn't show up at the rendezvous time Nana started feeling quite put out."

"Tell me about that?" asked Frances.

"Simon arrived just on time I believe, but once Maurice waltzed in later than four thirty, Nana started to take it personally. She said she couldn't believe the gall of some people, especially Americans. She said they were always so rude and arrogant, not caring for others. She said she didn't like Samuel and that he was up to no good. She could tell."

"Did she explain that further?"

Mahulda shook her head.

"No, I just don't think she likes him. She doesn't like Americans in general."

"Why is that?"

Mahulda looked around the room. She craned her neck to look behind her. Then she scrunched her mouth to the side and looked down at her lap, fiddling with her fingers. After a while she looked back up at Frances.

"You promise you won't tell?" she asked, her eyes pleading.

Frances nodded.

"What is it, dear?"

"Well, at the turn of the century, Nana had an affair with an American. He swept her off her feet. She was married then too, but things weren't going well. She doesn't know I know this. But my mother found out that Pops wasn't actually her father, the

American was. I think that's what led her to prostitution and all the other bad choices she made. She felt like her life was just one big lie. I think that Pops found out, but it was shortly after that time when Nana became bitter and sad. I don't think she ever quite recovered from having her heart broken."

"How do you know all of this?"

"Things I heard Pops and Nana argue about over the years, and a letter my mother wrote to me which one of her friends gave to me many years after she died."

"That's a terribly sad story," said Florence, "I'm sorry to hear it."

"It's all right," said Mahulda, "Nana raised me well enough, as did Pops. They tried their best. I'm just telling you so that you can understand Nana a bit better and why she doesn't like Americans much. She's not all that bad."

Frances smiled at Mahulda and rested her hands on the table between them.

"It's very brave of you to be that honest," said Frances. "Thank you."

Mahulda smiled.

"What were Lady Pompress and Captain Wainscott doing during all this time?"

"They were bickering on and off."

"About what?"

"Well, the captain wanted to go off exploring but Lady Pompress wouldn't let him. She was quite upset and adamant that he stay and take care of her. Though I felt sorry for him, I mean she seemed quite alright to me."

Frances nodded.

"They argued about that for a short while and then they started arguing about money. Lady Pompress was threatening not to marry him if he couldn't be the man she wanted."

"What did she mean by that?"

"Not entirely sure, but she kept telling him how selfish he was. He told her he'd spent his fortune on the engagement and the upcoming wedding, and so she said he was only marrying her for her money. He denied it strenuously and kept saying he wanted to marry her because he loved her, but I'm not terribly sure she was convinced."

"Did they discuss anything else?"

"Not really. If you'll forgive me for saying so, but I find Lady Pompress to be quite full of herself and self-centered. I tried to ignore them, but they weren't exactly being very discreet. But all they were arguing about was each other."

"Did she call the wedding off at all?"

Mahulda shook her head.

"One last thing," said Frances, changing subjects purposefully. "Does your grandmother have difficulty sleeping? Does she take sleeping draughts?"

Mahulda shook her head.

"No, I don't think so. I've never seen her take one or need any. Though last night, when Simon walked me down to my cabin, when I got inside I think I woke Nana up. She was glad I had come in before ten, but she started complaining about the heat. Like I told you before, I don't think she likes the heat terribly. Anyway, she said she was going to the icebox to get some ice for a face cloth."

"Did she come back with ice?" asked Frances.

"Yes, when I climbed into bed she had the damp cloth on her forehead and there was a cup of ice on the bedside table."

"And Simon," said Frances. "Did he go straight to bed last night?"

"I can't say for sure. He waited for me until I got into the cabin. He seems like quite the gentleman that way. I assumed he went straight to his cabin and off to bed, but like I said, he waited until I closed the door so I have no idea where he went."

"Thank you, Mahulda," said Frances. "You've been very helpful."

Mahulda started to leave but then hesitated. She looked at Frances and opened her mouth as if to speak, she stopped herself, then found her voice.

"Do you know who did it?" she asked. "Or why?"

"I have my suspicions," said Frances, "but I'd rather not say just yet."

Mahulda nodded her head quickly and then stood up and left. Fowler turned to Frances.

"She's quite different when she's not with her grandmother," he said.

Frances looked off after Mahulda and nodded her head slowly.

"Yes, she is. Though it isn't all that surprising how a flower might bloom when taken from the shade of a weeping willow."

"I like how you put that. Tell me, Frances, are you any closer to figuring out who did this?" asked Fowler.

Frances smiled at him.

"We're always getting closer, Perry. What about you?"

Perry smiled widely and flattened his mustache with his thumb and finger.

"Well, I can't say I've ever been involved with a homicide investigation. Like Florence here," he said, turning to look at Florence and then back at Frances, "I like the brother for it. Though to be honest, I think that American chap, Samuel, seems a bit dodgy to me."

"Yes, it's never a good sign when one of your suspects starts out by lying to you."

Seventeen

Fowler had wanted to interview Albert next, but Frances wanted to keep him until last. She wanted to get Maurice in to speak with him, knowing full well that he'd have spoken with Samuel. In fact, Fowler had seen them together shortly after lunch.

Anton came in with Maurice walking casually in behind him. Maurice was smiling, which was not something they had seen on him much at all. It seemed to soften his face and the creases carved into it by years of bad living. He sat down and smiled at them. He crossed his left leg over his right and pulled out a packet of American cigarettes from his shirt pocket. He lit one and inhaled deeply. Then he crossed his right hand which held the cigarette over his left, which was resting on his thigh.

"Maurice," said Frances, "I understand that you and Samuel are friends."

"I wouldn't say that, no."

"But people have seen the two of you together."

"We've shared a few words and a cigarette, but I wouldn't say we're close."

"I see you smoke the same brand of cigarettes," said Frances, nodding at the cigarette in his hand.

"Yes, fancy that."

"I imagine they might be hard to come by in England, if not impossible."

"Not if you know where to look."

"So you've never met Samuel before this holiday."

"Yes, that's correct."

Maurice took a puff on his cigarette and blew smoke off to the left.

"Listen," he said, "I want to help. This is a terrible thing that happened to that poor woman."

"That's very kind, Maurice. You can help us best when you tell us the truth."

"Of course," said Maurice, smiling and smoking his cigarette.

"What were you looking for when you headed off towards the Pyramid of Menkaure yesterday afternoon with your rucksack."

"It's more of a bag than an actual rucksack," he said. "I was going looking to see if there were any other spoils left inside. Perry's story about the jewels and riches in that pyramid fascinated me."

Maurice looked over at Fowler and nodded at him.

"Then why did you tell Simon you were at the western cemetery?" asked Frances.

"Just on a lark I suppose. I didn't feel like I had to explain myself."

"I see," said Frances. "And did you see anyone else at the Pyramid of Menkaure?"

"No, should I have?"

"I think so. Simon, Samuel and Nigel all went there too."

"You don't say."

Maurice puffed on his cigarette and looked at Frances for a while, straining to keep a smile on his face.

"I'm curious, Maurice. You all went to the Pyramid of Menkaure with bags and rucksacks, looking as if you were expecting to find something. Why is that?"

"Like I said before, I was hopeful after Perry's story."

"But you also knew that there was nothing left in the secret passages and the king's burial. What were you really looking for?"

"You can't rid of a man of his hopes and dreams, my Lady," said Maurice, "I thought I might find something that had been left behind, or overlooked."

"I would much prefer you spoke plainly and truly."

"My dear Lady, I do take offense to that remark. I am trying to help."

"Then stop lying."

"I'm not lying. If you're convinced I am, then why don't you tell me what I was looking for."

"I think you were looking for the artifacts that Abigail had taken back into the pyramid, perhaps to leave behind."

Frances watched Maurice carefully. She knew it was a gamble. She had no evidence that Abigail and Albert had actually gone in there to return stolen property, but she had her hunches. Maurice inhaled on his cigarette and looked back at Frances just as carefully as she looked at him.

"Now who's telling preposterous tales," he said. "Where are these artifacts then? Would you like to inspect my cabin? You're welcome to, and you won't find any such artifacts of the likes you speak of."

"We might yet do that."

"Feel free. If there's nothing else."

Maurice was about to stand up, when Frances spoke.

"There is actually. We have a witness who overheard you and Samuel talking in your cabin last night."

"And who was that?"

"Orpha Bendled."

"And what were we talking about?"

"About not finding it, and that Samuel's life depended on it."

"Fascinating."

"Is it true, Maurice? Would you like to confess?"

"Well I would, I certainly would like to confess that I had the radio on last night. That must have been what she heard. Ask Samuel himself, I'm sure he'll tell you he wasn't in my cabin last night."

"Yes, I imagine he would. Though the two of you have had a chance to get your stories straight, haven't you."

"You offend me again, my Lady."

"You can stop the pretense, Maurice, and Frances will do nicely thank you."

"As you wish."

"You were the first one to leave last night at right around nine thirty. Isn't that so?"

"I don't recall the time. If you say so. I'd had too much to drink."

"This gave you ample opportunity to get to the main deck and adulterate Ms. Abigail Beckles' milk. Isn't that so?"

"No, that is patently false," said Maurice, who as much as Frances tried, was failing to get angry. "I went to my cabin and I wasn't feeling very sober so I turned on the radio for a bit to listen to the music. The BBC news was being broadcast at that time, and that must have been what Orpha heard. I mean come on, Frances, Orpha is an old woman, and I don't mean any disrespect, but how good can her hearing be. In any event, where would I get the sleeping draught?"

Frances was getting infuriated by Maurice. He had an answer for everything and she couldn't get him riled up.

"You'd get the draught from your friend Samuel, the good doctor."

"As I've said before, we're not friends, and I doubt he'd give me any."

"How do you know he has sleeping draught."

"I don't, you just told me that's where I'd get it from."

Frances sighed and looked away for a moment. She didn't have anything to hang him by, but she could smell the reek of his lies. She looked at him with very stern eyes.

"I promise you, Maurice," she said, in a cold and calculated tone. "I will find the evidence and make sure you pay for your crimes."

"But I haven't committed any crimes, unless that's boundless naïveté for believing in dreams and possibilities."

He chuckled, took the last puff from his cigarette and put it out next to Samuel's. His laugh made Frances' blood boil.

"All right, Maurice. Did you hear any other sounds coming from the hallway or any of the other cabins?" asked Frances.

"Not much, I had the radio on like I told you. I heard a couple of people walk along the hallway. They walked past. A little while later someone entered the cabin across from me."

"You're certain it was the cabin across from you?"

"Fairly certain. Then later another cabin door opened and closed. That happened a few times over the next little while. I suppose everyone coming to bed."

Frances nodded thoughtfully.

"Will that be all?" he asked.

Frances nodded, and Maurice stood up. He pulled down his shirt and looked at the three of them.

"I do hope you catch him," he said, and he walked off, tall and proud as a monkey in a fez.

Frances groaned under her breath.

"That man annoys me beyond measure," she said.

"He is a pompous clot," said Florence, "I wanted to slap him across his smarmy face."

Frances chuckled. Florence had a way of making her feel better.

213

"I don't disagree," said Perry, "but did you hear the last thing he said?"

"Yes, he said he hopes we catch the bugger who did it," said Florence.

Fowler shook his head.

"No, he said he hoped we caught the man who did it. How would he know it was a man?"

"Because men are five times more likely to commit murder than women," said Frances.

"Or," said Fowler, "he knows who did it. Maybe it was him, or his friend Samuel?"

"I agree," said Florence.

"And I don't necessarily disagree," said Frances. "Maurice was lying about almost everything, though he seemed far too cavalier for a murderer."

"Or," said Anton, from behind her, "he's just that confident he won't be caught."

Eighteen

Nigel Durmott came walking in with his head held up, trailing behind Anton. He had a ready smile, which only made him all the more handsome. His black curly hair was immaculately styled and he looked fresh and eager as if he were about to head out on his first safari. He wore a white shirt with the sleeves rolled up to his elbows and khaki pants over brown hiking boots. He greeted everyone warmly with his honeyed voice and pleasing manner.

"This is an awful business," said Nigel as he sat down in the chair that had carried the bodies of four suspects before him. He casually tossed his left leg over his right knee and put his hands in his lap. He smiled warmly and openly at the four of them.

"You are quite correct," said Frances, "this is a terrible business. But I promise you that we'll get to the bottom of it."

"Good," said Nigel, nodding.

"Now you must understand, Nigel, that at this point, we can't rule anyone out. All of you left before Abigail returned to her cabin last night, which means all of you had an opportunity to poison her."

Nigel nodded.

"Of course," he said. "I understand. Though if I might be so bold as to inquire about the four of you."

He smiled at them non-threateningly. Frances could tell that he put women at ease with his manner, and encouraged an easy friendship with men.

"Fair enough," said Frances. "Florence and me were the last to leave the top deck last night and retire for the evening. Albert will attest to that fact if asked, because he and his sister were the second to last to retire. As for Perry and Anton, and in fact the rest of the staff of the Queen Nefertiti, they were in the mess playing cards and other things. That's not important though, as I have all but excluded them from this crime."

"Of course," said Nigel.

"You were the fourth to leave us last night from the top deck. Where did you go at that time?"

"I went straight back to my cabin and went to bed."

"Did you see or hear anything from any of the other cabins when you retired?" asked Frances.

Nigel took a moment to think about it.

"Not particularly, though I do remember thinking how odd it was that there were two voices coming from Maurice's room."

"Could you identify either of those voices?"

"No, I don't think so, they were murmurs really. I didn't stop to listen, that would be rude. I suppose that one of them must have been Maurice's voice, but the other I can't say."

"Could you tell if it was a man's or a woman's?"

"Certainly a man's."

Frances nodded and looked over at Fowler and Florence. Fowler turned his mouth upside down and nodded his head.

"I take it that's helpful?" asked Nigel.

"It certainly might be. Tell me, Nigel, do you sleep well?"

"Like a baby, why do you ask?"

"Have you ever taken a sleeping draught to help you sleep?"

"Once or twice, but not for quite some time now."

"So you don't have any on you at the moment, or in your cabin?"

"No."

Nigel kept smiling at Frances and the others.

"You're suspecting me of killing the poor woman aren't you?"

"We're trying to rule out the suspects, Nigel. And at the moment, everyone is a suspect."

"Yes, I suppose so."

"So if you don't have any Somunol then you won't mind us looking for any in your cabin?" asked Frances.

"Not at all."

Frances frowned ever so slightly and smiled thinly at him.

"Something I am curious of, Nigel, is why you went to the Pyramid of Menkaure carrying a rucksack yesterday afternoon by yourself?"

"I was looking for any mementos."

"And that's where Perry and Timothy found you?"

"It is."

"What sort of mementos were you looking for Nigel?" asked Frances, pointedly.

"I suppose there's no harm in telling, a woman has already been killed over it. I was looking for some of the stolen items from the Pyramid of Menkaure."

"But the pyramid has been emptied for decades and the bulk of the stolen items are deemed to be in England," said Perry.

"Quite right," said Nigel, "I was just hoping, dreaming, that's all."

"That's what Maurice said," mentioned Frances. "Don't you find that quite peculiar?"

"Not really," said Nigel, still smiling. "Egypt is one of the wonders of the worlds, doesn't it just fill the hopeful heart with dreams of grandeur and possibility?"

Nigel looked at the three of them and smiled at each in turn. He uncrossed his legs and crossed the right over the left this time. None of them smiled back so he let his smile go, gently, as if he had caught a butterfly by its wings.

"Did you find what you were looking for then?"

"No, I'm afraid I didn't."

"Why are you here, Nigel, really?" asked Frances.

Nigel looked at her and raised an eyebrow.

"The same reason I imagine that most of us here for. I'm taking a holiday."

Frances looked down at his hand. She hadn't seen him wearing a wedding ring, but she could tell he had recently worn one. A thin circle of pale skin contrasted with his otherwise quite tanned hands.

"Then where is your wife?"

Nigel looked down at his ring finger and rubbed the pale patch of skin and paused before answering.

"My wife and I thought that a bit of time apart might do us the world of good, if you must know."

He looked up at them and he wasn't smiling.

"I'm sorry to hear that, Mr. Durmott," said Florence.

He smiled at her and nodded.

"I'm confident this trip will give me the perspective I need in order to improve things when I get back."

Frances nodded, but she wasn't smiling.

"Thank you, Nigel," she said. "I don't have any more questions at this time. Do any of you?" She looked at the other two. Perry and Florence shook their heads.

Nigel stood up and nodded at them.

"I hope I've been helpful."

"You have been less than forthcoming, Nigel," said Frances, looking up at him.

Fowler and Florence both looked at her with puzzled faces. Nigel held Lady Marmalade's gaze for a moment, and then smiled at her.

"I'm sorry you feel that way," he said. "I hope you get the person who did this."

"I will, Nigel, you can count on that."

Nigel turned and walked away, as relaxed as he had walked in. Frances followed him out with her eyes. Florence looked at Frances and pinched her mouth together.

"Don't you think you were a little bit hard on him, after all he's going through?" asked Florence.

Frances shifted her gaze from the stairs that had just inhaled Nigel to Florence.

"Sometimes, my dear Flo," she said, "you have to be blunt in order to cut through the lies, or at least detect them. It's not personal but unless you can unsteady the suspect emotionally you haven't any chance of getting anywhere near to the truth let alone onto the greens of truth."

"But still, he's come here for some peace and reflection on his difficult marriage."

"My dear Flo, I think you're letting his good looks swoon your good judgment. I don't think for a moment his marriage is in trouble. He's either divorced or still quite happily married."

"How can you be so certain?"

"Because a man of his means doesn't spend a fortune on a trip like this if his marriage is falling apart. In fact, I don't think anyone would. You might pop over to the continent, France or Spain perhaps, but you wouldn't travel all the way to North Africa if your world was about to implode."

Florence nodded her head. Perry looked at her.

"How do you know he doesn't have much money?"

"On the form he filled out for you, he put civil servant at the Postal Service as his occupation, and his luggage was not an expensive brand, nor are his clothes of the highest cost. He's a modest man, and I make no judgment on that, it's just a fact."

"So you think he's lying to us?"

Frances nodded her head.

"I think he's lying to us about a lot of things. But he's not the only one."

"What's he lying about?" asked Perry.

"That remains to be seen. But through all of their lies, the pieces come together and we start to see the picture. Those jagged bits that don't fit. Those are the lies, and from where they should fit we find the truth."

Nineteen

Anton brought Simon in for an interview next. He looked a little nervous and he chewed on his fingernails before he sat down. In the wrong light, the scar on his left cheek gave him a menacing look. He sat down and folded his arms in front of himself and leaned back. He tried to smile but his mouth couldn't find the shape.

"Are you a bit nervous?" asked Lady Marmalade.

"I am a bit, yeah. I've never been a suspect in a murder before," he said, his voice losing its tone. He coughed at the end.

"Don't be," said Frances, smiling at him and trying to put him more at ease. "Everyone is a suspect at this stage."

"Except the four of you, I suppose."

"Yes, but that's because we have alibis. Florence and I were the last to leave the deck last evening, and Perry and Anton were playing cards downstairs in the officers' mess all night."

Simon nodded and bit his lip. He held his right hand out and looked at his fingers. He crossed his ankles but that didn't feel comfortable so he extended his legs under the table that was between them. That didn't make him feel any better so he tucked them under his chair and crossed his ankles and his arms.

"Tell me, Simon, why did you choose Egypt for a holiday?" asked Frances.

He looked at her and fidgeted in his chair.

"I took part in the Western Desert Campaign of the war," said Simon, nervously. He coughed to clear his voice. "Most of my time was spent in Egypt. I was part of the El Alamein campaign where we pushed the Germans and Italians back. Anyway, I had really enjoyed my time in Egypt, not the war part you understand, the brief moments of peace in between the war. And I always said to myself how I'd like to come back during peace times to explore the country more. That's why I'm here."

Frances nodded.

"I'm surprised you're nervous then," said Fowler, "you must have seen some action during that time in North Africa, perhaps even killed a man before."

Simon looked up Perry and scowled at him. He pinched his lips together and looked away.

"Listen," he said, getting noticeably upset, "I don't want to talk about that. That was war. All of us did things we had to do. It's not a point to be proud of, but we won didn't we?"

"Perry's only trying to understand why you're nervous talking to us about Abigail's murder when you've most certainly seen awful things during the war," said Frances.

"Because murder is a blight on the human soul. It's not something I wish to relive. Listen, I got out of the army as soon as the war finished. I might have earned the VC, but that doesn't mean I'm a hero. I just did what needed to be done. I've seen things I'd rather not see again and this whole nasty business with Abigail just brings it all back to the forefront. Killing during war for the protection of your country in the heat of battle is one thing. Murdering a woman for whatever reason during peacetimes is unfathomable and evil. That's why I'm nervous. It sends shivers down my spine to think that there is a cold hearted murderer amongst us."

Frances nodded and smiled kindly at him.

"I do thank you for your brave service during the war, Simon. We'll try and make this as easy on you as possible."

Simon glanced up at her and nodded. He had started chewing his nails again, his arms crossed over his chest tightly.

"Do you sleep well, Simon, or do you need sleeping draughts?"

He stopped biting his nails.

"I'll tell you right up front I didn't kill her, all right?"

Simon frowned and shook his head.

"Please answer the questions, Simon. You must understand that nine times out of ten a criminal will always deny their crime."

"Very well," said Simon, getting hot under the collar. "I barely sleep a wink most nights. Ever since I got out of the army. Insomnia is my constant companion most nights, he gets inside my head and plays games with me. I've tried sleeping draughts, and they don't help most times, and when they do I feel worse in the morning, so I don't use them."

"So you didn't bring any with you on this trip?"

"No. I'm telling you, I didn't kill her all right, and I'd be happier if you found out who did."

Simon brought his legs out from under him and he started tapping his right foot, his knee jumping up and down like a nervous ball.

"And perhaps you can help us with that," said Frances.

He glanced up at her and chewed at his fingernails. At this rate Frances thought he might chew them down to his first knuckle.

"Yesterday afternoon, after you left us at the Sphinx, you said you were going to explore the Pyramid of Menkaure."

"Yes, I did."

"Why did you want to go back to that pyramid when we'd seen it already?"

"We hadn't seen the secret chambers. Like I said, I was curious, and I wanted to explore the whole thing. I'd really like to get the whole experience of Egypt while I was here."

"But were you looking for anything in particular?"

"Well, you never know, but I was hoping that I might find some small trinket that had been left behind."

"Seems everyone's been looking for something like that," said Florence, looking at Frances. Frances nodded at her.

"And did you find what you were looking for?"

"Well I wasn't sure what I was looking for, but I didn't find anything. It was a little disappointing, only empty chambers and secret passageways. I would have loved to have seen it filled with treasures."

Simon was becoming more relaxed as he spoke of the pyramid and his imagination drew pictures of treasures piled high in his mind. Frances looked over at Perry and Florence.

"Did you see anyone else in there? Specifically Albert and Abigail?"

"No. Hang on. Albert and Abigail were turning north round the Pyramid of Menkaure when I reached the queen's pyramid. I remember Albert looking back and seeing me. He didn't look very happy."

"It seems then, that Simon entered the pyramid after Albert and Abigail had been in there, but found nothing," said Frances, looking at Perry and Florence.

"What does that mean?" asked Fowler.

"I think it means that they had a change of heart," said Florence. She turned to look at Simon. "Did you look pretty well for any trinkets you were hoping to find?"

"Quite well, but it would be hard to hide anything in there, I mean it's all open. The kings burial chamber and the room underneath where they say all the treasures were are all barren and empty."

Frances nodded.

"When you left, did you see anyone else?"

"Yes, the American chap, and Maurice were walking towards me. They stopped me and asked me if I'd seen anyone in there. I told them I thought Albert and Abigail had recently come and gone. They asked me if I had found anything in there. I told them I hadn't, that it was empty. Then they asked me if I had any water in my rucksack. I did, and they asked for some. I gave them some, and when we were done they told me not to tell anyone I was there. It sounded like a threat actually, and I decided to play along."

"Is that why you lied when you returned to the canopy?"

"Right, I don't know why, but I don't like that old woman. She doesn't treat Mahulda right and so I decided to lie to her. In any event, I don't know why she thought it was any of her business."

"Did Samuel and Maurice get a look in your rucksack when you went to find your water bottle?" asked Frances.

"They must have done, as I opened it in front of them."

Frances looked back at Fowler and Florence.

"On your way back to the canopy did you pass anyone else?" asked Frances.

"No, I don't think so. At least not that I saw, but I can't say I was looking."

Frances nodded.

"Thank you, Simon. Tell me about last night," said Frances.

"What about last night?"

"You escorted Mahulda downstairs to her cabin, didn't you?"

Simon nodded and looked furtively around the room.

"You left shortly after Lady Pompress did. Tell me what you did when you left the top deck."

"I don't know what you mean. I took Mahulda down to her cabin. She went in, then I went into mine and went to bed, and I tried to sleep."

"What I mean is, did you find anything suspicious when you took Mahulda back to her room?"

"No. I waited while she let herself into the room."

"Was Orpha inside already?"

"Probably, but I don't know. Mahulda snuck in quietly, just opening the door a crack so she could sneak in. The room was dark. I imagine the old lady was sleeping."

"You mean Mrs. Bendled," said Fowler sternly.

"Right."

"What about any of the other cabins? Did you overhear any conversations?" asked Lady Marmalade.

Simon looked up and gritted his teeth. His hands stayed folded across his chest.

"Well nothing that I'd find suspicious, though my cabin is right across from Lady Pompress' and Captain Wainscott's. Lady Pompress was in her cabin, the door wasn't closed and I could see in. She was looking in one of her bags for something and muttering."

"About what?"

"I don't know. I couldn't hear. She always seems to be muttering about one thing or another. She saw me by my cabin door. I smiled at her, and she came up to her door and slammed it shut. Before she did she said, 'can a woman not get any privacy at all?' That was it. I wasn't even spying on her, I only happened to notice because her door was open. Not my fault my cabin is across the hall from theirs."

Frances nodded.

"Your cabin is next to Maurice's. Did you hear anything at all from their cabin?"

"I heard two men talking and arguing about something intermittently until about midnight when the door opened and closed and then everything was quiet for the rest of the evening."

"Could you tell who it was or what they were talking about?"

Simon shook his head.

"No. I assume one of them was Maurice, but I couldn't swear on it. I don't know who the other man might have been."

"Do you think it might have been Samuel, the American?"

"I suppose so. Though like I said, their voices were murmurs. I couldn't identify them other than they were definitely male."

"Anything else at all during the night?"

"I heard Captain Wainscott come down to bed. I suppose that might have been around ten or a little before. He tried to enter the cabin as quietly as possible. You can tell, because he turned the key ever so slowly. In any event, it was all for naught. Lady Pompress was up and they had a fight for a few minutes. I couldn't hear any of it, just the ebb and flow of the heated arguments. It finished before Albert or Abigail came down to bed. I don't know which, because I heard their door open and close a couple of times within a few minutes of each other."

"Are you sure it was only twice that Albert and Abigail's door was opened."

"I think so. Might have been three times. I'm sorry, I wasn't counting. I just assumed that it was twice because I assumed they came to bed separately. At least that's what it sounded like."

"They did," said Frances.

"Then why are you asking whether it was twice or three times?"

"Three times would indicate the killer entered and would give a much narrower window to the timetable."

Simon nodded his head and looked down at his feet.

"Yes, I suppose so. I'm sorry I can't be of more assistance. I really can't say for certain if it was two or three times that the door opened."

Frances sighed heavily and nodded. That wasn't what she was hoping for. It would have helped to have a clearer time of when the murderer committed their dastardly deed.

"If you heard Albert and Abigail come to bed, then you must have heard Florence and I come down the hallway."

Simon shook his head.

"No, now that I think of it, I didn't hear the two of you. I must have nodded off during that time. I do get snatches of sleep here and there. What time would it have been?"

"Shortly after Abigail came to bed. Perhaps around ten thirty, though I didn't bother looking."

"Is there anything else you need?" asked Simon. "They're serving afternoon tea up on the open deck at three thirty." He looked at his watch. "Which is now."

Frances nodded.

"You've been helpful, Simon," she said, and then looking at Fowler and Florence. "Perhaps a break for tea would do us all the world of good."

They all got up, with Lady Marmalade grabbing all the documents they had strewn before them and shuffled them back into the folder.

"We don't want to leave this behind."

The five of them walked towards the end of the dining room and climbed up the stairs with Simon leading.

Twenty

Frances, Florence, Fowler and Pung all sat together at one table while Jafari served them tea. The spread was vast in its choices.

"I asked the kitchen to do up a good spread for tea this afternoon," said Fowler, "considering the sad matter at hand."

"It's very good of you," said Florence. "Nothing quite like a good tea to lift the spirits."

Jafari brought by a cake stand that had three levels on it. There were plates of freshly cut strawberries, clotted cream, crumpets, scones, jams, sponge cake, lemon bars and shortbread. Jafari placed two pots of tea in the middle of the table as well as four cups and saucers, a bowl of sugar and jugs of cream and milk. There was no lemon. Frances thought about asking for some but then decided against it. What she really needed under these circumstances was creamy, sweet tea, not tart lemony tea.

At a table close to them, Simon sat with Mahulda across from Orpha and Nigel. None of them spoke to each other. At the third table sat Lady Pompress, Captain Wainscott and Albert. The fourth and last table sat Maurice and Samuel. Nobody was talking to anybody else, except at the Lady Marmalade table. The tables were far enough spaced so that if you spoke in a lowered voice the other tables would be unlikely to hear you unless they craned their necks to hear it.

Fowler put a scone on his plate, which he broke in half and topped both sides with clotted cream and strawberry jam. He also put a lemon bar next to it. Pung took a warm crumpet and warm scone. On the crumpet he put a thick pat of butter with a dollop of marmalade and on the scone he put clotted cream and strawberry jam. Frances took a single piece of shortbread. Her appetite wasn't what it should have been. She was more concerned with clearing the fog regarding this murder which still hung like thick cobwebs around her. Florence took a piece of sponge cake and a lemon bar and two strawberries. Next to the strawberries she placed a pyramid of cream.

"The more we hear from everyone," said Florence, "the more it appears like Samuel and Maurice are hiding something."

"What do you mean?" asked Pung, cutting a piece of crumpet and stuffing it in his mouth.

"Well, look at what Simon said. He said he heard two men talking and arguing in Maurice's room when he went to bed. That must have been Maurice and Samuel."

"It could have also been Maurice with Nigel, Tim or Albert. They're the other two men onboard," said Perry, taking a bit out of his scone.

"No, it couldn't have been Albert, he went to bed just before Abigail, earlier than Simon," said Frances. "Same with Timothy."

"Do you remember the order in which everyone left the deck last night?" asked Pung.

"I do. It started with Maurice, then shortly after him Samuel left. A little while later it was Orpha and then Nigel. Lady Pompress left in a bit of huff some time after Nigel, followed by Simon and Mahulda. Then Timothy left, followed by Albert and then Abigail."

"Maurice could have had Nigel in his room then, I suppose," offered Fowler as he took the teapot and brought it to Lady Marmalade's cup. "Tea?"

Frances nodded her head, and Perry poured her a cup of tea, and then Florence, Pung and lastly filled his own teacup. That was the first pot finished.

"It certainly is an option, but I'm not quite convinced."

"Why not?" asked Pung, as Fowler sipped his plain black tea. Both he and Fowler had theirs black. Frances and Florence doctored theirs with cream and sugar.

"I haven't seen Maurice and Nigel share many words together since we've been on this trip. Samuel and Maurice, however, have. What's more, they both seem to be trying to hide something."

"Hide what?" asked Florence, taking a sip of her tea.

"That remains to be seen, but I believe that by the end of the day it is likely to be some artifact that was stolen from the Pyramid of Menkaure over fifty years ago."

"You really think Albert and Abigail brought stolen artifacts with them to Egypt, to return them?" asked Fowler.

"It has to be something like that. Most likely Abigail's doing. We'll find out, I'm sure. If I'm right, then I bet that Maurice and Samuel, working either together or alone, were after the same artifact. We just have to know how they heard of it and if they're working together or alone. And why Nigel is looking for it seems to be yet another piece of the puzzle I haven't quite figured out yet."

"Why bring it here though?" asked Pung. "Surely it would have been wiser if you did in fact want to return the stolen property to return it to the British Museum."

Frances took a sip of her tea, and nodded at Anton.

"Very true. The only reason I can think of, is that there are others who know the whereabouts or perhaps the general location of these stolen artifacts and if they'd have returned them in Britain, perhaps they felt their lives would have been in danger."

"And so what they thought was safer turns out to be just as dangerous."

"I haven't told you two this," said Frances, looking at Pung and Fowler, "but yesterday evening I told Albert that he looked like Arthur Vipond..."

"Who's that?" asked Fowler, finishing one half of his scone.

"He was believed to be one of the thieves who stole the treasures from the Pyramid of Menkaure."

Fowler nodded his head.

"Albert nearly choked when he heard that. It was a sure tell that he knew who Vipond was. At least to me he did."

"He certainly did react strangely," agreed Florence, eating her last strawberry peaked with white cream.

"He and Abigail went on to ask me about someone theoretically trying to return stolen jewels, and how unjust it would seem if that person was punished for trying to do right by it. I had the impression then, and I believe it still, that they were not talking in theory."

"I see," said Fowler, "then why haven't we interviewed him already?"

"I want to save him for last. I want him to sweat a bit so that he is more inclined to be forthcoming and tell us the truth. He knows that he's likely to be the prime suspect. Additionally, I want to get the liars telling their lies early so that come tomorrow they might not remember them as well."

"But Albert may very well have killed his sister. You said he was the prime suspect, and I, quite frankly, like him as the murderer," said Fowler.

"Me too," offered Pung, as he ate the last piece of his crumpet.

"I'm not dismissing him at all," said Frances, "and this whole affair is quite confusing still as everyone, it seems, continues to lie to us to some degree or another."

"Even Simon?" asked Florence, looking at Frances and sipping on her tea.

Overhead a colony of gulls flew quietly, staring down at the morsels and crumbs on the tables of the upper deck. The relatively flat, though rippled glass of the Nile's face rocked the Queen Nefertiti ever so slightly, and if you listened closely enough you could hear the water splash against the bow like playful mermaids.

"Now that you've mentioned it," said Frances. "Simon might be the only one telling the whole truth. At least that portion of truth that he's telling. I can't be certain he's told us everything he knows."

Frances took a small bite of her shortbread. Her first bite. It was crumbly and full in her mouth as it melted like flavored butter on her tongue. She turned to Fowler.

"Does this boat have a telegraph?"

Fowler nodded.

"It does. Would you like to make use of it?"

"Not just yet. But this evening, after we've interviewed everyone I'd like to send a telegram or two. There's one way to get the truth by morning, and that's from my friends in Scotland Yard."

"What are you trying to find out, and about whom?" asked Anton.

"I want to find the truth about some of the guests on this boat. Those that have lied to us so far."

Frances looked at her friend.

"I am so sorry, Flo, that this has happened on our holiday. We'll have to make sure to come out again sometime when nobody's killing anybody else."

Frances smiled at her and Florence nodded and smiled back.

"Jolly unfortunate," agreed Fowler.

"It is, but it can't be helped. I just hope we get to the bottom of this so we can determine who the bugger is that murdered poor Abigail."

"I'm certain we shall," said Frances.

"Speaking of which," said Fowler. "I have an announcement to make, if you'll excuse me."

Fowler got up from the table, dabbed at his mouth with his napkin, and straightened his mustache. He put the white napkin on the side of his place setting and walked into the middle of the upper deck so that he could speak more easily to all of those gathered.

"Ladies and gentleman," said Fowler. "If I can have your attention for just a moment. This morning, after we found dear Ms. Abigail Beckles murdered, I sent a telegram to the main office of Thoth Tours in London. From what we know currently, it appears as if we might all get off the Queen Nefertiti tomorrow at the latest. Unfortunately due to these unforeseen circumstances that were beyond our control, you are all eligible for refunds or if you'd prefer, future vouchers for this very same tour. The choice is yours. Please let me know when we disembark. Are there any questions?"

Fowler looked around at everyone gathered at their tables.

"When will we get off this boat? I'm getting quite claustrophobic, you know," asked Lady Pompress.

"My dear Lady," said Fowler, "just as soon as we can. Lady Marmalade needs to interview all of you, and we thank those who have already provided that information. Once that part of this investigation has finished, then it's just a matter of waiting for the Cairo police to come aboard and conduct their investigation. I'm sure that won't take long, as Lady Marmalade is doing much of their work for them. Once they've given us the green light, we'll be able to get you off and on your way back to Cairo."

"And when might that be, Perry? How come the police aren't here already. We're only nineteen miles out of Cairo. Surely they could have made it here already?" asked Captain Wainscott.

"There has been a terrible dust storm, called a simoom, blow into Cairo this afternoon. From what we know at this stage, they're hoping to get to us this evening. I'll keep you all posted. Please rest assured that we have enough water and food to last us several more days if needs be."

Fowler looked around at the faces at the tables and smiled at them all in turn. He was competent and inspiring at his job, and that eased everyone's nervousness. His warm and authoritative voice gave them all reassurance. After a few moments, when no new questions were asked, he sat back down with Lady Marmalade and made quick work of the second half of his scone.

Twenty-One

After a satisfying tea, Frances and the rest of them settled back down in the dining room.

"I think what I'd like to do," said Frances, "is interview Lady Pompress and Captain Wainscott separately."

"Who would you like to interview first?" asked Pung.

"Let's bring the captain in first."

Pung nodded and stood up and walked towards the stairs. The remaining guests were still on the top deck.

"I was thinking of bringing them in together, but then I thought better of it," said Frances.

"Why together?" asked Fowler.

"Those two have an interesting relationship and I thought it might be fun to see how they play off each other."

"If you ask me, I don't see their marriage lasting, even if they get that far," said Fowler.

"Yes, Captain Wainscott seems to have his work cut out for him," agreed Florence.

"Do you think they could have done it?" asked Fowler.

"No, not together anyway. I don't think they could agree on one thing long enough to commit a murder. But separately, perhaps."

"What would their motive be?" asked Florence.

"That's a bit of a pickle," said Frances.

"Lady Pompress has means, so I can't quite see why she would murder Abigail for what she would likely deem a trinket."

"Perhaps she has burnt through her wealth already," offered Florence.

"I don't believe so, Flo. Sir Stanley had a good sum, and from what I know of her and from what I've heard, she isn't a big spender. Additionally, Timothy said he paid for this trip and he's paying for the wedding, so her expenses here are hardly anything at all."

"Hmm," said Fowler, "I suppose there isn't a good reason for her to have done it then."

"Perhaps not, but you'd be surprised at the petty reasons that brings some amongst us to commit murder," said Frances.

"Such as?"

"Well, in Lady Pompress' case, it could be something as mean spirited as jealousy. But that would only work if Abigail were an attractive woman, but she's not. She quite plain really, and Timothy has shown no interest in her. You're right, I'm finding it hard to determine a motive for Lady Pompress."

"What about Timothy?" asked Fowler.

"That's rather straightforward I should think. As mentioned earlier, he is using up what small means he has to marry her. I think he's being a bit foolish about it, but perhaps he loves her and he likes the idea of living in relative luxury once they've tied the knot. However, finding out that Abigail and Albert had some artifacts here that they were carrying around, might have given him an idea. He might have thought it was better to hedge his bets and grab the spoils in case Lady Pompress decides to turn him down."

"But why would he do that if he's looking forward to marrying her and gaining access to her money?" asked Florence.

"Because on at least one occasion that I can recall, Lady Pompress has threatened to call off the wedding if he strays from behaving how she wants him to."

Florence nodded.

"Yes, I remember that now."

"He also has means," said Florence.

"Really?" asked Fowler, looking quite surprised. "How so?"

"We all overheard him tell us that she takes sleeping draughts to help sleep."

"Oh yes, I remember that now," said Fowler, "when she fainted."

Frances nodded.

"And now we know, at least to the best of our knowledge that there are only two people amongst us that have such drugs at their disposal. Dr. Samuel Newton and Lady Pompress."

"Right," said Fowler.

He looked off towards the stairs as Anton came back into the dining room with Captain Wainscott following. Captain Wainscott smiled nervously at them as he walked up. He was tall and handsome, but looked like he came more from Scandinavian stock than British with his blond hair and mustache. He licked his lips as he sat down and pressed his thin mustache against his lips with the index fingers of each hand. He crossed his legs over each other and folded his arms in his chest.

"I was rather hoping to be sitting there with you, than on this side," he said, trying to break the ice.

"I know," said Frances. "Unfortunately, we're the only ones with any alibis. Until we can remove you from the suspect list, I'm afraid you're a suspect."

"God, this is just awful. I've never been accused of killing anyone before. I even managed to escape that task during the war."

He smiled. Frances smiled back at him, and Fowler gave him a big grin. He was nervous and trying to calm himself with humor.

"No one likes to be accused of murder, Timothy, not even the murderer," said Frances.

"Good Lord, you're actually considering the thought that I did it. I'll tell you right now, I didn't. I swear to you I didn't."

Frances nodded.

"But I understand that you're under an enormous amount of debt at the moment with this trip and the impending wedding."

Captain Wainscott sighed.

"God, is it that obvious? Yes, you're right that I'm stretched fairly thin. But I'm mad about Abby. I've never met a woman like her. In any event, the wedding has been all but paid for."

"Except that Abigail has already threatened not to go through with the wedding at least once. And frankly Timothy, we find that understanding your relationship is quite difficult."

Timothy looked at them each in turn.

"Yes, I know she can be difficult. But you don't understand her like I do. She's really one of a kind, but she's had a difficult life and recently her husband died. She's still trying to come to terms with that."

"That may be, but she has threatened not to marry you."

Frances looked at him carefully, with a raised eyebrow.

"Oh hell," he said. "Yes, she has, and more than once actually. But I don't believe she's serious. And once we're together, and I know what you're really trying to get at, my situation will be much improved. But I can assure you that my intentions are pure. Anyway, if it really comes to it and we don't get married, I can always rejoin the army, and stay with them until I've earned my pension."

"That's one way of looking at it," said Frances, "the other way of looking at it, is that when you found out that Abigail Beckles was carrying with her some valuables on this trip, which had originally been stolen from the Menkaure pyramid you decided to pinch them yourself, and at the same time murder her."

"The horrors!" exclaimed Timothy, "Do you even hear yourself? Yes, I might have noticed those artifacts when they spilled from her case at the hotel, but so did others. I wouldn't stoop so low as to murder someone for money."

"But you do have access to the murder weapon," said Frances.

"Nonsense!"

"Are you denying that Lady Pompress has with her sleeping draughts?"

Timothy uncrossed his arms, gritted his teeth and put his hands through his hair.

"God, you aren't being very nice about it are you. Yes, Abby has sleeping draughts, but they're not mine. I don't use them."

"Then tell me this, Timothy, will Abigail admit that none of her sleeping draughts are missing?"

Timothy shook his head angrily from side to side and clutched at his head.

"I see where this is going. You've already convinced yourselves that I'm guilty. Look, somebody took a couple of sleeping draughts from Abby's medicine bag, and we got into quite a row about it last night when I got back to the cabin. But it wasn't me. Like I tried to tell her last night, why would I take them? I've never needed them to sleep in my entire life."

"The reason you might have taken them, Timothy, was to kill Abigail Beckles."

"I can't stand this anymore. I'm getting off this boat. I've told you I didn't do it. I swear to you I didn't. I'm leaving."

Captain Wainscott stood up as did Fowler and Pung.

"Captain," said Frances, "please sit down. We're not accusing you although you did have access to the sleeping draughts and motive. This emotional outburst is not going to help you. If you really didn't do it, then please entertain our questions a while longer. We're not the police. But when the Cairo police do come, they might not be as understanding."

Timothy stood there for a moment and then sat back down. So did Pung and Fowler.

"Let's get back to the row you had with your fiancée," said Frances. "Did Abigail say when she found the sleeping draughts missing."

"Well, she takes a draught every evening before bed. She took one on Wednesday night at the hotel, then she went to take her last one last night. That's when she found it missing. Why she has to accuse me is beyond comprehension. Besides, why would I take two, if indeed I did need some help sleeping, which I don't?"

"You would take two in order to murder Abigail Beckles," said Frances.

"Right," said Timothy, nodding his head, "I know that now. But last night I just thought the whole thing was preposterous. I asked her why would I take two, when one was all that was needed. I told her that perhaps she was mistaken. She went berserk at the thought that she might have miscounted. But she did recount them."

"And that only confirmed that they were missing?"

Timothy nodded his head.

"Yes, that's right. I don't recall how many she said she had, I was a bit drunk frankly, but she told me she was missing two, and I believed her. Abby is quite particular about those sorts of things."

"Does she take one every night?" asked Frances.

Timothy nodded.

"She does, as long as I've known her she does. As I told you, she's been going through a difficult time lately and this is the only way she can get any sleep."

"Then it would be fair to say that she likely had close to thirty sleeping draughts on her when she left England," said Frances.

"I couldn't say."

"Well, if she needs one every night and this holiday is four weeks long that's at least twenty-eight sleeping draughts."

Frances looked at Timothy for confirmation. He nodded his head.

"Yes, that would make sense. But as I said, I don't have any involvement in her prescription medications. I do give her an insulin injection twice a day though. She doesn't like to do that her self."

"I see," said Frances. "And her insulin isn't missing?"

"Not that I know of," said Timothy, "at least she didn't complain about that."

"And do you know how many vials of insulin she has with her?"

"No I don't, but it must be a few. If I recall correctly we get almost a week's worth out of a vial."

Frances nodded thoughtfully.

"You didn't go anywhere yesterday afternoon after we took Abigail back to canopy after she fainted, did you?"

"No, you'll recall I wanted to go with you three to see the Sphinx, fascinating sculpture, but alas, Abby wouldn't hear of it."

"Yes, I remember that. And you didn't sneak away after we left, did you?"

"Not at all, that would only have made things worse. Besides, were would I be sneaking off to?"

"The Pyramid of Menkaure," said Frances.

"What for? I had already seen it with Perry," said Captain Wainscott, looking at Perry.

"Perhaps you wanted to explore the secret chambers and find out if the artifacts had been returned."

Timothy grinned and then looked from Frances to Perry and then to Florence, grinning all the while.

"You don't say. You think that poor woman was going to return what was stolen right back to where it was stolen from."

Frances didn't say anything.

"That's the daftest idea I've ever heard. All the passageways and all the chambers we've seen in all of the pyramids are empty. There's no place to hide anything."

"Perhaps she thought there would be," said Frances.

"Poor dear," said Timothy, "I don't imagine Albert would have liked that idea."

"Why do you say that?"

"Well, come to think of it," said Timothy. "They left after you three had, and took their rucksacks and headed off towards the Great Pyramid of Giza. Their rucksacks weren't empty. In fact, they looked quite full. And they stopped to argue for a bit. Couldn't hear what about, but you could tell they were arguing. Then I lost them when they disappeared round the pyramid. So you think they were heading back to Menkaure's pyramid, eh?"

Timothy was smiling.

"I do think that her murder is related to these stolen artifacts that might not have been placed back in the pyramid."

"So you think they might still be onboard the boat then?" asked Timothy.

"Quite possibly."

"You don't say. This is turning out to be quite the intrigue. But it seems obvious to me then who did it."

"And who would that be?" asked Frances.

"Why the brother, of course. He seemed upset as I said before, and obviously he didn't want to return the spoils, so he stole them from his sister and then killed her before she could find out."

"And how did he get a hold of the sleeping draughts then, my dear Mr. Holmes," asked Frances smiling at him.

"That's elementary, my dear Frances. He stole them from my wife."

"Perhaps," said Frances. "He certainly does have the means and the motive. We'll be speaking with him later."

"But why? It's plain to see he did it. Why don't you just go and arrest him now, that miserable little fat man."

"In due time, Timothy, if you'll indulge me while I conduct this investigation," said Frances.

"Yes, of course. I'm just trying to be helpful."

"Did you hear anything at all last night before you fell asleep?"

"Well," said Timothy. "I did hear the door to the cabin next to us open and close a couple of times."

"That would have been Albert and Abigail's cabin then. Are you sure it was just twice?"

Timothy bunched his mouth up to one side and thought for a moment.

"Well, I wouldn't bet my life on it, but it could only have been twice couldn't it? Once for Albert and once for Abigail."

"Or thrice if you heard the killer enter before Albert and Abigail came in."

"Yes, I suppose so. To be honest, I'd wager it was only twice, but it could have been more. I had a bit more to drink than I should have," said Timothy, smiling.

"You or Abigail didn't see anything odd since you got onboard the Queen Nefertiti yesterday evening, did you? Did you see anyone trying to get into your room, or anything of that sort?"

Timothy shook his head.

"Not really. Though Abby came down yesterday just before dinner and she noticed Simon by our door. She thinks he was trying to get in, and he looked startled when she came up to him. But sometimes, if you don't mind me saying so, Abby exaggerates these sorts of things."

"Did he say anything to her?"

"He apologized profusely of course, said he forgot which side of the boat he was on for a minute."

"Did she notice her missing sleeping draughts at that time?"

"I don't think so, she wouldn't have been counting them at that time anyway, only in the evening when she was preparing for bed."

"Did anything look out of place in the room when she got in?"

"I asked her that and she didn't think so, but she was quite upset by it. I told her it was an honest mistake, and easy to make so early on in the trip. You see, Simon's cabin is opposite ours and I can quite easily see how you could get turned around and forget which side was yours. I almost did it myself when I came to bed last night."

Timothy chuckled at the thought.

"Poor lad with his scar. How awful. That must be quite embarrassing with the ladies, I imagine."

"Mahulda doesn't seem to mind," said Florence.

Timothy nodded his head slowly. He placed his hands together in his lap and crossed his legs over each other the other way.

"Yes, they are becoming quite friendly together. Good for them. Oh, but to be young and in love again."

"Is there anything else you might wish to share with us that could help?" asked Frances.

Timothy looked away for a moment, thinking if there was anything else he could think of.

"I can't really think of anything. There was some arguing last night though, coming from Maurice's or Samuel's room. Two men arguing about something. I couldn't tell what, and I just happened to notice as I walked by."

"Which room was it? Maurice's or Samuel's?"

"I can't say for certain. It was definitely one of the first couple on the port side."

Timothy closed his eyes, deep in thought.

"I'm just trying to think," he said. "I was walking towards the back of the boat, and the noise came from my right. The first couple of cabins are empty." Timothy still had his eyes closed. "It wasn't the next one, it was the one after. That's right, just before Simon's cabin. The room directly opposite Albert and Abigail's room. That would be Maurice's, I believe."

Timothy opened his eyes and looked at Lady Marmalade who was writing some notes down.

"Is that helpful?" he asked.

"It might be," said Frances, looking up.

"Well, that's all that comes to mind," he said.

"Thank you, Captain," said Frances. "I don't have any other questions for you. Do any of you?"

Frances looked at her colleagues, and they both shook their heads.

"Would you mind asking your wife to join us?" asked Frances.

Timothy stood up. He was ready to leave.

"Not at all, but go easy on her, she can be a bit temperamental."

Frances nodded and smiled at him. Timothy walked towards the stairs where he disappeared. Perry turned to Frances.

"What do you make of that?" he asked.

"Of what?"

"Simon hanging around the wrong cabin. Sounds quite suspicious to me," said Fowler.

"Me too," said Florence.

"It certainly does require an explanation. But as Timothy said, it could easily have been an honest mistake."

"But he failed to mention that to us," said Fowler.

"Or he forgot, or he didn't think it was important," said Frances. "Could you give me a motive."

She looked at both Fowler and Florence.

"The classic motive," said Fowler. "Greed. He wants the stolen jewels and other objects so that he might become rich."

"But how would he know that there would be such things on this trip?"

"He probably didn't, unless there is some hidden relationship between him and Abigail that we don't know about."

"That's an interesting idea worth exploring further."

"In any event, why does he have to know in advance. Couldn't this just be a crime of opportunity. He sees the spilled spoils from the bus when Abigail's bag opens and he fancies trying to get them for himself. He notices that Albert and Abigail have just come from the Pyramid of Menkaure and he goes into the secret chambers to find out if they had left the stolen goods there. They haven't, so he decides he'll take them from Abigail on the boat. He sneaks into their room and decides to poison Abigail and retrieve the artifacts."

"So you think he has them now?"

"I do."

"And if he doesn't?"

"Then he'll continue to look for them."

"Then tell me this. Why doesn't he just poison both Albert and Abigail to make it easier on himself? Murdering only the one of them could make it more difficult to access the artifacts if he hasn't got them yet."

"Not necessarily," said Fowler. "He only killed Abigail because that puts Albert as the prime suspect. He doesn't want to draw any attention to himself."

Frances nodded her head.

"I think you might have a great theory there, Fowler. I'm just not sure it applies to Simon."

Twenty-Two

Lady Pompress descended the stairs with elegance and walked towards them as if she were gliding upon cotton clouds. She wore a pale yellow dress, and in her right hand she carried a yellow fan. From a certain distance she was quite a vision. Frances had no doubt that she had entertained many suitors in her youth. But the more intimately you got to know her, the less attractive she became.

And now, being in her mid-forties, her beauty was starting to sallow, which only gave her unpleasant personality more opportunity to shine brightly. Captain Wainscott was both a handsome and patient man. Additionally, he was a good decade younger than her and still within the warm embrace of youthful vigor. Frances wondered if, in quiet moments, Lady Pompress realized that this was her last chance at love, or was she so self-involved to be oblivious to anything beyond her own navel.

Frances smiled at her as Lady Pompress sat down. Lady Pompress didn't offer a smile back. She was stingy with both happiness, which one realized she didn't have much of, and social etiquette which, for a woman in her position she would hold much, she nevertheless doled out stingily.

"Thank you for joining us, Abigail," said Frances.

Lady Pompress rolled her eyes.

"I would like it so much better if you would use my title."

"And I would like it so much better if the likes of you never received courtesy titles at all," said Frances. "Unfortunately, neither of those situations is going to change."

Lady Pompress flicked her short curly brown hair in disgust as she glanced upwards.

"Timmy has told me everything," she said, "so you shan't be able to pull the wool over my eyes."

Frances felt bold. She didn't want to waste time beating about the bush. Rather than a warning shot across the bows, she decided a pointed blow right into the bowels was more appropriate. If she could rattle Lady Pompress' cage, she might have a chance of getting to the truth a little big quicker.

"Why did you kill Abigail Beckles?" asked Frances with a straight face.

Lady Pompress' eyes widened and her jaw slackened causing her mouth to open.

"Why I... I... I didn't," she said.

She fumbled around for the words for a moment, and the affect that Lady Marmalade had been hoping for had been achieved.

"You had the opportunity and you had the means," said Frances, not wanting to add motive, because she wasn't sure what the motive was.

"I... Good Lord, you can't be serious."

Lady Pompress looked at the three of them with incredulity.

"Here's what I think, Abigail," said Frances. "You used two of your sleeping draughts to murder Ms. Beckles so that you could steal her artifacts. You then complained to your fiancé that two had gone missing to try and place doubt on the fact that you had taken them to kill that poor woman. What I don't understand, Abigail, is why you are so greedy and heartless that you needed to steal from those who have so little."

Frances knew she was being sharp and pointed, but she wanted to get beyond the severe façade that Lady Pompress wore, and to her inner vulnerability where the truth lay hidden.

Lady Pompress, was vigorously fanning herself as she listened in outrage to what Frances was alleging.

"So because I have sleeping draughts, I'm now the suspect," she said.

"You're only the suspect until I have the evidence required to convict you in court. It is apparent that you didn't like Abigail. You greatly disdain anyone who you think is of lower class than you. You go to great lengths to be spiteful to those around you. You are, in other words, Abigail, a horrid woman."

Frances wasn't enjoying this anymore, and she wondered if she'd gone too far. Lady Pompress started to tear up. She was fanning herself faster and faster as her anger turned towards hatred and then into a deep sadness. Florence glanced over at Frances in concern. As did Fowler. She ignored them both, she kept her eyes on Lady Pompress.

"You don't know what it's like," said Lady Pompress, as tears rolled down her cheeks. "I was a widow at forty six. The man I loved with all my heart, who had cared for me for over twenty-five years left me with nothing except this title and a modest inheritance. I am still grieving, and now I have a second chance with Captain Wainscott, and I fear he will leave me just like my dear Stanley did."

Lady Pompress choked on a sob.

"I was a lowly charwoman when Stanley fell in love with me, and he changed my life for the better. You might think I'm a mean-spirited woman, but everything I've loved has been taken from me and this is the only way I know of to protect myself. I'm sorry if my social etiquette isn't up to your fine standards Lady Marmalade. You who has not known a day of sadness in your many years."

That last bit was untrue, but Frances had pushed her hard and now was the time to back away.

"You might as well put me in jail and throw away the key. Timmy will have nothing to do with me now, I'm sure. Even though I'm innocent of this atrocity you sully me with."

Fowler offered her his clean handkerchief. She took it and dabbed at her eyes.

"Captain Wainscott loves you a great deal Lady Pompress," said Florence.

Lady Pompress looked up at Florence but couldn't afford a smile.

"I can tell. He is just as fearful as you that you might leave him."

Lady Pompress shook her head.

"I couldn't bear to lose him. He's my only chance at love. My only hope of coming to grips with the sadness that has plagued me this last year."

Frances looked at Lady Pompress and recognized the sincerity in her eyes.

"My grandmother used to say that you'll attract more bees with honey than with... well I think you get the gist of it," Frances said, smiling. "You've shared a great deal with us, and for that I'm grateful, but I fear that if you continue to act hardened and acerbic towards others, that will only alienate you further and bring about that which you fear most."

Lady Pompress dabbed at her eyes again, and handed Fowler his handkerchief back.

"Thank you," she said to him.

"I hope you'll forgive me, Abigail, for my direct and perhaps blunt manner with you just now. You must understand that time is of the essence in finding out who committed this awful murder, and I was afraid that we didn't have the time beating around the bush with you while we tried to dance around the issues that are right at hand."

Lady Pompress nodded her head. She was fanning her face at a much more moderate pace.

"I understand."

"Now yesterday evening, Timothy told me that the two of you got into quite a row about your missing sleeping draughts. Is that correct?"

Lady Pompress nodded her head.

"Yes, I'm embarrassed to admit it now, but we did. I don't know why I blamed him, I guess because there was no one else to blame. He couldn't have taken them anyway, he's such a heavy sleeper, I've never known him to need any help sleeping. It gives me great comfort too, if I'm to be honest. He falls asleep within minutes, and when I'm having the devil of a time in sleeping, I'll watch his chest rise and fall. I find it soothing."

Lady Pompress was looking off in the distance in a sort of reverie, as if she were right at that moment, watching Timothy's chest fall and rise as he breathed slowly and deeply, like the peaceful sleep that only babies seem to enjoy.

"How many sleeping draughts were missing?"

"Two. I know it doesn't seem like many, but you must understand, I was in quite the state last night. You see, I only brought enough with me to last the trip. I'm very careful that way. I knew that when we arrived on Wednesday in Alexandria that I had thirty sleeping draughts with me. You see," said Lady Pompress, biting her lip as she thought carefully for a moment, "that the holiday is twenty-eight days long, additionally Timmy and I will spend a night in Naples before we head back home to London. That means twenty-nine nights abroad. I put an extra one in just for good measure. And then last night, with two of them gone, I feared I'd be one short at the end of the trip. You can't imagine the fright that gave me. I can't sleep a wink without them. Now of course I suppose it doesn't matter."

"How so?" asked Florence.

"Well, the poor dear is dead isn't she, so we'll be leaving here within the next day or two."

Florence nodded.

"Timothy tells me that you also saw Simon by your cabin yesterday evening before dinner," said Frances.

Lady Pompress nodded her head vigorously.

"That's right, I found it quite odd. Timmy and I had gone upstairs for dinner, but I realized I had forgotten my purse so I went back downstairs to fetch it when I saw Simon standing by my cabin with his hand on the door knob."

"What did you say to him?"

"I told him that was my cabin, his was across the way. He looked up at me quite puzzled. Then he blushed and apologized profusely and disappeared into his own cabin."

"Do you think he had gone inside?" asked Florence.

"No, I don't think so. If he did, he didn't disturb anything. I made a thorough look just to be sure."

"Do you know if your sleeping draughts were missing at that time?" asked Frances.

Lady Pompress shook her head.

"No, I didn't think to look at those at the time. Only when I got back and before bed did I need one, and that's when I check."

Frances nodded.

"That's understandable," she said. "Did you notice anything else unusual yesterday evening after you retired?"

"Well, Simon came down the hall and stared into my cabin when he did so. I find him quite unsettling to be honest."

"Did he say anything to you when you saw him looking into your cabin?"

"No, I noticed him, so I went to the door and closed it. I asked him why a woman couldn't get any privacy, but he didn't say anything."

"Could you hear if he went into his cabin right away?"

"Yes I think he did. I heard his cabin door shortly after I closed mind."

"Your cabin is right next to Albert's and Abigail's on the starboard side..."

"I don't understand all this port and starboard nonsense, but we are next to them, that's true."

"Did you hear anyone coming and going from their room?"

"Twice," said Lady Pompress.

"You mean when Albert and Abigail came down to bed?" asked Frances.

"Well no, I meant before that. Once after I had just arrived, then a few minutes later again. And then after Timmy came into the cabin I heard their cabin door open and close a couple more times in rather close succession."

"How do you know it wasn't Albert and Abigail coming to bed?"

"Timmy told me who was still upstairs when he had left." Frances nodded.

"Is that helpful?" asked Lady Pompress.

"Quite helpful," said Frances.

"Who do you think did it?" she asked.

"I have yet to determine that, but I feel that I am getting closer. Who do you think murdered her?"

"I don't know, it seems quite obvious to me that it must have been the brother though."

"Most of you pointing a finger at Albert. Why would you choose him?"

"He just seems closest to her than any of the rest of us."

"Do you know why he might have wanted to kill her?"

"No, not really."

"I believe that it had something to do with the theft of the jewels from Menkaure's pyramid back in the late 1890s."

"Interesting."

"You didn't see what was in Abigail's bag when it fell open as we were all boarding the bus?"

"No," she said, "but Timmy told me he thought he saw some sort of trinkets or valuables inside."

"He did. What if I told you that Abigail and Albert were going to return the stolen artifacts to the pyramid yesterday?"

"I'd ask you how they got them in the first place," said Lady Pompress.

"That my dear, is at the heart of this matter. Once I've sorted that out, I'm sure the culprit will come into much sharper focus. I have a suspicion that Albert wasn't onboard the returning of said stolen artifacts."

"Then he's the perfect candidate for it, isn't he!" exclaimed Lady Pompress.

"He certainly does look like one."

"Do you have any other information that might be of help?"

Lady Pompress stopped fanning herself for a moment and thought about it.

"I'm afraid not. I think I've been quite selfishly self-involved all this time, and I obviously couldn't have been bothered in anyone else."

Frances nodded.

"Well, thank you for your honesty, dear."

Lady Pompress stood up and looked back at them.

"I do hope I've been helpful," she said quite eagerly.

"You have Abigail, don't worry about that, you have."

Lady Pompress walked away from the group at the table and magically disappeared after being swallowed up by the staircase. Florence looked over at her friend.

"I was going to say I thought you were a bit hard on her at first. But then you seemed to have changed her, how shall I put it, for the better."

Frances nodded.

"I've found there's often a reason for the prickly exterior of most people like her. We uncovered it, and from there we were able to move that much quicker to the important things at hand. Whether she's able to maintain her softer side has yet to be determined, but we've given her a chance and we were kind to her with it. I hope she gives it a good go."

Florence nodded.

"It will make things so much better for her and Timothy. I do hope she can open up to him more."

"If you don't mind me changing the subject back to the matter at hand," said Fowler, grinning. "But what about this comment of hers that she heard the next door's cabin open not just twice, but four times."

"That is very interesting," said Frances.

"Just interesting?" asked Fowler.

Frances smiled at him.

"The pieces are coming together rather nicely as I knew they would."

"Could you be less cryptic and more clear?" asked Fowler. "I'm new at this."

Frances nodded and chuckled.

"Yes of course, my dear Perry, of course. What it means in the simplest terms, is that without knowing directly, Lady Pompress heard the killer enter and leave Albert's and Abigail's room."

"I don't understand. She said she heard the cabin door open four times. Albert and Abigail use up two of those. Why would the killer need to enter twice?" asked Fowler.

"He or she didn't," said Frances, "I believe the first time was the delivery of Abigail's warm milk. The second time was the

259

killer who then placed the sleeping draught into it and likely looked for the stolen goods."

"That means," said Florence, "that the killer must have been one of the first six who left the top deck for the cabin quarters."

"Quite right, Flo, and that narrows it down nicely."

"I don't see how narrowing it down to six is all that helpful," said Fowler. "We have Samuel, Maurice, Orpha, Mahulda, Simon and Nigel then. Now that I think about it perhaps it is helpful, I can't see Orpha or Mahulda doing it, so that leaves four."

"And you've always liked Samuel or Maurice for it," said Frances, grinning at him.

"Yes, and I still do."

"And let's not forget that we don't know what Simon did after he dropped Mahulda off and then got to his cabin."

"Are you suggesting that he went straight into Albert's cabin to doctor the milk before going to bed?"

"I don't want to suggest anything at the moment, but let's not discount anybody yet. He was found at Lady Pompress' door earlier in the evening. He could have just exited it with two sleeping draughts in his hand."

Fowler thought about that for a moment, then he scratched at his chin. He didn't have an answer for her, and he realized he might not be cut out for sleuthing after all.

"So you mean it couldn't have been Albert?" asked Florence.

"Not if he were acting alone. But I have a hunch that the relationships between many of the guests are not all that they seem."

"How can you know that?" exclaimed Florence.

"The lies, Flo. The lies make up the veil of truth if you look closely enough. And everyone has been lying to us. It started with Samuel and carried on up to Simon. Most of the guests are hiding something from us."

"How will you find out what?" asked Fowler.

"Once I've received the answers to my telegraphs all will fall into place, I'm sure. In the meantime, I think that we should wrap this up before dinner and interview, who up until this point, was the prime suspect and the victim's sister. Anton," said Frances, turning to face him, "could you bring Albert down to us please?"

Anton got up and left them for the top deck. Florence turned to Frances.

"My dear Fran, you say there are only six suspects now, but what about Lady Pompress, surely she could have lied about what she heard. She might have done it herself," said Florence.

"I think that's a slim chance," said Frances.

"What makes you so sure?" asked Florence.

"Well, my dear Flo, part of trying to unnerve her and unmask her was to put her on the defensive. At least that was the goal. Instead she folded like a flower in this dessert heat. She opened up and became quite transparent. I don't see any reason to doubt her testimony she gave today. I mean, if you really think about it, do you feel she was hiding something from us like the others were?"

Florence thought for a moment, putting her index finger to her lip.

"No, I suppose you're right, she was rather forthcoming. I must say, having been with you on a few of these murder investigations, I am constantly amazed at the things you see that I continually miss."

Frances smiled at her friend.

"Perhaps I have a gift."

"I think you do," said Florence, smiling at her.

"Additionally, my dear Flo," said Frances, "tomorrow morning, or perhaps even later this evening if I'm lucky, Scotland Yard will send the details I'll be requesting, and I'm certain that will bring this whole terrible affair into clear focus."

Twenty-Three

Anton followed Albert into the dining room. Albert was clutching his rucksack in front of him like a swaddled baby. He wore khaki shorts and a khaki short sleeved shirt. He had on khaki colored knee high socks and his feet were tucked into brown leather walking boots. He looked like the stereotypical British safari explorer, though he was not as confident. In fact, he looked scared. Very, very scared. He looked around the room nervously before he sat down, clutching his rucksack as if someone wanted to snatch it away from him.

His receding brown hair, badly colored, was slicked back, and he had a brown comb stuck in his shirt pocket. He sat bolt upright, and his nose seemed to throb an almost glowing red. His face was clammy, and his small beady eyes rolled around in their sockets like the last pickled eggs in a pickling jar.

"You know I didn't do it," he blurted out. "I didn't kill my sister, even though you think I did."

"Why do you think we believe you killed her?" asked Frances.

"Well, that's easy. I'm her brother, I ordered her milk for her, and I was the last person to see her alive."

He looked at them and swallowed hard.

"Why would you kill her, Albert? Why would you kill your sister?" asked Frances.

"I wouldn't. I didn't. I loved my sister, and now I think someone is out to get me."

Florence and Fowler looked at Frances. She returned their gaze and then looked at Albert.

"You are a primary suspect," said Frances, lying to him.

"But I didn't do it!" he exclaimed.

"Then you must help us in proving that you're innocent. You have to be terribly honest with us."

Albert nodded his head vigorously and some of his hair started to flop forward over his forehead. He didn't seem to notice.

"Right, right. That's why I brought this," he said, hugging the rucksack ever closer as if it were his last chance at holding it.

"That contains the stolen artifacts from the Pyramid of Menkaure. Doesn't it?" asked Frances.

Albert nodded his head more vigorously. More hair fell across his forehead.

"How did you know?"

"I saw them. Most of us saw them when Abigail's bag fell open at the bus yesterday morning."

"Oh God," he said. "I knew, that's why they must have known, that's why they killed her."

"Who killed her?" asked Frances.

"I don't know," he said, his voice trembling, "but someone here must have done it."

"Let's take a moment to calm ourselves, Albert, and let's start from the beginning. Take a deep breath," said Frances.

Albert opened his mouth and sighed more than breathed, but it was a start.

"Tell us why you and your sister were here on this holiday," said Frances.

Albert looked around nervously, but there was no one in the room except for the five of them. He undid the top flap of his rucksack and emptied its contents onto the table in front of them. Jewelry, trinkets, an ankh, golden bowls and other precious artifacts fell onto the table. There were dozens of items, from four inch diameter bowls to a six inch golden ankh all the way down to small inch-sized jewelry.

"We, I should say Abby, wanted to return the stolen items to their rightful place. They've been nothing but a curse to our family for years."

Fowler's jaw slackened as he looked at the small pile of valuables sitting right in front of him. Frances kept looking at Albert.

"But you weren't onboard with that course of events were you?"

Albert put the soft, crumpled rucksack over his legs and placed his arms on top of it. His hands held each other in sympathy and he frowned and shook his head.

"No, we needed the money. Me more so than her, but they have been given to her for safe keeping and she wanted to return them. I should have let her. She wouldn't be dead if I'd just let her put them back."

"What happened when you went to return them, Albert?" asked Frances.

He looked up at her for a moment before speaking. His mouth trembled and for a moment, Frances thought he might burst into tears, but he didn't.

"We had a bit of an argument. I tried to convince her that this wasn't such a good idea, but she wouldn't hear of it, so I pretended to go along. We went to the queen's pyramid and found the room beneath the king's chamber. I asked Abby to stand guard, while I hid the stolen items. Abby was so naïve," he said, "and gullible too. She believed I had done it."

"She didn't ask to look in your rucksack?"

"No, she took my word on it. You see I'd never lied to her before, and she had no reason to disbelieve me. I told her I still didn't think it was a good idea. Now it might have been the only thing that would have saved her life."

"Perhaps," said Frances, "but then we wouldn't be able to return these artifacts to their rightful owners."

Albert nodded his head sadly.

"And I have lost everything," he said, sounding more upset. "I have lost my beloved sister and I have lost any opportunity at wealth."

"It was never yours in the first place."

"Yes, but if we'd not come on this bloody trip in the first place. If Abby had only listened to me, we could have kept both the goods and our lives."

"I don't know how you would have expected to part with them without notifying the authorities," said Frances.

"I had lined up a private buyer."

"Who was that?"

"I don't know, but the groundskeeper for the late Howard Trenglove knew someone who was very discreet and would be willing to pay £250,000."

"That's not near their value," said Frances.

"Yes, I know, but as you said, it's hard to find a buyer for these items lately and I didn't particularly care."

"You said earlier that you fear for your life. Do you mean that you fear for your safety now?" asked Frances.

"I do."

"Why is that?"

"Because everybody knows I brought this rucksack in here, and the murderer must know that I have these artifacts with me. I'm sure they'll come looking for them."

"I wouldn't worry about that now, Albert," said Frances. "Perry is going to safeguard these items until they can be returned to their rightful owners. Whether that be the British Museum or the Museum of Cairo."

Albert nodded.

"On our first night here, at the hotel," said Frances, "you spoke with Orpha. Do you remember what you said to her?"

Lady Marmalade knew, as she had overheard them speaking, but she wanted to see how truthful he'd be.

"Yes, I do remember that. I asked her if I knew her, as she reminded me of someone. But I was mistaken."

"Who did she remind you of?"

Albert shook his head slowly.

"I'm not sure why this is important. It's so stupid now that I think of it. I thought she might have been Lottie. Lottie Hutchings."

"Who is she?"

"Part of the Trenglove clan which I'll get to in a bit. She lives in Howard Trenglove's mansion. Only Orpha couldn't have been her, she seems too old, if you'll pardon me. And besides, now that I think about it, Orpha was quite pleasant to me, whereas Lottie had never wanted to have anything to do with me. I also haven't seen Lottie in several years. It was an honest mistake. I just thought for a tiny moment, how interesting it would be to have an acquaintance on the trip with you. You know, small world and all."

Frances nodded.

"Last night I mentioned to you that I thought you reminded me of Arthur Vipond. Are you related to him, Albert? The truth now if you don't mind."

Albert looked down and slowly nodded his head.

"Yes, you're right. He was my uncle. My mother's brother."

"Had you always known that he was one of the thieves of the Pyramid of Menkaure?"

Albert shook his head, and kept looking down.

"No, not for a long time. My sister and I were always close to him growing up. He was our only uncle, but he would have been our favorite if we had more. Our mother didn't like us spending much time with him but we did anyway."

"Why was that? Did she know what he'd done?"

"No, I don't think so. But she knew he didn't earn his money honestly. He lived well. He had a large mansion and the finest cars, and he always spent lavishly on us."

"When did you learn that he was one of the Menkaure thieves?"

"Shortly before his death. In 1927, that was three years before he died, his health started becoming quite poor. He called on Abby and I and he confessed to the whole thing. But he wasn't seeking forgiveness, he was proud of what he'd done. He'd spent most of his fortune from selling almost all the stolen artifacts, but he had some left that he wanted to leave to us. It wasn't a lot, what you see here before you is Abby's share. I had spent mine."

"How had you managed that?" asked Frances.

"Well, those of you who are law abiding think that just because something is known to be stolen that there aren't buyers for it. I can tell you, that there are many wealthy men, and women, who don't care how an item was obtained. They'll pay good money for it to have it in their private collection. I sold all of mine, and Abby had decided to sell none of hers."

"But at the time she didn't mind taking the stolen items," said Florence.

Albert looked over at her.

"No, she didn't. Her change of heart took some time. I think mostly it was because she didn't want to believe that our beloved uncle was a thief."

Frances nodded.

"It took many years after his death for her to come round to the fact that he was a thief and a liar, and that's when she decided she wanted to get rid of them. To try and return them from where they came. She was naïvely sweet natured and innocent that way. I tried to convince her to give them to me or to sell them to me but she wouldn't hear of it."

"I take it you had run through your share quite quickly?"

"I had. I guess there was some of Arthur in me."

"What do you mean?"

"Well, when he died, my mother found out the truth. Abby told her that he was one of the thieves, but she didn't tell her that he'd given us the remaining spoils. This ruined my mother and father. It shook her world, really turned it upside down. She felt she had been living a lie all this time. I'm not really sure why. But in any event, her health failed and she died the year after he did, but not without first confessing to Scotland Yard."

"So nobody could get any of his estate then?" asked Fowler.

Albert nodded his head.

"Yes, that's right. But it was more than that. I told you I was a bit like Arthur, well, he was a spendthrift and had overextended himself. There were more debts than assets at the time of his death."

"I see," said Frances. "And what about Howard Trenglove's share?"

"Trenglove died many years before my uncle did. It was in 1907, I believe. What happened was that Arthur stole what was remaining from Howard's share, before his family knew what had happened."

"Did they know about that?"

"I'm sure they must have suspected," said Albert, "but Howard wasn't very close to most of his family, so I don't know they knew the full extent of Howard's share at the time of his death. From what I recall my uncle telling me, what Howard had left when he died was roughly equivalent to this amount of Abby's."

"Do you know much about Howard's family?" asked Frances.

"I know he had a nephew, the last I heard, the nephew was living in the United States. He also had a niece who moved into the mansion after he passed. She's still there. The Trengloves are generally not very good people, much like their uncle."

"He was never married then?"

"No, not that I heard of."

"And what about the niece or nephew?"

"Well, the niece is a spinster, as for the nephew I don't think he ever married. Rumor suggested he was queer."

"I wonder, then," said Frances thinking out loud, "who could have known you'd be out here with all this treasure."

Albert looked at her and shrugged.

"The only person who knew we were coming to Egypt besides Abby and me was the groundskeeper who I had to tell, because I was no longer able to let the buyer purchase Abby's share."

"What did you tell him exactly?"

"I told him just that. That Abby wanted to return the stolen goods to Egypt and we were going there to do just that."

"And you thought nothing of that?"

"Oh God," said Albert, pulling at this hair with his hands, "I didn't. He seemed like the harmless sort. You don't think he would have told, do you?"

"Quite likely, it seems. I can't see of any other way that this trip of yours got out. What was his name?"

"Pascal."

"Did you get his surname?"

Albert shook his head.

"Well, I think that shall still help. What was the niece's name. Do you recall?"

"Yes, she was Lottie Hutchings. From what I heard, she was the daughter of Howard's sister."

"What about the nephew. Do you know his name?"

"No, he was sent to boarding school. Last I heard he finished his studies and then went to America. I don't think anybody's heard from him since. To complicate things a bit further, this is how sordid the Trengloves are, there was a second niece who I believe was given away when a baby."

"I'm not quite sure I'm following all of this, I'm afraid," said Fowler.

"Let me see if I can help," said Frances. "Albert, correct me if I'm wrong. Howard Trenglove had two sisters."

Frances looked at Albert and he nodded.

"Do we know their names?"

"I'm afraid I only remember the name of the youngest sister. Her name was Hortence, Hortence Hutchings."

Frances smiled.

"That helps a great deal. All right, let's try and knit this sordid family all together. Was Howard the oldest, or the middle sibling?" asked Frances.

"He was the oldest from what Arthur told me."

"Howard Trenglove was the oldest of three siblings. He never married and never had any children from what we can tell."

Frances paused to look at Albert, and he nodded his affirmation.

"Howard Trenglove had two sisters, both of whom were younger than him, obviously. The youngest sister had a daughter..."

"I believe she was the one who had both daughters," interjected Albert.

"Right, Howard Trenglove's youngest sister who we know as Hortence Hutchings, which must have been her married name, had two daughters. We know the name of one of them as she's the niece, Lottie Hutchings who lives in Howard's mansion. She also gave up a daughter. I would presume that daughter was the first born."

Frances looked up at Albert and he nodded.

"Yes, quite right. I believe she was quite young and unwed at that time. As you can imagine that wasn't spoken about much in those days, so I'm afraid I don't know what her name is."

Fowler nodded as did Florence.

"I think I'm getting a clearer picture," he said. "So Howard Trenglove had two sisters, the youngest one of which had two daughters. These were Howard's nieces. We know the youngest niece lives in his mansion, but we don't know what happened to the second one, as she was given away. Correct?"

Frances and Albert both nodded.

"So what about the nephew?" asked Fowler.

"Let me try," said Frances. "Howard's oldest sister, the middle child must have had a son, Howard's nephew."

Albert nodded.

"That's correct, but we don't know as much about her as we do about Hortence. She sort of went her own way. We do know her first name which is Edna. But Arthur didn't know if she ever got married or who she married."

"So how do you know she had a son and he moved to America?" asked Frances.

"Howard was apparently paranoid, and had Edna investigated periodically just to keep tabs on her whereabouts. He was fearful that he'd be found out or told on by his sisters."

"Did they know what he had done?"

"Arthur got the sense that they didn't know for certain, but one has to suspect that they had some gleanings about it as he did make quite a show about his money."

"This piece puzzles me," said Frances. "You said that Howard kept an investigator looking into Edna periodically, and he found out enough that Edna had borne a son and that the son eventually moved to America, and yet he didn't find out her surname or even if she married."

"No, that's not quite true," answered Albert. "I didn't say Howard never knew that, just that he didn't share it with Arthur, so I don't know that information. You see, Howard, much like my uncle was a thief and a liar. Thieves are often untrustworthy and as such they don't trust others. I don't think Howard and Arthur trusted each other much at all. That's the impression I got. Most of this information that Arthur got was gleaned from remaining close to Howard and listening carefully over the decades of their friendship if you can call it that. The gaps in knowledge are because Arthur didn't know and Howard wouldn't tell."

Frances nodded.

"That makes more sense. So," she said, "we have the middle sister with her name of Edna who had a son and we don't know his name, is that correct?"

"Quite correct," said Albert, "I was never told his name."

"There are three offspring from Howard's two sisters," said Florence. "We only know much about Lottie who lives in Howard's mansion. We know that Lottie's mother was Hortence, Howard's youngest sister, and she had another daughter that she gave up but we don't know that daughter's name. Then there was the oldest sister named Edna who eventually had a son who left for America. Am I on the right path?"

Albert nodded, and grinned at her.

"I told you it was quite the sordid family."

"More like confusing," said Florence, sighing. "I honestly can't make head or tail of it. Neither do I know whether this is important or not."

Florence looked over at Frances, and then at Fowler.

"I'm with you," said Fowler. "This all makes my head spin and I can't fathom why we're even wasting our time on it."

"Because it is crucially important," said Frances.

"Could you explain simply for those of us not versed in the dark arts of detective work," said Fowler, grinning.

"Certainly," said Frances as she smiled back at him. "There has been one thing that has puzzled me from the beginning with this particular murder. We have twelve strangers all gathered for a holiday and one of them gets murdered for stolen goods from 1895. That seems highly coincidental."

"I always thought it was a crime of opportunity," said Fowler. "Ever since Abigail's bag spilled open showing it's contents at the hotel, everybody would have seen the artifacts."

"That's quite true," agreed Frances, "but that's because both you and I know where those valuables came from. To someone not very well versed with ancient Egyptian history and archaeology, they would look like nothing more than trinkets. No, I don't believe in coincidence, at least not usually. And that has puzzled me up until this time. And then all the lies that most of the other guests have been feeding us. I've always felt that there must have been more to it than meets the eye. Albert has just given us that missing piece."

"I'm afraid I still don't quite understand," said Fowler.

"I believe by tomorrow you will. I believe there are relationships amongst us that we have yet to uncover. Or at least relationships that stretch back to Vipond and Trenglove," said Frances.

"If you say so," said Fowler.

"Frankly, Fran, my head aches just trying to keep all of this together."

"I understand. Never have I come across such a complicated crime before. But I think the light of day tomorrow will reveal the truth."

Frances turned to Albert.

"Is there anything else you might like to add?" she asked Albert.

"I'll need a new room if you don't mind," Albert said, looking at Perry.

"Already done," said Fowler.

"I think that will be all then," said Frances. "I would advise you not to mention what was discussed here with any of the other guests. We don't want to tip our hat, however little it appears that we know at this stage, to the murderer it could be everything."

Albert nodded and stood up. He shook hands with all of them.

"Could you leave the rucksack, Albert?" asked France.

He placed it on top of the stolen artifacts.

"You will make him pay for this, won't you?" asked Albert. He looked intently into Lady Marmalade's eyes.

"I will," she said with certainty, and watched him walk across the dining room and climb the stairs to the upper deck.

"Well," said Fowler, "I think my work here is done. I'm not going to worry about who did it until you hear back from Scotland Yard. I'm afraid my little gray cells are overtaxed."

He grinned at her.

"I quite agree, it's been a jolly difficult few hours," said Florence, "and I still don't feel that we're any closer to uncovering the murderer's identity."

"I understand," said Frances. "I imagine dinner will be ready about now."

Fowler looked at his watch.

"Actually, we're a bit late," he said. "I make it past six. Shall I have dinner served on the upper deck?"

"No, I think everyone could probably benefit from a good meal in the dinning room. I think we've made good use of it. Perhaps you could let me send the telegram now?"

Fowler nodded and stood up. He gathered up the papers in front of him and then put the stolen jewelry and other artifacts into the rucksack.

Twenty-Four

Fowler returned from the officers' quarters and found Frances and Florence waiting for him on the upper deck. Everyone was up there, but it was a quiet and somber environment.

"Ladies and gentlemen," said Fowler, "if I may have your attention."

He waited as they guests gathered around him.

"Firstly, I'd like to thank you all for your cooperation in this investigation. We have had the opportunity to interview you all, and we thank you for your patience. I know it has been a trying day. As such, I have instructed the kitchen to provide you all with a memorable five course meal. You make your way down to the dining room at your leisure and dinner service should start at six thirty. That's in about ten minutes."

"When are the Cairo police going to get here," asked Orpha, "so that we can put this horrid incident behind us?"

Fowler looked at her and smiled.

"I haven't heard yet from the captain, but I should imagine that they're unlikely to get here until after midnight. I'll inform you all as soon as I'm able."

There were no more questions as everyone made their way downstairs towards the dining room. Everyone except for Fowler, Frances and Florence.

"Come with me Frances," said Fowler, "and let's get that telegram sent."

Frances and Florence followed Fowler to the stern of the boat and up a flight of stairs to the helm, where the captain greeted them with a broad smile. His black beard was still impeccable.

"Lady Marmalade would like to send a telegram. Quite urgently, if you don't mind."

"Of course, my Lady," he said, bowing slightly at Frances.

"Have you heard from Cairo?" asked Fowler as they moved toward the telegraph machine which was operated by one of Captain Badawi's officers.

"We just received information earlier. The storm was one of the worst in recent memory. All their mechanical systems, in their boats, and cars have been clogged by the dust and sand. They're working round the clock to fix them, but they don't imagine they'll be here until early in the morning. They're hoping for six," said Badawi.

Fowler nodded.

"That's a pity," he said.

"It is," agreed Lady Marmalade, "we'll have to remain vigilant tonight."

"Hasani," said Captain Badawi.

A young and slim Egyptian stood up erect as if someone had just poked him with a sharp pin.

"Yes, sir."

"Lady Marmalade needs to send a telegram. It is of the highest importance. Make sure it gets to its destination, and report immediately when the reply comes in."

"Yes, sir," Hasani answered. "My Lady."

He looked over at Frances and sat down at his telegraph machine. Fowler brought up a hard wooden chair for Frances to sit on. She thanked him and sat down. He offered one for Florence but she declined. She stood behind her friend. Hasani looked at her. He placed the headphone over his head and readied his finger to tap the code out.

"Send it to Scotland Yard, care of Chief Inspector Devlin Pearce."

Hasani started tapping away. When he was finished he looked back at Frances.

"All information related to individuals below, stop. Samuel Newton, American, New York, Dob 12 January 1885, London, stop. Maurice Gabberdeen, British, London, Dob 7 May 1902, Bristol, stop. Nigel Durmott, British, London, Dob 29 April 1912, Swansea, stop. Simon Gragg, British, London, Dob 9 October 1923, Grimsby, stop. Orpha Bendled, British, London, Dob 15 March 1878, London, stop."

Frances paused for a moment to allow Hasani's vibrating finger to catch up with her.

"Specifically, relations, any all, Arthur Vipond et alia, Howard Trenglove et alia, stop. Solving murder, stop. Urgent, stop."

Frances paused again and looked at her friend. Florence looked down at her.

"What about Mahulda?" asked Florence.

"I don't think she did it. In any event I think Pearce will look into her as she's related to Orpha. We'll see."

Florence shrugged.

"Then I can't think of anyone else."

Hasani stopped his tapping and looked up at Frances.

"That's it," she said to him smiling.

He nodded and finished the message. Frances stood up. Fowler came across the room having spent the time talking with Captain Badawi.

"You must be starved, Frances," he said. "Shall we go to dinner."

"Nothing would please me more," she answered, looking at Florence.

PHANTOMS OF THE PHARAOH (A LADY MARMALADE MYSTERY)

"Splendid idea," said Florence.

Twenty-Five

Everybody was on the upper deck enjoying the warm late evening. It was about nine, and the stars were twinkling and the inky black Nile was as still as glass. Frances looked off the starboard side and looked over at the ruins of Memphis. Not that she could see them, they were about a mile inland, past the lush vegetation that drank deeply from the river. There weren't many lights on that side of the embankment and they weren't exactly docked. But she felt badly for her friend Florence.

What should have been a memorable month long holiday for the two of them had turned into a blasted murder investigation. Frances was tiring of investigating murders and other crimes. Looking at the dead, and more specifically the murdered was becoming wearisome. Having to deal with human foibles and atrocities was taking its tolls. And yet it seemed she couldn't travel far before the grim reaper knocked on her door and delivered another murdered body for her perusal and solution.

"Lovely night, isn't it?" asked Florence.

"It's wonderful, Flo, just wonderful. I only wish we were still following the itinerary for the holiday."

Frances kept her gaze out of over the plains of Saqqara. It was still and quiet. By this time the ruins would have been closed to visitors for the day. Florence put her hand on her friend's shoulder.

"It can't be helped," she said, looking at Frances and smiling at her. "I would have preferred that no one had been murdered frankly, but now that has happened, I'm more interested in finding justice for poor Abigail."

"Yes, the poor thing. Naïvely trying to do what's right. She shouldn't have been punished for that. You know what I'm going to do?"

"No," said Florence.

"I'm going to ask Perry to see if he can't spare a couple of men to watch the cabin hallway during the night to ensure that nothing nefarious takes place once we've all gone to bed."

"I think that's a good idea."

"Shall we get a drink?" asked Frances.

"I could use one," said Florence. "It's been quite the grueling day."

They walked over to the bar where Jafari was making up drinks for whoever wanted. Even though they had only arrived a half hour or so onto the upper deck, most everyone was making liberal used of the beverages Jafari was happy to offer.

Samuel had drunk two whiskeys already and Maurice had matched him. They were looking out over the port side towards the city of Helwan. The lights from that city were more enchanting, like the flickering beads of a belly dancer as she danced under the moonlight. The two of them stood close together, speaking in whispers that no one else could hear.

Towards the bow of the ship, the same band from the night before played. Only this time they played more somberly, more carefully, as if not to wake the dead. Nigel sat on a divan by himself, withdrawn, and with a long face that nursed a brandy. Likely his second. Jafari smiled at Lady Marmalade, and Florence as they approached him.

"Two sherries please, Jafari," said Frances.

He poured them and offered them to Frances and Florence. They both took a sip.

"I think this is just what we need," said Frances.

Florence nodded and they went over to a divan on the starboard side, where they had sat the night before and placed their Sherries on the table in front of them. Albert was sitting at a divan that was ninety degrees to theirs. He moved up to the starboard corner so that he could be closer to Lady Marmalade. He was quickly finishing his second brandy.

On the same side as them, but towards the bow sat Orpha, Simon and Mahulda. Simon was drinking a beer, his second one, and Orpha and Mahulda nursed Sherries. Their first.

Towards the stern of the boat, though it was just past the middle, sat Captain Wainscott and Lady Pompress. Lady Pompress was nursing a second crème de menthe as Timothy sipped on his second brandy.

"Do you mind if I enjoy a cigar, darling?" asked Timothy.

Lady Pompress nodded her head, and smiled at him. It appeared as though she were trying to be softer and kinder since her interrogation earlier in the day.

"I'll go and smoke by the band," he offered.

Lady Pompress nodded at him. He stood up and went over to the bar where he asked Jafari for a cigar and a refill of his brandy. With his lit cigar and freshened brandy he walked outside the canopy and leaned against the starboard railing and watched the band play with less eagerness than they had just the night before. He was opposite where Maurice and Samuel stood with their backs to him.

Albert leaned in towards Lady Marmalade and took the last sip from his brandy. It warmed him from the inside, and he felt less frightened and bolder.

"Do you know when the authorities are going to make it here?"

He looked around nervously at the other guests, and they all ignored him.

"I'm sure Perry will make an announcement shortly, but they'll be here first thing in the morning at the latest."

"Good," said Albert, nodding his nervously. He brought his snifter up to his mouth and took another sip, forgetting that he had already finished.

"I think I'll have just one more before bed," he said, as he got up and walked over to the bar.

"Everyone is certainly imbibing quite liberally," said Florence.

"Can't necessarily blame them," said Frances, "after all, it has been a very trying day, and I'm sure they all just want to have this behind them already."

Maurice and Samuel walked up to the bar behind him. They gave him quite a fright as he turned around. He jumped ever so slightly, gave them a stern look up and down and then came back and sat down next to Lady Marmalade. Frances watched Jafari refill Samuel and Maurice's whiskey. Jafari gave them two fingers worth, and as he brought bottle away from the glasses, Samuel took it from him, and poured himself and Maurice another two fingers' worth. He gave the bottle back to Jafari without saying anything and the two of them walked back to the port side railing. Maurice grinning and licking his lips, before he took a good sip.

"I don't like those two," said Albert, looking at Maurice and Samuel walk to the far railing. "Do you think they did it?"

France looked over at Albert and patted him gently on the knee.

"It is possible," she said. "Though I am reserving my judgment until the evidence comes in."

Albert turned to her.

"Bloody hell," he said, louder than needed. "When will that be? What if they murder again."

Frances looked away, but didn't speak.

"Sorry," said Albert. "I'm nervous. I can't stand the thought that the murderer still walks freely amongst us."

"I understand," she said. "We'll have everything we need by the time the police are here tomorrow morning. Just a little more patience."

"But what if they try to murder me while I sleep?" he asked, and he felt his question was a legitimate one.

"Don't worry about that," said Frances. "I'm going to ask Perry to station guards at the end of the hall all night so that we may sleep secure that nobody will be able to leave their cabin without being noticed."

"Oh good, jolly good," said Albert. "That does give me great comfort. Thank you."

Frances smiled at him. Fowler came down from the helm and came over to Frances. He stood behind the table that was in front of her and faced her.

"I've just received confirmation that the Cairo authorities will be here by six tomorrow morning."

"Good," said Frances. "Any word yet from Scotland Yard?"

Fowler nodded, and handed Frances a faded yellow slip of paper. She looked at it, and this is what it read.

WORKING ALL NIGHT STOP REQUIRED INFORMATION ARRIVING SHORTLY STOP HAVE ALERTED CAIRO AUTHORITIES STOP WILL SEND INFORMATION ASAP STOP REMAIN VIGILANT STOP.

It was signed Chief Inspector Pearce. She was comforted that he was personally taking on her request. She nodded at the paper in her hand and then tucked it into her purse. She looked up at Fowler and smiled at him.

"Thank you," she said. "I was hoping you might be willing to do one more favor for me."

"Of course," he said.

"I think it might be prudent if we have guards posted at the end of the hallway once we've all gone to bed. Just as a precaution so that the killer doesn't think they have free reign to terrorize anyone else."

Fowler nodded thoughtfully.

"I'll do it myself. I'll speak to Anton and we'll conduct the shifts ourselves."

"That's very kind. I'm sure it will put to rest any residual fears of the other guests."

Fowler nodded.

"I'll tell them."

He walked over to the band and spoke with the singer. They stopped their music. Everyone glanced over at the band and saw Fowler looking at them. He put up his hand.

"Ladies and gentleman, if I can have your attention please."

He looked at the each in turn to be sure they were paying attention to him.

"I have good news. Tonight will be your last night on the Queen Nefertiti. The Cairo authorities have assured me that they will be here by six tomorrow morning. As such, I urge you all to try and have an early night. Additionally, Anton and I will be setting up shifts to stand guard all night once you've all gone to bed. None of you will be able to leave your cabin this evening without Anton or I seeing you. So please rest assured that you will not be harmed overnight and that you'll be able to get a good night's rest. As an additional precaution I recommend that you lock your cabin door once you're safe inside. Lastly, we have received word that Chief Inspector Devlin Pearce of Scotland Yard is looking into this murder at Lady Marmalade's request. I am certain," said Fowler, looking over at Frances, "that we will have the murderer exposed as soon as we hear back from Scotland Yard."

There were murmurs of appreciation, and Fowler stood for a moment in front of them all for any questions. There were none, so he walked back to Lady Marmalade.

"I'll go and speak with Anton, and let him know we'll be standing guard all night."

He smiled at her, nodded his head and left. Albert looked back at her and took a big sip of his brandy.

"That makes me feel a lot better," he said.

"Additionally, you have a new room I imagine," said Frances.

"That's quite right," he said. "The second one on the left as you enter onto the main deck."

"That would be starboard side then," added Lady Marmalade.

"If you say so."

"That's right next to me," said Florence.

Albert nodded and smiled at her.

"You haven't told anyone, have you?" asked Frances.

Albert nodded and Frances smiled at him.

"Good," she said. "Don't tell anyone either. That way no one will know where you're sleeping, and it will ensure your safety."

"Ah," said Albert, nodding his head slowly. "I hadn't thought of that, but it's a very good point."

He smiled. With that knowledge and his third brandy starting to give him courage, he was feeling much better about the whole situation. He only had to make it through one more night, and surely the killer wouldn't dare try anything tonight, what with the guards. It would be utter madness.

Orpha finished up her small glass of sherry and went over and had words with Mahulda. Then she came towards Frances, Florence and Albert. She paused briefly.

"I'm off to bed. It's been a very strenuous day. Good night," she said.

They all responded in kind, and Orpha walked away down the stairs. Nigel finished his brandy and sat morosely with his hands folded in his chest, his feet thrust out straight in front of him and his head bowed down. His chin was almost resting on his chest. He looked quite upset and removed from the very environment he was in. Lady Pompress finished her crème de menthe and got up and walked over to Captain Wainscott. They chatted for a few minutes, then she kissed him on the cheek and walked back past Frances.

"I'm off for the evening too. It's been absolutely ghastly," she said. "Good night."

"It has been exhausting," replied Florence. "Good night."

They all wished her a good evening and she left too. Frances was not surprised to see the ladies off to bed early. She too was drained, but she was trying to stay vigilant and sort through all the lies and the interviews that she had conducted during the day with Fowler and Florence. There would be time for rest when she had confronted the murderer and gotten a confession out of him, or her.

Captain Wainscott came by and ordered another brandy from Jafari. By this time, Jafari was being more liberal with his pouring. This was Timothy's fourth. He walked back towards Frances, Florence and Albert, with the springy step of a man walking along the plank of drunkenness, before he falls completely off. His arm swayed left and right in front of him as the brandy danced seductively up at the rim but never actually spilling off. The cigar, now a stub, was still lit and tucked into one corner of his mouth. He pulled it out with his free hand, and grinned at them.

"I don't know what you did, Frances," he said to her, swaying ever so slightly on his feet, "but ever since her interview she's been absolutely marvelous."

"You're talking about your fiancée," asked Frances.

Timothy grinned and nodded. He was a man teetering on the edge of drunkenness, where he fumbled with the words in his mouth, but managed not to spill any.

"As much as I hate to say it, I think this murder's been the best thing for our relationship," he said. "'Scuse me, I'm going to go and listen to the band."

Frances smiled politely at him and watched him weave his way towards the bow where the band had recently started back up. His weaving might have been forgiven, for they were on a boat, but the Nile was still. These were hardly heavy seas.

"I don't think he'll last much longer," said Florence.

"I agree," she said, "we might even find him sleeping on one of these divans tomorrow morning."

The two of them shared a small chuckle. Albert stood up and looked at them both.

"Well," he said, "before I decide on another one which is bound to do me no good, I'll bid you goodnight."

"Good night, Albert," they said in unison.

Frances watched him walk off towards the stairs. He was just as unstable as the Captain. He didn't seem to hold his liquor as well as the military man.

"Are you going to have another?" asked Florence, looking at their sherry glasses. They were both half full.

"Not likely," she said, "not from what it's been doing to this lot."

Frances looked at her watch. It was almost ten in the evening.

"Are you getting tired?" asked Florence.

"A little, but I'm trying to put all the pieces of the puzzle together," she said, smiling at her friend.

"But you don't have all the pieces yet do you?"

Frances looked at her quizzically.

"Well, you don't have the information you're waiting for from Pearce at Scotland Yard. Perhaps a good night's rest will be in order to help you make sense of it all tomorrow morning with a fresh mind."

Frances nodded at her.

"I think you're quite right. Though I think I'll stay up for another half hour or so. We still have half our sherry to finish," she said, looking down at their sherry glasses.

And in spite of it all, the air was warm, and the scents were fresh. It was a wonderful evening, and the band played soothing, melodic songs. Frances looked over at them, and saw Captain Wainscott swaying to the music by himself. Nigel finally got up from his chair, picked up his snifter and went over to the bar. He made a gesture to Jafari that he wanted a refill, which Jafari gladly obliged. Nigel didn't say anything to him. He took a big gulp of it, coughed and spluttered, cursed under his breath and went back to his divan, where he sat just as morosely as he had before. Only this time he held onto his snifter with one hand.

At a little after ten, Fowler came back up to the top deck and took a seat next to Lady Marmalade. He surveyed the rest of the group, leaning his forearms on his thighs, and then he turned to look at her.

"Looks like we lost a couple," he said grinning.

Frances nodded.

"I think it's likely to be an early night for most of us," she said.

On the port side of the boat, Samuel finished with his whiskey and went back to the bar. He placed his empty glass on the bar, and walked off towards the stairs. He nodded at Fowler, Frances, and Florence but didn't say a word, nor did he stop.

"Not a very happy chap is he?" asked Fowler.

"Not at all. He was quite rude to Abigail as I recall, as was Maurice," said Frances.

"Are you confident Scotland Yard will be able to help?"

Fowler leaned back and put his left arm on the back rest between them. He looked at Lady Marmalade kindly, smiling softly.

"Chief Inspector Pearce is the best policeman I've met. I'm sure he'll have the information for us by morning."

"Good," said Fowler, nodding, "because I'd rather not leave it up to the Cairo authorities, I can't promise they wouldn't mangle it."

He smiled at her and she smiled back at him.

"By the way," he said. "I'm taking first shift. I'll be standing guard until two, and then Anton will come and relieve me and stay until six, when the Cairo police get here."

Frances nodded.

"That's very kind," she said, looking out over the port side of the boat towards Helwan.

"Not at all," said Fowler, "I'm aghast I've had one murder, I'll be damned if I allow anymore."

His good natured confidence was inspiring.

"It would take a very brazen killer to try any more tricks, now that they know we've got a thorough investigation going on," said Florence.

Fowler nodded and smiled at her. Maurice turned away from the railings and walked towards the bar. Once there he took the last sip of his whiskey, and just like Samuel before him, he strode off towards the stairwell, barely nodding as he passed by Frances and company, and certainly not stopping.

"I must know what's going on with those two," said Fowler, "they're quite the pair. More than meets the eye I'm sure."

Frances nodded.

"I know. Their lying has intrigued me. I'm sure Devlin will shine some light on that. They are an odd couple, even though they both swear they hardly know each other."

Simon got up and offered his hand to Mahulda who took it. They had finished their drinks. It was ten fifteen. They both walked up to Frances and stopped for a moment.

"I'm taking Mahulda to her room, then I'll be off to bed myself. Awful day we've all had," said Simon. "Wouldn't you agree?"

Frances nodded, as did Fowler.

"Very trying indeed," said Florence.

They all exchanged their evening farewells and Mahulda took Simon's elbow as he helped her towards the stairwell.

"At least the whole tour wasn't wasted. Perhaps with those two, some love can come out this hateful violence," said Fowler.

"I'd like to think so," said Frances. "They do seem happy together."

There were only five of them left on the upper deck at this point. Nigel, still staring at nothing on the floor in front of his feet. Captain Wainscott who was still swaying in front of the band as they continued to play, and the three of them, Frances, Florence, and Fowler sitting quietly on a divan at the starboard side of Queen Nefertiti.

"I don't imagine it will be too long before the stragglers head down to their cabins," said Fowler, looking at the remaining two men.

"No, I don't imagine it will be long at all," said Frances. "Though I wouldn't bet on Captain Wainscott actually making it down to his room at all. He might end up here all night."

Fowler nodded.

"I suppose I can't stop him, can I?"

Frances looked over at Captain Wainscott, he was turning towards them now, his brandy snifter almost empty. He stumbled towards them, grinning.

"Wonderful music. Anyone want to dance?"

He was starting to dribble vowels out of his mouth as he spoke, slurring on the roomier words. They all smiled politely at him, and he made his way towards Jafari who filled him up for a fifth time.

"I think that seals it," said Florence, "I don't think he'll make it downstairs. Not on five brandies, I shouldn't think."

Frances nodded, and Fowler chuckled to himself. Captain Wainscott turned and headed back towards the band. As he did so he raised his glass towards the three of them, and almost tripped over his own feet but managed somehow to remain upright. The stub of his now unlit cigar was tucked back into the corner of his mouth.

"The band finishes up at eleven, Captain," said Fowler.

Timothy nodded as he walked back up to the bow of the ship. On the port side of the boat, Nigel stood up and placed his empty glass on the table in front of him. He walked towards them with his head down, heading towards the stairs.

"Nigel," called out Frances.

He stopped and looked at her. He didn't look nearly as handsome as he did when he was in a happier mood.

"Is everything all right?" she asked.

"No," he said.

"Would you like my help?"

Nigel looked at her for a few moments, not speaking.

"Perhaps tomorrow, when I have a clear head. Good night," he said and headed towards the stairs, not waiting for their response.

They all watched after him. Fowler turned after a while towards Lady Marmalade.

"Never in my career have I seen a group of holidayers turn from happy to sour so quickly and with such consistency," he mused.

"It can't be help, Perry," said Frances. "I wouldn't take it personally. You're very good at this I must say, and I know that Florence and I will be back to actually finish this marvelous tour that you and Thoth Tours have put together."

"Thank you," said Perry, grinning as he usually did.

Frances took the last sip of her sherry and turned to watch the band play. They were playing European classics now. Dancing songs, though the only one in front of them dancing was Captain Wainscott. They were currently playing the Bing Crosby version of "Don't Fence Me In". One of Lady Marmalade's favorites from the last couple of years.

Captain Wainscott was dancing slowly with an imaginary partner, singing along softly. She smiled at him. Once the song was finished, Lady Marmalade stood up.

"Ready for bed, Fran?" asked Florence.

Frances nodded.

"I think I am," she said.

"Give me a moment, won't you?" asked Fowler.

He stood up and walked over to Captain Wainscott. The two of them exchanged words. Fowler smiled at him, nodded his head and walked back to Frances and Florence.

"I told him everyone was heading to bed if he wanted to come along. He said he was enjoying the music and would be down shortly. I told him, once he was in his cabin to stay in there for everyone's safety."

"Will you be all right for first watch?" asked Frances. "I wouldn't mind doing it either."

"Good heavens no," said Fowler. "I could never permit that. What if the killer wants to get out and cause a ruckus in the middle of the night? I would hate to think that something might happen to you."

Frances smiled at him and the three of them made their way down to the main level.

Twenty-Six

Frances was out of her cabin at six a.m. on the dot. A tired looking, but awake Anton greeted her. She had slept restlessly, tossing and turning thinking of who might have committed the atrocious murder of poor Abigail Beckles.

"Anything untoward happen last night?" she asked him.

Anton shook his head.

"Not a peep. You all sleep quite silently. Although," said Anton, thinking about it for a moment, "when I relieved Perry this morning, he said that Captain Wainscott had not come to bed, and he still hasn't"

"Thank you, Anton. Any word from Scotland Yard?"

"Not yet, at least not that I know of. I know that Captain Badawi was asked to wake you as soon as anything came through the wire, but I don't believe there has been anything yet."

"That's a pity," said Frances. "I'll go up and see what's going on. Would you mind waking everyone. I'm sure the Cairo police will be here any minute."

Anton nodded, and as Lady Marmalade made her way up the stairs she heard him knocking loudly on the first door across from hers, which was her dear friend Florence's.

Frances made her way all the way up to the helm and knocked on the door. Captain Badawi smiled at her and came and opened it up for her.

"I have just gotten on shift myself," he said to her.

"No word from Scotland Yard then, I take it," she asked.

Badawi looked across at the telegraph operator. He started to look through the papers at his station.

"Hasani has just come on shift with me too, at six this morning."

"Sorry, Captain," said Hasani. "It appears as if this came in within the last couple of hours ago."

Badawi looked at him sternly, as he took the sheets of telegram paper from him. He handed them to Lady Marmalade.

"I do apologize," he said. "I left strict instructions for them last night to wake me if any telegram should come for you or me. I will have strong words with Moswen."

"It is quite all right, Captain," she said. "From all accounts the evening was quite uneventful."

Lady Marmalade looked out over towards the bow of the ship. On the upper deck, under the canopy she could see a stirring, and disheveled Captain Wainscott. Fowler was already coming up the stairs and crossing the upper deck towards the helm. He waved at them as he approached. Lady Marmalade smiled in return. At last he entered the bridge, smiling at everyone.

"You look well for a man who hasn't had much sleep," said Frances.

"There'll be sleep enough when we're dead," he said, and then winced at what he'd just said. "Pardon me, I didn't quite mean it like that."

He grimaced, but Frances smiled kindly at him.

"It's quite alright," she said, "and even so, there is some truth to it."

"You're very kind. Did you get any word back from Scotland Yard?" he asked.

Frances nodded and waved the telegrams in front of him.

"I'll need some time to mull over what I've been sent. When is breakfast being served?"

"I've asked for it to be served by six thirty," said Fowler.

"Good, I'll just pop out on the deck and have a read then. Anton is waking everyone as we speak."

Fowler nodded at her. Frances looked back at Badawi.

"Have you received word from the Cairo authorities?" she asked.

Badawi nodded.

"They are on their way. They've sent two boats. One with the coroner and one with the police. They should be here by seven at the very latest they promised."

Frances nodded.

"All right then," she said, "I'll go have a read of my telegrams and meet you all in the dining room for six thirty?"

Fowler and Badawi nodded in agreement.

"From my quick perusal, I am delighted to inform you that I know who our culprit is."

Fowler grinned.

"That is a relief."

Frances smiled at them both and made her way from the helm and down the stairs to the top deck. Captain Wainscott was yawning and stretching, tucking in his shirt. He sat back down and started to massage his temples. He looked up at her when Frances strolled across the deck towards the divan she had sat in the night before. He tried to put on a smile, but it obviously pained him.

"Did we survive a typhoon last night?" he asked, grinning sheepishly.

"Not we, but I think you went a few too many rounds with brandy," she replied.

"That must be it," he said.

"You might want to get ready," she said encouragingly. "Breakfast is at six thirty and I'll be outing the murderer."

"You don't say? That's jolly good news."

Frances nodded at him.

"Your fiancée might have some aspirin for that nasty headache of yours."

"You're right. I had forgotten about that. All is right with the world this good morning."

Timothy slowly got up and steadied himself for a moment before walking towards the stairs. He stopped close to Lady Marmalade.

"I shan't be drinking that much again, I daresay."

"You're getting wiser as you get older, Captain," said Frances, smiling at him.

Captain Wainscott left Lady Marmalade to her telegrams and gingerly headed down to the main deck all the while holding tentatively to the railing.

After a few minutes, Florence came up to the top deck and saw Lady Marmalade just as she was finishing reading her last telegram. A wise smile had swept across her lips. She looked up to see her friend walking towards her.

"Did you sleep well?" asked Frances.

"As well as one would expect with a killer on the loose," answered Florence, smiling.

"That will all change moments from now," said Florence. "I have determined who did it."

Florence sat down next to her friend and looked at her.

"Who was it?"

Frances leaned in and whispered something into her ear. Florence pulled back and looked at her friend with a furrowed brow.

"You don't say? I can't see how that could be," she said.

"You will soon," said Frances. "It all makes perfect sense now."

"Well, I'll be glad to have this behind us. I didn't realize how much of a dour pall a murder can case over this whole experience."

"Yes, I'm terribly sorry it happened during our holiday. We will come back again and do it properly."

Florence smiled.

"I'm not really complaining, it's just awful, that's all. I wish there was more kindness and understanding. Then we might not turn so quickly to violence and murder."

Frances nodded.

"Me too, my dear Flo. Me too. That's why I can't help but to try and find justice for the victims. The less chance they have of getting away with it, perhaps the less crime these ne'er-do-wells will commit."

Florence nodded and looked out over the port side towards Helwan. She smiled a sad smile that had seen too much misery but not enough to temper the humors. Florence turned back to Frances.

"That city over there," she said, nodding towards Helwan with her head. Frances nodded back at her. "I thought how odd it was that we'd come to Helwan where murder was committed. I got nervous about it frankly. Silly, I know, but sometimes one can't help but be a little superstitious."

"What do you mean?" asked Frances.

"Well, I thought that perhaps hell had won, as in Helwan. But you've broken that silly little superstition now that you've determined who did it."

Florence looked away, back at Helwan and rebuked herself gently for even putting the two together. Frances smiled slightly. It was no surprise to her that the innocent and optimistic human mind wished to make sense of what were sometimes irrational acts, like this murder. We comfort ourselves by trying to explain things, make sense of things that hammer away at our belief in a safe world. When so often, things are left to chance, and sometimes humans just act badly when left to chance.

"There are more things in heaven and earth, Flo, than are dreamt of in our philosophy."

"Hamlet was wise," said Florence, looking back at her friend.

"Or the bard was," said Frances smiling. "In any event, it's not a sin to try and make sense of madness."

Florence smiled sweetly and patted Frances on the knee.

"I saw something quite peculiar this morning, though I don't think it's all that important to you anymore," said Florence.

"Even the smallest fulcrum can move the world with a lever long enough."

"Is this becoming a classics quiz?" asked Florence, laughing with her friend. Frances nodded.

"No. But never doubt the importance of small things in explaining the largest ideas."

"Very well then," said Florence, continuing. "As I was getting ready, I thought everyone had left the cabins before me. Then, just as I was getting ready to leave my cabin, I heard another cabin door open and close. I took a look through my peephole, and I saw Maurice leaving. Then moments later, I heard what seemed to be the same cabin door open and close and then Samuel walked by. Now I couldn't quite see up towards Samuel's cabin, but I'm fairly certain that's where they both came from. That or Maurice's. It sounded like it was the same cabin."

"I know," said Frances. "And it likely was the same cabin to be sure."

300

"Oh well, perhaps it wasn't important just like I thought."

"Oh no, my dear Flo, it explains a great many things."

Just off to their right, Frances and Florence heard great bounding of someone coming up the stairs in a great hurry. They looked to see what all the commotion was. It was Anton. He rushed up to them.

"Thank God, I found you. Please come quickly. Lady Pompress has been murdered."

Florence looked back at Frances in horror. Frances gritted her teeth and cursed under her breath.

"This shouldn't have happened," she said to herself.

Anton hadn't even waited for their response. He ran up to the helm, waving and gesticulating like a madman. Fowler came rushing out as Anton explained to him what had just happened.

"How can it be?" he asked, looking at Anton. "We never saw anyone leave their cabins during the night, did we?"

Anton nodded.

"I don't understand," he said to Perry.

"It happened before," said Frances, as the two men rushed passed the women and headed downstairs.

"What?" asked Anton, as he started after Perry who was in the lead.

Frances followed him and Florence followed her. They made quick work down to the main deck where the cabins were. On the third last cabin on the starboard side they all entered and Frances saw Captain Wainscott on the floor. He was up against the bed and his legs were at all awkward angle with his feet pointing to the door while his head faced the side table. In his lap he cradled Lady Pompress' head. She was looking towards the door with dead eyes, her right ear resting on his thigh. He was inconsolable and rocking gently back and forth.

"My dear sweet darling," he kept saying over and over again between the sobs.

He was stroking her brown hair with his right hand which was now stained with blood. Frances went up to him but he didn't acknowledge them at first. Lady Pompress' head was a mess of wet and clotted hair and blood just above her left ear.

On the carpet just where Lady Pompress' head must have lain before Timothy picked it up and put it in his lap was a large pool of burgundy blood on the sandy colored carpet. Next to it, up against the bedside table was the lamp which should have been on the table. The base end of this brass lamp stand was dented slightly and tinged with the blood of Lady Pompress. The lamp shade was ruined and the bulb broken.

Florence looked at Frances and brought her hands to her mouth.

"Surely not?" she asked, looking at Frances with wide eyes.

Frances gritted her teeth and slowly nodded her head. Captain Wainscott looked up at her, his eyes wet with tears, his mouth upturned, a pink gash of sadness.

"If I hadn't gotten drunk. If only I'd have come to bed when I should have."

Frances bent down and squeezed him on the shoulder.

"You can't blame yourself for this," she said. "I'm sorry to say it was planned for before you got to your cabin."

"I don't understand," he said, looking up at her, the pain still vibrant red rivers in his wet eyes.

"You will."

Frances turned to Anton.

"Is everyone else counted for?" she asked.

He looked at her and frowned.

"Well, yes, I think so."

"Do you know so, or do you think so?" she demanded, more forcefully this time.

"Well I... I think so."

"Please make sure, Anton. Make sure everyone else is alive and well."

He nodded and ran out and started counting those guests he could find. He went up to the second deck where the dining room was and he went to the top deck too.

"We're going to have to put her into the other bathtub in the main suite," said Frances, looking at Fowler.

Fowler nodded and walked up to Captain Wainscott. He was slowly beginning to regain his composure. Frances walked up to him.

"Could I have a word, Captain?" she asked.

Addressing him by his title she hoped that he would act the part. And it helped, to some degree. He slowly laid Lady Pompress' face down on the carpet and stood up. He took out his handkerchief and wiped the blood that was on his right hand onto it. It smudged like streaks of rouge lipstick. He clumped up the handkerchief and put it into his trouser pocket.

"Can you tell me exactly how she was when you found her?" asked Frances.

She was trying to take his mind off of the emotion and steer him towards facts. She wasn't doing it for her own good. She could see plainly how the poor woman had been murdered. She had likely been taken by surprise by a blow to the back of the head, and more than one from the looks of it. She also knew who had done it. The purpose of this line of questioning was to help Captain Wainscott get a hold of himself.

"I... um, I uh, found her lying there," he said, pointing at the spot where she still lay. "Almost exactly like that."

"And the bed?" asked Frances, looking over at the bed which was immaculately made. "Was it undisturbed as it is now?"

Captain Wainscott turned around to look at the bed. He nodded and turned back to face Frances.

"Yes," he said.

"Have you had a look everywhere else in the cabin to see if anything is missing?" she asked him.

He shook his head.

"I... I didn't think to."

"It's all right," she said. "This has been quite a shock. Where did Lady Pompress keep her medication?"

"In the bathroom, I think."

"Would you mind coming with me?"

Captain Wainscott followed Frances into the bathroom. Everything was neat and tidy except for the sink and medicine cabinet above the sink. There were vials of insulin that had fallen into the sink. One was broken and its contents gone. Another was whole and as Frances picked it up she noticed that it held very little insulin. A syringe was in the sink too, along with several envelopes of Somunol. The medicine cabinet door was still ajar. Frances looked inside it.

"Can you tell if anything is missing?" she asked him.

He looked into the medicine cabinet and started counting the vials of insulin and the syringes and needles. He looked down at the sink at the broken one and Frances passed him the other one she had picked up from the sink. He nodded at her.

"I can't tell about the Somunol," he said, "but there is one syringe and needle missing and this vial of insulin should be full."

"Are you sure?"

Captain Wainscott nodded. He took another vial out of the medicine cabinet and showed it to her.

"This is the one I used last night before dinner to give her her injection of insulin. You can see there is about a third of it left. I had started using this one on Monday."

Frances nodded. She didn't like the thought of where it was going. Why was insulin missing? Frances looked at one of the

304

vials, and she guessed that the empty syringe lying in the sink before her could likely take most of the insulin in a single vial.

"Do you think somebody stole a syringe and some insulin?" asked Captain Wainscott.

Frances nodded at him as they walked out of the bathroom.

"But why on earth would someone do that. Diabetics are very careful about making sure they have their medication with them at all times. Worse case, they should have just asked if they needed some. I know Abby wouldn't have minded helping a fellow diabetic. They didn't need to kill her for it."

Timothy looked down at Lady Pompress as her lifeless body lay on the floor in front of them. Frances gently took him by the elbow and led him towards the door.

"She wasn't killed by a diabetic looking for a shot of insulin," said Frances.

"But then why?"

Their conversation was interrupted by Anton barging into the cabin. He look flushed and breathless.

"What is it?" asked Frances.

Anton paused for a moment, leaning over with his hands on his knees, taking in great big, quick breaths. He looked up at her.

"I can't find Mr. Warrant," he said, in a gasp.

"Albert?"

Anton nodded. Frances shook her head. Perry had joined them by this time.

"What's going on?" asked Fowler.

"Albert is missing," said Frances.

Anton started to straighten up now, getting a handle on his breath.

"We need to search all the cabins for him," she said.

Fowler and Anton nodded. They all exited the cabin and walked to the bow of the ship. On the port side was Lady Marmalade's cabin and starboard held Florence's.

Moving up towards the stern of the ship, the next cabin on the port side was empty. The one on the starboard side just past Florence's cabin had been designated as Albert's new cabin for the night before. Fowler tried the door and found it open. He walked in tentatively expecting to see something. Anton followed in after him, then followed by Frances, Florence and Captain Wainscott. The room was empty, the bed still made. They looked into the bathroom. It too was empty. The whole cabin looked like it had been unused. The only telltale sign of any life was Albert's suitcase on the bed. It was unopened.

"I don't understand," said Fowler, "where could he be if not in his room?"

"We're going to have to search from stem to stern," said Frances. "He must be here somewhere."

"Unless he's been thrown overboard," said Anton.

Frances shook her head.

"He hasn't been thrown overboard."

"I mean, if he's ended up like Lady Pompress, God forbid, they might have thrown his body overboard," said Anton.

Frances shook her head quickly.

"No. If, God forbid, he has been murdered, he'll be onboard."

"How can you be so sure?" asked Fowler.

"Because I know who committed these first two murders."

"I see," said Fowler, moving past Frances and heading back into the hallway. "We best search quickly then."

Fowler moved across the hallway towards Samuel's room on the port side. He opened it and walked in. The room was immaculate. It was clear that no one had slept in the room the night before. The bed was still made. Samuel's suitcase was at the foot of the bed and in the bathroom his toiletries were nowhere to be found. There was also no sign of Albert.

Fowler crossed back to the starboard side and entered Orpha and Mahulda's room. Both beds had been slept in and the covers pulled back over in haste. The bathroom contained toiletries of both Orpha and Mahulda and their suitcases had been unpacked. In the closet were their clothes. There seemed to be nothing unusual about the room. There was also no sign of Albert.

Fowler, leading again, exited the cabin and crossed the hallway, heading stern and port he entered into Maurice's room. This room was a mess. The bed was unmade and a pile of clothes was crumpled up in the corner of the room by the entrance to the door way. The closet contained Maurice's clothes and his suitcase was up against the end of the queen sized bed. The bathroom contained two toothbrushes, two colognes and two jars of pomade. But there was no sign of Albert.

"This is getting ridiculous," said Fowler. "Perhaps he threw himself overboard, riddled with grief about the loss of his sister."

Nobody said anything to that. They followed him out and across the hallway towards Albert and Abigail's original room. Fowler hesitated for a moment before entering. He turned to Frances.

"Surely he wouldn't be back in here," he said.

"One never knows. We should be thorough nevertheless," she said.

So he opened the door, but something caught it halfway. He pushed at it more vigorously but it wouldn't budge. He squeezed himself in through the crack. He took a quick breath.

"My God," he said, "I've found him."

"Don't move him just yet," said Frances, squeezing herself into the room.

Albert lay on his stomach with his head facing the door and his arm outstretched as if he were reaching for it. His face was bloated and ruddy, and turned to his left. Anton came in after her, followed by Florence and then Captain Wainscott.

"Would you mind pulling him into the room so we can turn him over?" asked Frances.

307

Fowler grabbed his ankles and pulled his heft back into the room. Frances looked around the room. It was in disarray. All the doors that could be opened were. The only one that was closed was the closet door by the entrance, and that was only likely due to Albert's body having bumped against it to close it. The doors and drawers of the side tables at both beds were opened and rifled through. The main closet in the room had its contents flung out onto the floor, and the bottom drawer pulled out. The contents being mostly Abigail's clothes.

Frances walked into the bathroom. The medicine cabinet door was opened and most of the contents pulled out where they had crashed into the sink. In the wastebasket was the item that Frances was looking for. It was the missing syringe with needle attached.

Frances came back out and waited until Anton and Fowler had turned Albert onto his back. She kneeled down by his body, looking for any telltale signs.

"What happened to him?" asked Anton.

"He was murdered," said Frances, "with this."

She handed the syringe to Perry.

"Please keep it safe."

"My God," said Timothy. "So that's what happened to the syringe."

"This is yours?" asked Fowler.

"No. It was Abby's. I noticed it missing from the bathroom when Frances asked me to take a look."

Frances looked carefully around Albert's torso and on his right side just under his ribs was a small red stain against his shirt. Frances lifted it up and against his bloated skin she saw a small red dot of blood. It marked the injection point. She pointed at it.

"This is where he was stabbed with it," she said.

Fowler and Anton kneeled down and looked at it.

"Murdered by insulin?" asked Fowler, looking at Frances.

Frances nodded. It was what was available.

"But why?"

"He wasn't supposed to be here. If he hadn't have been, he might still be alive. I think whoever was in here, wasn't expecting to see him, or at least, that wasn't their primary goal."

Frances looked at her watch. It was six thirty.

"Can we get everyone upstairs, please. The Cairo police will be here any minute and I want to insure that they are given the murderer by the time they arrive."

Frances got up and started to walk out of the cabin.

"What about the bodies?" asked Fowler.

"They'll be all right for the next little while. The coroner is coming along with the police, and he'll take over when he gets here. It's time to catch this unrepentant criminal."

They followed her upstairs to the second floor where everyone was seated and making good work on their breakfast. They all looked up at her as she entered.

Twenty-Seven

Fowler leaned in to Lady Marmalade and whispered in her ear.

"Do you want to have something to eat?" he asked.

Frances shook her head.

"There isn't time," she said. "But you'd be a friend for life if you could manage a cup of tea for me."

She smiled at him. He nodded at her, grinning. They walked together to the stern side of the dining room.

"Ladies and gentleman," said Fowler, pausing to meet with everyone's gaze. "The Cairo police and coroner are on their way. In fact," he said, looking down at his watch, "they should be here any minute. If you'd give us your attention, Lady Marmalade has some words."

Fowler turned to her and she smiled and nodded at him. Behind her was a dumb waiter. Her friend Florence stood to her left. Frances took a small step towards the room. She took her time not saying a word, looking at each of them in turn.

"I'm angry," she said. "In fact, I am very angry. My dear friend, Florence, has wanted to holiday in Egypt for over fifty years. And here we are in Egypt, finally fulfilling her wish, and I get dragged into a murder investigation by the most selfish, childish and unrepentant murderer I have ever had the misfortune of meeting."

Frances looked around the room. She was met with blank faces for the most part. Samuel was eating his bacon, and Maurice was toying with his scrambled eggs. Nigel sat defiantly, looking at her with his arms crossed over his chest. Simon was frowning slightly, as was Mahulda, while Orpha sipped on her tea. Captain Wainscott had just sat down and was being served a plate of sausages and eggs. Ishaq was pouring him a full cup of dark coffee.

"More appalling than the murder of Ms. Abigail Beckles which occurred on Thursday evening is the discovery of the bodies of Lady Pompress and Mr. Albert Warrant, Ms. Beckles' brother."

Frances paused for a moment to judge the crowd. Bewilderment stung most of the faces as if a nest of hornets had just been released amongst them.

"Good Lord!" exclaimed Nigel, his façade softening.

Frances nodded.

"What happened?" asked Orpha.

Frances looked at her.

"Lady Pompress was bludgeoned to death with a lamp stand and Albert was injected with a lethal dose of insulin."

"That's awful," she said.

Frances nodded solemnly.

"What has been upsetting to me, above everything has been the constant web of lies that most of you have fed me. I came here to holiday with my friend, and instead I got a web of lies from most of you, even those of you not related to the murder, which only made things that more difficult. In fact," she said, "if you had been honest with me, I might not be here discussing three murders with you, but rather just the one. One, mind you, which is still too many."

Fowler came over to Frances and handed her a teacup and saucer. The tea was orange and unadulterated. He asked if she needed cream or sugar, which she declined. Frances sipped on her tea and then put the cup and saucer on the dumb waiter behind her.

"At first," she said, looking at them one at a time, "I couldn't quite fathom the motive. I had my suspicions early on that it must have had something to do with Ms. Beckles' jewelry and artifacts that most of us must have seen fall out of her bag when we were all getting ready to board the bus at the hotel. But it seemed odd to me that she would have been murdered over what at that time seemed more like a crime of opportunity."

Fowler came back with a cup of tea for Florence. She thanked him and walked behind Frances to a side table where she added cream and sugar. She came back and stood to the left of Frances and sipped her tea, cradling the saucer in her left hand.

"Things became more complicated when we arrived at the pyramids. I knew, from having helped Scotland Yard on previous occasions, that the jewelry and artifacts that fell out of Ms. Beckles' suitcase were in fact stolen property."

Frances looked around. She knew that this was not news to most of the guests seated in front of her.

"Stolen from where?" asked Mahulda, timidly.

"From the Pyramid of Menkaure. Perry had discussed the theft of most of the artifacts that were buried in the secret burial chamber of King Menkaure. This occurred in the late eighteen hundreds. 1895 to be exact. But then most of you knew about that, didn't you, Dr. Durmott?"

Frances looked at Nigel. He coughed and spluttered for a moment as she caught him off guard.

"I beg your pardon," he said.

"The time of charades and games is over," said Frances, quite sternly. "Three amongst us are dead already."

"Well I... I didn't have anything to do with that," he said.

"Yes, I know, but what you are all forgetting is that I have friends at Scotland Yard, and I have received word from them this morning."

Frances took some time to carefully extract the telegrams from her handbag. She did it with measured pause for emphasis. She looked at them for some time, shuffling each one in turn. Then she held them up and waved them in front of the group.

"On your registration form for this trip, Nigel, you failed to include your salutation as doctor. Instead you checked the mark for Mr. But you are, in fact, a doctor, are you not?"

Nigel looked away.

"Yes, well, I suppose I am."

"And would you like to tell us what you're a doctor of?" asked Frances.

Nigel looked back at his plate and then back at her, and held her gaze for a moment, not saying a word. Frances looked at her telegrams for a moment.

"Doctor Nigel Durmott, born at Swansea. You are in fact a doctor of archaeology. You are the chief investigator of stolen artifacts at the British Museum. Am I correct, Nigel?"

Frances looked at him and held his gaze for a long while.

"Yes, I suppose I am."

"And because of your lies, at least to some extent, two other guests are now dead."

"I beg your pardon," he said. "I must strongly disagree with that. This was a very important and sensitive investigation. Those artifacts are extremely valuable and rare, and I need to get them back to the museum at once."

"And yet you lied about your reasons for being here. That your marriage was in a shambles and that you were just exploring the pyramids of Menkaure on the off chance that you might find some stolen treasures. But you did in fact know that

Abigail Beckles was planning on returning the stolen artifacts that she had in her possession to their original home."

"Listen," said Nigel, getting visibly upset. "I didn't want anyone to get murdered over this. I had reached out to her in London and said she could return them to me and I'd make sure they were safely stored in the British Museum. I told her I wouldn't involve the police. But she didn't believe the British Museum had any right to them either. She told me she was going to return them to their rightful place. I knew that meant she was coming to Cairo. I made inquiries and followed her itinerary. Look, after she was murdered, I knew you'd be investigating, and I knew your reputation preceded you. All I thought was that I'd wait until you'd identified the murderer and then have a word about obtaining the stolen property. I am as shocked as you are that Albert and Lady Pompress were also murdered."

Frances put her handbag down by her feet and turned around and took a sip of her tea with her free hand. She replaced the teacup and looked back at Nigel.

"How did you come to know that Abigail Beckles owned the remaining stolen property?" she asked him.

"Well, I didn't, at least not with any certainty. My man at Scotland Yard had informed me that Abigail's mother had told them that her deceased brother, Arthur Vipond, was one of the thieves who had stolen the property of King Menkaure. Scotland Yard had investigated, but of course there was no hard evidence, and Abigail's mother had died shortly after, so they couldn't press her for more information. I took a gamble as I felt that if Arthur no longer had any of the property he probably dispersed it to his surviving heirs, Albert and Abigail. Investigating them both, I felt that Abigail likely had some of this property left, as she didn't live as ostentatiously as her brother did. I reached out to her and she told me the British Museum wasn't the rightful owner. Instead of coming all the way to Egypt, I thought I'd try to set myself up as a buyer. I contacted Lottie Hutchings' groundskeeper and told him I was interested in purchasing the property no questions asked."

"I'm not following," said Captain Wainscott, looking up from his half finished plate of food. "Who are all these people?"

Frances looked at him, and smiled mildly.

"Yes, I forget that there are indeed a couple of us who don't know who everyone is around here. I'll try and explain it briefly for you, Timothy. In 1895, two Englishmen named Arthur Vipond and Howard Trenglove, found the secret passageways that led from the queen's pyramid into the Pyramid of Menkaure where the valuables were stored under the king's burial chamber. They ransacked the place, pillaging it of millions of pounds worth of artifacts and valuables. They were never caught for their crime, though they were suspected."

Frances looked around the room. Everyone was looking at her in between bites of food or sips of tea and coffee.

"Howard Trenglove died in 1907. At that time he had no family other than two sisters, Edna the older sister, and Hortence the younger sister. He wasn't particularly close to either of them, but before they could obtain his unsold share of the spoils, Arthur Vipond swooped in and snatched it out from under them. In 1930, Arthur Vipond died, but before he did he left what was remaining of the Menkaure treasures to his niece and nephew, Abigail and Albert. Albert, at his own admission, was a bit of a spendthrift and managed to sell what was given to him and used up all the money. That left only Abigail with any remaining artifacts of the theft, which she wished to return to Cairo and the pyramid from whence they came."

Captain Wainscott frowned, his fork hovering with a piece of sausage like a bomber over the battlefield ruins of his eggs.

"So you're saying she was killed for those artifacts?" he asked.

"That's exactly what I'm saying."

Captain Wainscott shook his head sadly and put the sausage into his mouth where he chewed it thoughtfully. Frances turned to Nigel.

"So you were pretending to be the buyer that Albert spoke of?"

"I suppose I was. Then Pascal, the groundskeeper told me that Albert couldn't fulfill our agreement, and that his sister was taking the stolen property back here to Cairo."

"And did you tell anyone else this?" asked Frances.

Nigel shook his head.

"I told Pascal not to tell anyone else about it either. He said he wouldn't."

"He lied to you," said Frances.

Maurice looked at Frances steadily, as did Samuel and everyone else.

"What do you mean?" asked Nigel.

"Did you ever get Pascal's surname?" asked Frances.

"No, I didn't."

"And here is where we start to get closer to the truth," said Frances. "I had wondered about why all the lies, Nigel. Now I know why. It would have been much better if you had confessed to me instead. But one can't cry over spilled milk."

Frances turned back to her tea and took a long sip. She looked back at the group gathered in front of her. Almost everyone had finished eating by now, and they were carefully nursing their drinks.

"Everything started falling into place yesterday, especially after we spoke with Albert. He was most forthcoming, helped obviously, by his grief at the loss of his sister."

"So who did it?" asked Simon, looking at Frances and then around at the others.

"We're coming to that. But it is true, that a few of you were caught like flies in a spider's web of deceit and lies. You amongst them, Simon," said Frances. "You see, it all came down to the stolen property of the Pyramid of Menkaure. Other than for Simon, Captain Timothy Wainscott, Mahulda and Lady Abigail Pompress, everyone amongst you is involved."

Frances looked around at the group of them. There was nervous clearing of the throat and shuffling in position.

"Poppycock," said Maurice, looking at Frances with his arms crossed over his chest. Frances smiled at him.

"Poppycock indeed, Mr. Gabberdeen," she said. "The only thing about all of this that is poppycock is your feigned ignorance."

Frances looked at her telegrams again.

"Mr. Maurice Gabberdeen, born in Bristol in 1902. It seems you like to spend a lot of time in America."

"That's none of your business," he said.

"Yes, it seems here, that for the past seventeen years you've been making more than one trip to America each year. Specifically it appears that you travel to New York. Why is that?"

Frances looked at him, and held his gaze.

"I like the Big Apple," he said, "not that it's any of your concern or related to this case."

"You also have a brother who lives in London, isn't that so?"

"What of it?"

"It's his name that intrigues me, Mr. Gabberdeen. Would you care to tell us his name?"

Frances looked at him, and Maurice held her gaze without saying anything.

"Very well, I shall out you myself," said Frances, watching him swallow hard. "Your brother's name is Pascal, and Mr. Pascal Gabberdeen has been employed as Lottie Hutchings' groundskeeper for some time."

He remained silent and kept his gaze on Lady Marmalade as everyone turned and looked at him.

"Our Maurice has also been visiting New York all these years, as his lover is there. Isn't that right?"

Frances looked at him and again he said nothing.

"Now listen here," said Samuel in his American accent, "this is none of your concern, and I've heard quite enough."

Samuel stood up from his chair as if to give emphasis to his statement. Fowler stepped forward and spoke to him sternly, his smile was no longer present.

"Mr. Newton, you'll sit down, if you don't mind."

After a bit of posturing, Samuel sat back down. Frances nodded.

"Yes, Mr. Newton, I'm quite sure you've had enough. You and Maurice have been lovers for years, haven't you?"

"Listen!" said Samuel, getting quite hot under the collar. "You can't just go rummaging through other people's intimate lives if you know what's good for you."

"I'm afraid I must, Mr. Newton, especially when said people have been lying to me related to a murder investigation."

"That's because you aren't the bloody police."

"So they did it, did they?" asked Timothy. "He has the medicine to have poisoned the poor gal."

Frances shook her head.

"Outrageous lies!" said Maurice, "we had nothing to do with the murder. With any of them."

"Perhaps you'd care to explain then," said Frances. "Why the lies? I knew you were lying when you told me you had gone to see the Tomb of Hemon and you agreed that the reliefs showed him emaciated. Hemon was not emaciated, Samuel, in fact, he's fat."

Maurice and Samuel looked at each other for a moment.

"The Cairo police will be here any moment, gentlemen, and I can assure you that a Cairo jail is the last place either of you would want to find yourselves."

"Very well," said Samuel, looking over at Maurice who nodded at him, "Maurice and I have known each other for many years. Our relationship however, is none of your business."

"But you helped Maurice's brother become the groundskeeper at your cousin's estate, didn't you?"

Samuel nodded.

"I'm confused. Who is Samuel's cousin?" asked Timothy.

Frances looked over at him.

"Howard Trenglove was one of the original thieves. He had two sisters, both younger than him. The older of the two sisters was Samuel's mother. Her name was Edna Newton."

Frances looked back over at Samuel whose head hung low.

"The younger of the two sisters was Hortence, Hortence Hutchings. Hortence had two daughters. The youngest daughter got Howard Trenglove's estate when he died. Her name is Lottie Hutchings, and she employed Maurice's brother Pascal as the groundskeeper. Isn't that so?"

Frances looked at Samuel. He looked back up at her and nodded slowly.

"That's right. But murder was never part of the agenda. All Maurice and I were planning on was to get back what was rightfully mine. Albert and Abigail had no right to what had been my uncle's. It belonged back with us, the Trengloves. We had come here to steal it from them when Pascal had informed Maurice that Abigail and Albert were coming here to return the treasures. We were going to take it back."

"Only it's not really yours, Samuel, it was stolen."

"So they didn't murder Abigail, or my darling Abby?" asked Captain Wainscott.

"We didn't murder anyone," said Maurice, feeling quite exasperated.

"All three murders were committed by the same person," said Frances.

"We followed Abigail and Albert into the pyramid, but we saw Simon come out just as we were getting there. We asked him if he'd found anything, and he said he hadn't. However, we couldn't just take his word for it, so we asked him for some water and he opened up his rucksack in front of us and we could see he didn't have any of the artifacts," said Samuel. "We went into Menkaure's pyramid but when we got there we realized that Albert and Abigail hadn't left any of the jewelry and other goods behind. Our plan was to wait until the day after, yesterday, when Maurice would feign heat stroke at Memphis and come back to the boat and see if he couldn't find the stolen goods in their room. Obviously, the murder put those plans on halt."

Frances nodded.

"Finally," she said, "we are starting to get some truth out everyone."

"Then who killed all these people and for what reason?" asked Timothy.

"The reason is obvious. Abigail Beckles was killed for the stolen goods, and the person who killed her didn't want her to be alive to notice that the artifacts had been stolen. The problem was, the stolen goods were never found. You see, what the killer didn't know, was that Albert had decided to keep the Menkaure artifacts for himself after his sister had tasked him with returning them. The killer thought that the goods were still with Abigail. The Somunol was added to the milk first, and when the goods weren't found she left the cabin for fear of being found..."

"She?" asked Captain.

Frances nodded.

"Yes, the woman who murdered both Abigails and Albert is Orpha Bendled."

Everyone turned to look at Orpha, the old woman who despite being a little curmudgeonly seemed like anyone's grandmother.

"This is preposterous," she said.

"Why?" asked Timothy.

Frances looked at Orpha but she kept her mouth shut.

"Would you like to tell us why you did it?" asked Frances.

"I didn't do it, and I don't appreciate your tone."

Orpha looked off and pushed her chair away from the table.

"All right then," said Frances, "I'll tell you all why. I first started getting suspicious about Orpha at the hotel when Albert walked up to her during dinner and asked if he knew her. Orpha of course denied knowing him..."

"Because I didn't," snapped Orpha.

"Well, actually you did. Albert might have been much younger, but he recognized you as one of the Trengloves. He remembered meeting you when Arthur had invited him round to Howard Trenglove's home where you were. This was many years ago and he thought he must have been mistaken, but I believe that made him a liability, and when the opportunity presented itself to murder him, she took it."

"I still don't understand," said Captain Wainscott. "Who is she?"

"I mentioned the Trengloves before," said Frances, looking at him. "Howard had two sisters, the older one was Edna and the younger was Hortence. Hortence had two children, the youngest of whom was Lottie who now lives in the Trenglove estate. The oldest daughter was given up for adoption, and she is Orpha Bendled."

Frances paused and looked at Orpha. Orpha remained mute.

"You carried with you a great umbrage, didn't you, Orpha?" asked Frances.

Orpha still remained mute.

"Not only had you been cast aside as not being worthy of the Trengloves, but after you found out who your real mother was you spent years ingratiating yourself with Howard Trenglove in the hope that you'd one day find yourself in possession of the stolen artifacts he still had."

Frances looked at her and waited.

"If anyone deserved them, I did," said Orpha. "Cast aside as I was from the bosom of my mother, I've had to claw and scrape my way back to any sense of decency. I was so close to Howard trusting me when he died suddenly when that ungrateful bastard, Arthur, stole what was rightly ours right from under us. And he gave it to that stupid niece of his. She didn't deserve it, she didn't even want it."

"Why did you have to kill her?" asked Frances, softly.

"Because she wouldn't let me have them. I sent her a letter telling her that they belonged to me. She rudely told me that she was going to return them and that if anything should happen to her before then she would send my letter to the police. I couldn't chance it. She was better off dead then."

"But surely you didn't use your own name?"

"Didn't matter, the address was the same if anyone had cared to look."

"But you didn't find the treasures you were looking for did you?"

"No I didn't, but like you said, I had already poisoned the milk and I thought that everyone would think it was the brother. I was hoping to have another look in Albert's bags the following day."

"Except your plans went very wrong," said Frances.

"How do you know?" asked Orpha.

"Because this morning when I saw how Lady Pompress had been murdered I knew it must have been you. Finding Albert poisoned after the fact was easy to put two and two together."

"How did you know it was her?" asked Timothy. "She's a frail old grandmother."

"That's deceiving," said Frances. "Mahulda had proudly told me how her grandmother is the oldest woman to have summited Ben Nevis just last summer. No, Orpha is hardly a frail old woman, and I noticed that at dinner at the hotel, the first night we were all here that she was left-handed. None of the rest of us are, and Lady Pompress was murdered by a left-handed person. I believe what happened, was that Orpha had gone back into Lady Pompress' room to get the insulin just in case, when Lady Pompress came in quite suddenly. You," said Frances, looking at Orpha, "were startled and tried to apologize for an honest mistake, but Lady Pompress wouldn't have any of it. After she identified you as the killer of Abigail, she turned to leave, threatening to expose you, when you grabbed the lamp stand off the bedside table and struck her across the left side of the temple from behind, killing her."

Frances looked at Orpha and she nodded.

"She wouldn't have died if she'd just have minded her own business."

"I think rather she wouldn't have died if you had minded your own business," said Lady Marmalade.

"It doesn't matter," said Orpha, "as my granddaughter told you, I'm quite athletic and you'll never capture me."

With that, Orpha sprung up like a startled gazelle and ran swiftly between the tables before anyone realized what had happened, and darted upstairs. Fowler finally realized what was going on and chased after her. She was surprisingly nimble for an old woman, and she had just gained the element of surprise.

Everybody made their way up the stairs after her and Fowler. Fowler arrived on the top deck as Orpha sprinted to the end and jumped over the railing of the bow like a graceful diver.

They all made their way to the bow and peered over the railing, only to see a wet Orpha surface just a few feet away from the Cairo police boat moving up to board.

"Detain her," shouted Fowler.

He turned around grinning at Lady Marmalade.

"It looks like justice will be served after all," he said.

Frances peered over the railing and watched a couple of Egyptian policeman help a disgruntled wet rat of a woman onto their boat. She looked up at Frances with an upturned mouth and furrowed brow full of anger.

Twenty-Eight

Lady Marmalade and Florence were amongst the first off the boat after it had docked alongside the two Cairo boats on the west bank of the Nile. Fowler had told everyone that the Queen Nefertiti would likely be docked for most of the morning if not for the day, but that he was happy to give them a tour through the ruins of Memphis for those who wished.

Alternatively, he had called for an additional bus for those who wished to make their way back to Cairo or Alexandria in order to return home as quickly as possible.

Samuel and Maurice were debarking from the boat with their suitcases. There was nothing left for them on the Queen Nefertiti and having not found what they had come for they were determined to return home. However, that wouldn't happen for a couple of hours as the Cairo police still needed to collect everyone's statements.

Mahulda came off the boat not carrying any bags with her. She smiled at Frances and Florence as she debarked.

"I'll take your picture alongside the boat if you'd like," said Florence.

"Oh, thank you," said Mahulda, "that would be wonderful."

Mahulda walked several paces towards the stern of the boat where the boat's name was painted in an Arabic looking script. Florence readied her camera and looked at the young woman through her viewfinder. Mahulda put on a brave smile and the picture was taken. And for a moment, if ever so briefly, Florence had captured a small slice of effervescent innocence and optimism in Mahulda's face. A brief chance to cherish the reason for coming all the way to Egypt. A last, fleeting taste of what this holiday should have been for her. Mahulda walked back up to Florence and Frances. They were both smiling at her.

"I take it you're going to take the boat back to Cairo, rather than the bus?" asked Florence.

Mahulda nodded.

"Yes, I should think so. Perhaps it will give me just a chance of trying to enjoy what this trip should have been about."

"Good, dear," said Florence, "I think it will be helpful. Remember to give me your address so I can mail the photograph to you."

Mahulda nodded absentmindedly and turned to Frances.

"Why did she murder Albert?" she asked. "You never clarified that for us."

Frances looked out over the Nile. If it was true that you could never step into the same river twice, then you could never undo anything once it had been done. And perhaps that was the greatest tragedy that befell mankind. There were always second chances, but never retakes.

"I believe my dear," said Frances, "that the murder of Albert was unplanned and accidental. You see, Albert had been given a new room, and I don't believe your grandmother knew about that. She went into Albert and Abigail's original cabin hoping to find the stolen goods, not knowing that Albert had moved cabins and that he also no longer had the stolen artifacts. I believe she was surprised by Albert when he entered. She probably hid in the bathroom until she had her opportunity to stab him with the overdose of insulin. This whole affair is just an awful and terrible mess. Why Albert had returned to the cabin is something we'll never know. But I suspect he wanted to say goodbye to his sister one last time."

"Thank you for solving it for us," said Mahulda. "I feel so awful that my grandmother would do something so appalling."

Mahulda left Frances and Florence and walked over towards her grandmother who was being guarded by two Egyptian policemen. Frances and Florence watched after her.

"Poor girl," said Florence, "it's going to leave a mark, I'm sure."

Frances nodded.

"Why did you do it, Grandmother?" asked Mahulda, looking at her grandmother.

Orpha looked up with feigned pleading eyes.

"I did it for you. I wanted a better life for us. Those treasures belonged to us."

"They never belonged to us," said Mahulda. "And they were never worth harming anyone."

"You don't understand," snapped Orpha, her tone turning sharp ever so quickly. "You've always been an ungrateful and spoiled child. I spent everything on you trying to make sure you had a decent life and decent opportunity at something better."

That was a lie and Mahulda knew it. Her grandmother had spared as much as she could from any expense for Mahulda's enrichment. The only thing she hadn't spared was the rod.

Mahulda turned away from her and walked back towards the boat. Simon walked off and came up to her. His scar was shiny in the Egyptian sun, like someone had melted wax onto his face, but Mahulda thought it made him ruggedly handsome. He took her hands in his and kissed her on the lips. They walked over to where Frances and Florence were still standing.

"You two are taking the boat back with us to Cairo, Mahulda tells me," said Simon.

Frances smiled at them.

"Somebody needs to chaperone the two of you," she said.

Simon laughed heartily and Mahulda giggled.

"Is it that obvious?" she asked.

"What is obvious," said Frances, "is that perhaps something beautiful can come from this trip."

Mahulda and Simon smiled at the two of them.

"We're very happy to have the company," he said.

Fowler walked off the boat and approached the group of them. He was grinning as he had the first time she had met him.

"I think it's just the two of you for the tour of Memphis," he said. "Have you given the authorities your statements."

Simon and Mahulda nodded.

"I'll be joining them back in Cairo to give them my full account of the investigation," said Frances.

"I wanted to ask you what I should do with the artifacts," said Fowler. "Nigel is adamant I return them to him."

"I think not," said Frances. "They belong to the Egyptian people. Hold onto them until we return to Cairo when we can give them to Dr. Abubakar Haddad of the Egyptian Museum."

Fowler nodded.

"That sounds about right," he said, grinning.

Captain Wainscott came off the boat carrying his suitcases as well as Lady Pompress' with the help of Jafari. He walked up to them.

"I wanted to thank you, deeply, for finding justice for my Abby," he said, through wet eyes. "My life will never be whole again, but it brings me some comfort that justice will be served."

Frances smiled at him and patted him on the forearm.

"When we are broken it is hard to find the beauty that's still there. Yet it is by the fixing, and the putting back of the pieces that the light shines more brightly from within us. You will find that light again, Captain, you will shine more brightly than before."

About Jason Blacker

Jason Blacker was born in Cape Town but spent most of his first 18 years in Johannesburg. When not grinding his fingers down to stubs at the keyboard he enjoys drinking tisane, calisthenics and running. Currently he lives in Canada.

Under his own name he writes hard boiled as well as cozy mysteries, action adventure, thrillers, literary fiction and anything else that tickles his muse. Jason Blacker also writes poetry and daily haikus at his haiku blog.

You can find his haikus and other poetry at his website **www.haiqueue.com**.

To stay up to date and learn about new releases be sure to visit **www.jasonblacker.com** where you can find more information about his writing and upcoming projects.

If you enjoy space opera in the tradition of Star Trek then take a look at Jason Blacker's pen name "Sylynt Storme". It is under the name Sylynt Storme where you can find both sci-fi and vampire fiction written by Jason Blacker.

"Star Sails" is the space opera series and "The Misgivings of the Vampire Lucius Lafayette" is his vampire series.